I'M ONLY ME WHEN I'M WITH HIM

BY AMANDA SCHIMMOELLER

Royal Hearts Series
A Royal Obligation
A Royal Competition
A Royal Arrangement
A Royal Promise
A Royal Possibility

Sweeter Than Fiction Series
I Knew He Was Trouble
How He Got the Girl
I'm Only Me When I'm With Him

I'M ONLY ME WHEN I'M WITH HIM

AMANDA SCHIMMOELLER

3
SWEETER THAN
FICTION

ISBN: 979-8-9926045-2-8 (paperback)

Cover Design by Melody Jeffries
Edited by Caitlin Miller
Proofread by Alicia Whitaker

Visit www.authoramandaschimmoeller.com for more information.

CONTENT WARNING

While the overall tone of this story is lighthearted, this book contains a few heavy themes, including anxiety (panic attacks depicted on page), a character stuck in a burning building, and self-doubt.

But, rest assured, a happily-ever-after is guaranteed.

CHAPTER ONE

SHAYNA

RUNNING THROUGH THE AIRPORT in my pajamas is not how I saw my morning going.

Unfortunately, that's my current state as I sprint through the crowd, trying to catch my flight. It's not even one of my cute matching pajama sets. No, I'm in the ratty high school sweatshirt I stole from my best friend's older brother nearly a decade ago and a grungy pair of sweatpants I sleep in that probably should be retired.

There's a solid chance the booty region is see-through from how many years I've worn them. But I can't think about the thousands of people who might be seeing my cute floral underwear. All I can think about is how I *must* make my flight home.

I had the best week attending the Northwest Flower and Garden Festival in Washington. I can't wait to implement all the helpful tips I learned about growing cut flowers and integrating underused blooms into bouquets. But the whole traveling across the country part…that I could do without.

Heights are my greatest fear, so let's just say flying and I are *not* a match made in heaven. Seriously, who thought it was a smart idea to add wings to a giant chunk of aluminum and put it in the air? I'd like to personally *not* thank them for this utter disservice.

But I'll admit, it is nice that I can get home to Louisville, Kentucky, in mere hours rather than a thirty-four-hour road trip. And I know, statistically speaking, I'm more likely to get in a car accident than a plane accident…but there isn't a fact out there that will calm my anxiety around flying. I already worked myself up enough last night, fretting over today's travels. If I have to wait in the airport for hours or—heaven forbid, overnight—I don't think my body could handle that level of nerves. Which is exactly why I *need* to get on that plane, see-through sweatpants and all.

"This is the final boarding call for Flight 7613 to Louisville. Final boarding call." The announcement comes through the speakers. I huff, picking up my pace as I drag my carry-on behind me.

"Sorry, excuse me," I rasp out between sharp breaths as I squeeze between groups of people, not slowing my pace. Even if I'm running way late, I'll never lose my manners.

Stupid phone alarm. But I'm the one who accidentally set it to vibrate rather than a sound, so I guess that makes me the stupid one. I would've won the Olympic gold for how quickly I threw my remaining items into my suitcase and caught a shuttle from my hotel to the airport.

But there isn't a gold medal that can save me if I don't make my flight.

Sweat forms on my forehead and upper lip, and my armpits are definitely damp since I didn't have time to apply deodorant this morning, but there's no stopping to take a breather. I shout an internal *hallelujah* when I finally spot my gate.

I frantically wave my phone in the air as I approach the desk. "I'm here. So sorry. I didn't hear my alarm go off this morning, and I woke up with, like, negative minutes to get here." I let out a dramatic sigh. "But I made it."

The woman drags her eyes from my hair, which probably looks like a rat's nest, to my old sweatshirt and grungy sweatpants. I reach up, readjusting my signature pearl-studded headband. I wouldn't feel like myself without it. So, even though my hair is in a messy ponytail that I slept in and didn't bother redoing in my rush to get to the airport, at least I have my headband that makes me feel the slightest bit put together.

But I don't think the gate attendant sees the effort. She purses her lips, looking like she's debating quitting her job just so she doesn't have to let me on the plane. "Boarding pass?" She sounds both unamused and annoyed.

"Right." I pull it up on my phone, thankful I at least remembered to charge it last night. She scans the pass and gestures to the jet bridge without another word.

I slide my phone into my large sweatshirt pocket. "Thank you. Have a beautiful day." Even when I don't receive kindness in return, I always try to leave the world and people better off than I found them. Sometimes that requires biting my tongue when I'd rather say *bless your hateful heart*. But maybe my kindness will help turn her day—and attitude—around.

"Welcome aboard," a flight attendant greets with a tight smile as I step onto the plane. She's probably frustrated at my tardiness, too, and I don't blame her.

I offer her as much of a grin as I'm able to muster with the anxiety building in my chest before walking down the aisle, looking for an open seat. Of course, the only one available is at the very back of the plane, next to a man who has his hood pulled low over his face and looks to be asleep.

Thankfully, he's next to the window, so I'm able to sit down in the aisle seat without bothering him.

I hear the sound of a toilet flushing, followed by some running water. When the poor soul who was in there opens the bathroom door, the stench of a dirty porta-potty hits my nostrils, and I grimace. Now it makes sense why the only open seat was in the back of the plane…it's right next to the restroom. Wonderful. Just when I thought this day couldn't get any worse, I'm going to have to smell *that* for the entire flight home. I blame past me for not recognizing the importance of paying the extra charge to pick my seat on the plane so I didn't get stuck sitting where no one else wanted to.

I slide my purse under the seat in front of me and click the seatbelt into place over my lap as the flight attendants go through their usual safety spiel. I half listen, not wanting to hear about worst-case scenarios when my brain is already reeling with them.

The engines roar to life, and I realize yet another reason why this seat was empty. Who knew that sitting near the back of the plane makes the engines sound even louder? Not me. I tap my fingers in a random rhythm on my worn sweats to distract myself as we begin to taxi.

Takeoff and landing are always the worst for me. But especially takeoff, thanks to the one time I flew with my parents to the beach as a child. While we were ascending, our plane shook and bobbed like it sometimes does with turbulence. It didn't feel normal, though. It felt like the pilot wasn't in control and we were going to careen back down to the earth. People around us screamed and vomited as the violent shaking continued while I clung to my mom for dear life. After several nerve-wracking minutes, the turbulence finally stopped, but the damage was done. Ever since then, I've hated flying.

Scratch that, I've hated anything where my feet aren't firmly planted on solid ground.

My heart races faster than the sound of the plane's wheels barreling us down the runway like we're in a high-speed chase. I try to practice a breathing exercise I learned from my therapist. I inhale for four seconds, hold for seven, and slowly release for eight. But the second we're in the air, my belly swoops like I'm on a roller coaster. I feel weightless, but not in a good way. In a I'm-very-aware-that-I'm-no-longer-on-the-ground-and-I'm-freaking-out kind of way.

My breathing strains as I grip the armrests on either side of me, accidentally knocking the arm of the man next to me off the one between us. Normally, I'd apologize, but I'm unable to form complete sentences. Fear grips my chest, constricting it. I can't breathe. Can't think.

Suddenly, a hand grasps mine, grounding me.

"Breathe. Just breathe, Shayna."

The familiar voice pulls me out of my panic just enough that I'm able to suck in a sharp breath, filling my lungs with precious air again.

"There you go. Keep going, just like that."

I focus on my breathing exercises. It's only once my breathing has slowed and my heart rate feels as close to normal as it's going to get while on a plane that I'm finally able to form coherent thoughts.

Like why the voice next to me sounds familiar.

And how he knows my name.

I slowly drag my eyes from the hand holding mine up his sweatshirt with a Seattle Station 7 logo to the face I memorized when I was in middle school. With his hood now pulled back, I can see that his blond hair is standing up in the same way it used to all those years ago. He has always run his hands through his hair as a nervous tic. I guess some things never change.

"Connor?" I whisper his name in disbelief, as if my mind conjured him. But I feel his hand in mine. And I heard his voice, the one I'd know anywhere.

This is really happening. I'm sitting next to Connor Porter. My best friend Mallory's older brother. The same Connor I've had a giant crush on since I first met him when I was eleven and he was thirteen. The same crush I've convinced myself time and time again that I was over, only to see him again and have all those prepubescent feelings come rushing back.

I've never told another soul about it. I just deny, deny, deny whenever any of my best friends—lovingly referred to as the Long Live Girlies—ask me if I'm interested in anyone. Mallory, Alyssa, Kelsey, and I all met in the sixth grade when we were in the front row at a Taylor Swift concert, and we've been besties ever since. They're my ride or dies…but just not people I can share my massive crush with.

From the weekend we met onward, the four of us alternated having the others over for a sleepover every Friday night. The first time we slept at Mallory's house, she introduced us to Connor, and I immediately thought he was cute. But when we became friends, we all agreed we'd never let a guy come between our sisterhood, so we swore off dating each other's exes and siblings. It sounded simple, a way to protect our friend group from fighting over boys…until I met Connor.

I'm not the kind of person to break girl code. So, I've sucked up my feelings for him like the last precious sip of a strawberry matcha and just lived for every inkling of a moment I shared with him.

It felt wrong back then. Over ten years later, as I stare into his hazel eyes, it still feels wrong.

I mean, it's not one of the Ten Commandments or anything, but maybe it should be.

Thou shalt not kill, steal, or covet thy best friend's older brother.

CHAPTER TWO
CONNOR

My eyes lock on Shayna's. They're such a deep brown that they're almost black in certain lighting, just like the way I enjoy my coffee. They're warm and inviting, a stark contrast to the death grip she currently has on my hand.

My gaze drops to our joined hands as a tingle shoots up my arms. It's probably just a lack of blood flow from how hard she's squeezing it. Nothing to do with the way she said my name or the fact that she's the first woman who has touched me in years, aside from my family.

What are the odds that Shayna would end up on the same plane as me, thousands of miles away from her home? Not to mention the fact that we unknowingly ended up sitting beside each other.

I inhale sharply, clenching my free hand into a fist in my sweatshirt pocket. I should've continued to pretend I was asleep with my hood pulled low over my eyes. If I had, I wouldn't be stuck in this predicament. One where I'm holding the hand of my little sister's best friend.

It was purely instinct. My firefighter training kicked in the second I heard the woman in the seat next to me start to hyperventilate during takeoff. There was no way I could morally *not* help.

But the second I saw it was Shayna with a white-knuckled grip on both armrests, my stomach dropped. It's one thing to help a stranger in a moment of need and never have to see them again, but it's something else entirely to help someone you know. Someone my path will inevitably cross with again.

"What're you doing here?" she whispers.

For some unexplainable reason, I find myself rubbing the pad of my thumb along the back of her hand. "Flying home."

The plane shakes from some minor turbulence, and Shayna squeezes my hand so hard, I'm worried she might break my fingers. She inhales a shuddering breath before digging through her purse.

With the way her hand is shaking, she can't seem to find what she's looking for.

"Shrinking violet," she mutters under her breath.

I'm not sure what that means, and I don't feel like asking. Not when I can see how much she's struggling.

A memory pops into my brain of Shayna using an inhaler after a particularly elaborate dance routine she and her friends made to a song back when they were in middle school. "Do you have asthma?" I ask.

She nods. I lean down and grab her purse from under the seat and quickly rifle through it until I find her inhaler. I take the cap off and pass it to her. She grabs it and inhales a few puffs while still squeezing my hand with a strength I didn't know she possessed.

Shayna slides her inhaler back in her purse, and I try to recall what I learned in my training about helping someone through a panic attack.

"Tell me five things you can see," I say, desperate to help her calm down for the sake of my poor fingers.

"What?" she squeaks, shutting her eyes as the plane jolts again.

"Shayna." I say her name softly. Her eyes slowly open and find mine. I wish I could take away the fear I see in them, but I have to settle for doing what I can to help her feel safe. "Tell me five things you can see," I repeat.

She inhales through her nose and slowly exhales through her mouth before looking around her. "The flight attendant. The plane seat in front of me. The safety instruction pamphlet." Her eyes drop to her lap. "My seat belt." Then she turns to face me. "And you."

My mouth goes dry, but I push forward. "Good. Now, four things you can feel."

"My butt on the plane seat. The vibrations of the plane. The armrest. And the calluses on your hands."

I try not to feel self-conscious about my rough hands. When I'm not working with my hands at the station, I'm usually doing one of the three hobbies that help me feel relaxed: working out, fishing, or woodworking. All things that probably only contribute more to my calluses.

It doesn't matter if she feels them, I remind myself. It's not like this is a romantic moment. I'm helping Shayna come down from her state of panic. I have a job to do.

"You're doing great," I encourage. "What about three things you can hear?"

"Why are you doing this?" she asks, eyeing me warily.

I press my thumb against the pulse point near her wrist and feel her heartbeat finally starting to slow to a normal pace. "Just keep going."

"Fine. The loud sound of the jet engines. The flight attendant talking to someone about the drink options. And your voice."

I don't know why she keeps mentioning me. We'll go with the fact that she's in a state of panic and I'm the only person on this plane she has a history with. Er, not a *romantic* history. But just someone that knows her.

I nod. "Now, two things you can smell."

"The smell of the Clorox wipes I'm sure you cleaned your seat down with before I got here. And the disgusting stench coming from the bathroom. I think they're going to need a biohazard team for whatever happened in there."

I bite the inside of my cheek and wrinkle my nose. She's not wrong about either. "How about one thing you can taste?"

Her gaze drops to my lips, and I really wish I had used the beard grooming kit my sister's boyfriend—also known as the famous actor, Griffin Reynolds—bought me for Christmas. I've been wearing my beard longer than usual, and it's gotten a little unruly, but the way Shayna is examining my mouth makes it seem like she doesn't mind.

Why is she looking at my lips? A rush of heat spreads up my neck.

I swallow hard as she slowly drags her eyes from my mouth up to my eyes, her cheeks flushed. "Does my horrible morning breath count?"

A small laugh slips out before I can stop it. It sounds dead coming from my lips, like it needs a good dose of happiness to bring it back to life.

Shayna finally smiles, making her look more like the girl I remember. "Did I just hear Connor Porter *laugh*?" She loosens her hold on my hand but doesn't fully let go. "I don't think I've ever heard you laugh before."

She probably hasn't. I don't laugh. Or even smile. It's not that there aren't things in life worth being happy about, but I've learned that the more stoic and quiet you are, the fewer questions people ask you. And the fewer questions people ask, the fewer opportunities for me to mess up or say the wrong thing.

I school my features. "I'll allow morning breath to count."

"You forgot the horrible part." She smiles again, making it look easy.

"I'll allow *horrible* morning breath to count."

"Thank you." Shayna blushes. I'm not sure why. Morning breath is nothing to be embarrassed about. Happens to the best of us. She finally grants my captive hand its freedom. I let it fall back into my lap. "Now will you please explain why you just asked me a bunch of random questions?"

"Learned it in my firefighter training. It's an exercise to help someone feel more grounded when they're experiencing a panic attack." I slide my hand back into my pocket. "Do you get them a lot?"

"Not too often anymore. Mainly when I'm dealing with heights or feeling super stressed or overwhelmed about something." She pulls at the collar of her sweatshirt but suddenly stops, dropping both hands and her gaze to her lap. I follow the movement, and my eyes catch on the logo of her hoodie.

Or should I say, *my* hoodie.

On the right side of her chest are barely legible words that read *Waggener Wildcats Baseball* with the faded outline of our school's mascot underneath. It's the sweatshirt I wore every game day of baseball season, but I lost it my senior year before I left for college. Or, at least, I *thought* I'd lost it.

"Is that mine?" I ask.

Shayna worries her bottom lip as her eyes slowly drag up my torso before finally meeting my eyes. I shift uncomfortably in my seat. "I'm sorry."

I look at her, waiting for her to continue. That was a tactic I learned early on in my life, when words were hard for me to come by. If I stay quiet, most people will continue to fill the space, either giving me time to figure out what I want to say or letting me not say anything at all.

"I should've given it back, but…" She shoves her hands into the oversized pocket. "I'm sorry. I know you didn't give it to me to keep."

"Give it to you?" I think I'd remember giving my favorite sweatshirt away.

"Yeah." Her brows furrow. "You let me borrow it at one of your baseball games in your senior year. Remember?" I keep my mouth shut, and she continues. "It started raining and your game was delayed partway through." When I don't say anything, she leans forward and keeps explaining. "I was there with your mom and Mal. They both thought ahead and brought rain jackets, but I was only wearing a T-shirt and got soaked."

The memory—one I'd apparently blocked out of my mind—comes back to me in an instant.

We're in the middle of the fourth inning against our biggest rival when the gray sky dumps buckets onto everyone. My team runs back into the dugout as the umpire calls a delay of game. When I look at the bleachers, I see Shayna sitting next to my sister and mom. They're huddled together, but I can see Shayna shivering, even from this far away. Then I notice how her light gray T-shirt clings to her skin. My mom and Mallory are fine in their rain jackets, but I can't let Shayna freeze.

I go to my bag, digging through it. I don't have a rain jacket or umbrella to offer her, but I do have my lucky sweatshirt. The one I wear before every game, regardless of the temperature. I grab it and run out in the downpour. My uniform sticks to my body within seconds. Drops roll off the brim of my baseball hat as I carefully make my way up the bleachers to them.

I extend the sweatshirt to Shayna. She looks up at me with her big brown eyes as her dark hair sticks to her face in clumps.

"You sure?" she asks, hesitant.

I nod, and she takes it from me, her cold fingers brushing mine. Shayna pulls it over her head, takes off her pearl headband, repositions it back on her head, and pulls some of her hair back from her face. She slides her hands into the large pocket and sighs happily, even as the rain continues to fall around us.

"Thanks." She smiles up at me, looking like the sun amidst the storm around us. I half expect a rainbow to appear.

I dip my chin again and turn around, returning to my teammates in the dugout as the rain begins letting up. We start playing again soon after, but I can hardly focus. I make more errors in this game than I've ever made in my life. My eyes keep drifting to her in the stands, cheering me on in my *sweatshirt.*

My teammates razz me for the rest of the season, but I don't care. Seeing Shayna smiling in the bleachers and no longer shivering is worth all the teasing.

"Right," I grumble, and avert my gaze, keeping my expression neutral. Guess I didn't lose my sweatshirt after all.

CHAPTER THREE
SHAYNA

THERE'S NOT AN OUNCE of recognition of the memory in Connor's eyes. I'd even take a smidgeon. I glance at him again because I'm an idiot.

No, scratch that. I'm not an idiot. I'm an optimistic person. A firm believer in true love. A hopeless romantic.

But whatever I am, it doesn't matter, because he's unreadable. His face is a stoic mask that I can't see past.

I guess that makes me an optimistic idiot.

Why did I ever think he'd remember giving me his sweatshirt?

Just because it's a core memory in my mind doesn't mean it meant anything to him. He probably was just trying to be nice to his sister's friend, especially in front of his mom.

I used to think I was an expert at reading Connor Porter—that I could see through the mask he wears—but I think I've lost my touch. Or maybe I never knew him as well as I thought I did. That thought stings like the prick of a thorn from a rose stem.

I fidget with my hands in the sweatshirt pocket. I don't want to give up the one piece I have of Connor, but it doesn't seem like I have much of a choice now. "I'll make sure to wash it and get it back to you. How long will you be in town?"

He presses his lips into a firm line.

I was embarrassed before about my appearance, but now that Connor has seen me in *his* sweatshirt, my ratty sweatpants, and my panic-induced state, I'm not embarrassed. No, I'm *mortified*. It's becoming more obvious by the minute that he doesn't want to talk to me. I wish his obvious indifference would knock this silly childhood crush out of me, but it hangs on like the last petals on a flower in a spring breeze.

I like to think it's because I'm resilient…but it's probably just because of the optimistic idiot thing.

I'm so lost in my own mortification that I barely hear his delayed, whispered response. "Indefinitely."

"What?" My eyes shoot to his, searching for any other explanation for his answer. Because there's no way he just told me he's going to be staying in Louisville *indefinitely*.

Connor swallows hard. "I'm moving back."

I take a deep breath, trying to stay calm. "To Louisville?"

He nods.

"You're moving back. To Louisville." I repeat the words slowly, trying to let them sink in as truth.

My childhood crush is going to be living in the same zip code as me again. I should be thrilled. Overjoyed. Ecstatic. And I would be…if I thought I stood a chance at being with him.

It's already hard enough to see Connor when he visits around the holidays. To have small blips where he returns to my life and serves as a very muscular, very handsome reminder that all other men are ruined for me because all my heart seems to want is this off-limits, indifferent man.

Connor cups my face. The rough calluses on his palms brush my skin. My mind creates images of him in his turnout pants held up by red suspenders and wearing a tight muscle tee, a fire hose in his hands. No, better yet, an axe. Like a hot-lumberjack firefighter.

My body tingles with awareness. If his hands weren't in the way, I'd reach up to make sure I'm not drooling.

No more thinking about his hands. Or his muscular body. Or Connor in general.

Although, that's a little difficult to do with him sitting right next to me, his hands on my face.

"What're you doing?" I ask.

He tilts my chin up with his thumb with a gentleness I wouldn't expect from a man who runs into burning buildings for a living. "You're repeating everything I say. I think you might be in shock."

"I *am* in shock. But not the medical kind." I reach up and wrap my hands around his, lowering them to my lap, though he quickly pulls them back into his own space. "Mallory didn't mention you were moving back, is all."

When Connor doesn't respond, I look up to find his eyes fixed on the lavatory behind me. I can't think of a reason he'd rather be looking at that biohazard than me, unless…

"Your family doesn't know?"

No response.

"Where are you going to work?"

No response.

"Where are you going to live?"

No response.

I open my mouth, ready to continue my inquisition, but he cuts me off.

"Are you done interrogating me?" One of Connor's eyebrows rises slightly, almost as if he's amused.

"If you start answering my questions."

His lips twitch, not quite a smile. Mrs. Porter always complained about how he never even smiled for family photos. No one's getting a smile out of Connor Porter unless he wants to. So this little twitch of his lips? I consider it a win.

He sighs. "They don't know."

"Why doesn't your family know that you're moving across the country?"

"Didn't tell them," he says matter-of-factly.

"Why?"

He rubs the back of his neck, his mouth a firm line.

"Let me guess," I say. "In case you changed your mind?"

Connor grunts. "Something like that."

Looks like I still know *some* things about him. "I'm guessing you already have a job lined up?"

He nods. "It was a long process to obtain my Kentucky fire certification. I won't bore you with the details, but I recently accepted a position at Station 13."

I gasp. "Did you know—"

"Yes, I know it's Taylor Swift's favorite number."

"So you actually listened when the Long Live Girlies talked to you about her."

"Against my will and better judgment," he grumbles.

I grin. "Yet you're the one who still remembers her favorite number."

He shakes his head. "Looks like you're back to your normal self."

Connor's not wrong. He brought me down from the height of my anxiety. Part of it was because of his training and whatever that senses method he used was, but also because of who he is. Because he makes me feel alive.

"I feel a lot better." I tuck one leg up under me, trying to get more comfortable in the stiff plane seat. "Tell me all the hot gossip. What are you going to do at Station 13?"

Connor quirks a brow. "Are you calling it hot gossip because I put out fires?"

"It's a phrase people use. Try to keep up."

His jaw ticks. "I'm fine being left in the dark."

"That's fair." I laugh. "When Mal tells me some of the words the next generation comes up with, I feel the same way."

He runs a hand over his face. "I don't want to know. I'm still trying to get over YOLO."

I giggle. "Okay, tell me about this new job."

"I'll just be a probie."

"English, please?"

"It's what they call the new firefighter at the station. The actual term is *probationary firefighter*, but no one calls it that." Connor sighs. "I was up for lieutenant at my station in Seattle, so it will be a major step down the ladder."

"So you're basically starting over?"

He nods.

"But?" I prompt, my voice softer. Getting Connor to open up is like a fine art, one I'm trying to relearn after these years apart.

"But I thought it was time for me to come home."

This is it, my heart whispers. My chance to finally land the only man who has ever occupied my dreams. But my head tells me I need to let this silly crush go before I get burned by a fire not even the best of firefighters can put out.

CHAPTER FOUR

SHAYNA

I THOUGHT LIFE WOULD feel different, knowing Connor was back, but I've been home from the flower exhibition for a little over a week, and nothing's changed. Just like my unchanging dream: working with flowers.

When I started working at Shirley's Florist in my senior year in high school, it was surreal. I love what I get to do, the smiles I get to see on people's faces as they pick out bouquets for their loved ones. The people I get to bring together through the flowers I help them select.

I glance up from the bouquet I'm making to the photo hanging on the wall. The store's owner, Shirley, and I are surrounded by floral arrangements we crafted for a wedding and both smiling wide. She's become like a grandmother to me over the past six years. We have the kind of relationship now where she fully relies on me to take and make all of our orders while she sits and talks to me. I love listening to her regale me with her memories and share life advice.

It still feels unreal that, in just one short week, Shirley will be leaving this flower shop to me, and I'll be the owner. It will be the perfect distraction from the fact that Connor is back. Mallory told me that his parents were shocked when he showed up at their weekly family dinner. She even said her mom cried when Connor said he was back for good.

I grab another daisy from the table. Instead of adding it to the bouquet, I pluck the petals off one at a time.

He loves me. He loves me not. I continue until I pull the last petal. *He loves me.* I sigh, knowing it doesn't mean anything. It's just the silly daisy game I've played since I was a child. I'm a grown woman now who can't mistake Connor's kindness for infatuation, regardless of what the petals indicate.

I pick up another daisy and add it to the bouquet. In flower language, they're said to represent innocence and new beginnings. It's exactly what I need. A fresh start. To stop getting swallowed up in the past and hoping that Connor and I will ever be anything.

Inhaling a deep breath, I move to grab another bloom, but a burning smell tickles my nose. It's an old building, so I'm always hit with a gross burning scent whenever the heat kicks on, but I didn't know it was supposed to be cold enough today for that.

I attempt to keep making the bouquet. Shirley isn't in the shop today, so I'm on my own finishing this order. I add a few more flowers, but then I'm hit with another strong whiff of the burning smell that makes me cough. My heart pounds in my chest as I begin to panic.

Something isn't right.

I drop the unfinished bouquet on the worktable and cover my mouth with my elbow as another cough wracks my body. My eyes start to burn as I rush toward the door. What did they teach us to do when we were kids if there might be a fire? Now would be a really good time to have Connor's number so I could ask him.

I cough as the burning stench grows stronger. Looks like I don't have time to research it, either. I think I'm supposed to feel it with the back of my hand, so that's what I do. It's cool, so I move and quickly tap the back of my hand against the doorknob, relieved to find it's not hot either. If there's a fire, at least it's not too close to block my only escape.

"Please work for me, baby," I sweet-talk the doorknob. It's been finicky lately, so I jimmy the knob like I usually do, lifting it slightly while pushing against the door with my shoulder, but it doesn't budge.

I groan, which makes me break into another coughing fit. I told Shirley we needed to get this fixed.

The opening verse of "This Is Why We Can't Have Nice Things" by Taylor Swift begins to play over my Bluetooth speaker. If my future career—and potentially *my life*—is about to go up in flames, at least it's happening with my favorite singer playing in the background. I have to keep joking, even if it feels a little macabre, because it's the only way I'm keeping myself from full-on panicking right now.

The burning smell grows stronger as the pre-chorus hits. I pull my floral-patterned cardigan up over my mouth and nose with one hand as I scramble back to the worktable. My head pounds as I grab my phone and I clumsily unlock it to dial 911.

"911, what's your emergency?"

"Hi, I hope you're having a good day," I quickly say, despite my panic. "I'm at work and think there may possibly be a fire in my building. I smell something burning." I look back at the door and see a faint plume of smoke coming in. "And there's some smoke." I suck in a ragged breath, but it only makes me cough again.

The dispatcher gets my name and location and then says, "Okay, Shayna. The fire department is on its way. To your knowledge, is there anyone still in the building?"

"I am," I rasp, coughing harder.

"You need to leave immediately, ma'am. It's not safe for you to remain in the building."

"I would love to do that, but you see, I'm in the back room and the door is jammed. I can usually un-jam it, but it's not budging this time." I do my best to sound optimistic, despite the present circumstances and my internal panic. "I'm a little stuck, but I'm sure I'll figure something out."

The dispatcher's voice sounds slightly more alarmed as she says, "Stay in the back room, ma'am. The fire department should be there shortly, and they'll get you out. If you're able, get as low as you can on the ground and cover yourself with a blanket or a sweater as a barrier from the smoke."

"Okay, I will." My voice comes out raspy, my lungs burning from the smoke inhalation. I take my cardigan off, wrapping it around my head before pulling it back over my nose and mouth.

"I can stay on the line with you, if you'd like. They're about three minutes out."

"That's okay," I say, not wanting to be a bother. I'm sure there are other calls she needs to answer. I swallow hard, taking another shallow breath. "Thank you so much for your help."

"Okay, just try to stay calm, Shayna. Help will be there soon."

After I've hung up the phone, I grab all the current order tickets from our cabinet, stuffing them in my bag before sitting on the hardwood floor, as far away from the door as possible.

Shirley doesn't believe in using the internet, so she's always made me handle orders the old-fashioned way. It was nothing short of a miracle when I finally convinced her to have a landline installed for call-in orders and questions from customers. One of the first changes I had in mind when the business officially became mine was to implement an online order system. But who knows if there will even be a business left for me to inherit after this.

My body trembles and I begin feeling lightheaded. I grab my inhaler from my large work bag and slowly breathe in as I press down on the top of the canister. Smoke typically is the worst trigger for my asthma, so I repeat the action, hoping it helps until the fire department arrives.

Wrapping my cardigan more tightly around my mouth, I try to focus on my breathing, but each breath becomes more difficult. There's a loud crackling sound from outside the door, then a popping noise that makes me jump and break into another coughing fit.

The fire department will be here any minute. Then I'll be out of here. I'm not trapped. I'm just temporarily stuck.

Stating the facts doesn't seem like it's doing much to slow my racing heart, so I try to think back on the questions Connor asked me on the plane. I think the first one was five things I can see. The smoke coming through the door is an obvious answer. My unfinished bouquet on the table. The water stains on the ceiling. My cardigan pulled over my face.

A pounding on the door breaks my concentration. "Louisville FD. Anyone in there?"

"Yes," I croak. "Help." The two words are small, but they make my chest feel even heavier. I cough from the effort of speaking and wrap my free arm around my knees, praying they heard me.

"Stand back," a masculine voice shouts. I think I'm going crazy because I hear the firm command in Connor's voice.

A second later, a tall figure dressed in tan turnouts comes barreling into the room. I need to figure out what workout routine he does at the fire station because he just knocked that door down with only his body like it was nothing.

There it is, the fifth thing I see: the firefighter here to save my life. He looks around the small space before finding me. The firefighter takes fast steps toward me.

I try to stand, but the small exertion sends me into another coughing fit. He rushes forward, wrapping one arm around my middle and the other under my legs. The way he scoops me up like I weigh nothing is impressive.

I look at his face to thank him, but the words get lost in my mouth because there's no mistaking those hazel eyes. Not even the mask he wears is enough to hide the fact that the concerned eyes that are looking at me right now are the same ones that looked at me on that plane.

I wasn't going crazy from smoke inhalation or thinking I was on the brink of death.

Connor Porter is my firefighter in shining tan armor. The man here to save my life. And after seeing him in his turnouts in the flesh…I'm not sure I'll ever be able to get this image out of my mind. And I'm not sure I want to.

CHAPTER FIVE

CONNOR

I PRIDE MYSELF ON being levelheaded on the job. When you're the one running into fires rather than away from them, you kind of have to be.

But the second I spot Shayna cowering on the hardwood floor in the back room, fear grips my chest. The kind of fear that feels suffocating and makes you lose all common sense.

I knew she worked at a flower shop, but I didn't know she worked at *this* one.

It feels like I'm having an out-of-body experience as my feet carry me toward Shayna. I lift her into my arms and look into her eyes, hoping that she can see what I'm unable to say with the fear overwhelming me.

Everything's okay now.

You're safe.

I've got you.

I jog through the building, and we pass two members of my crew who are actively putting out the fire in the main room. The scent of burning flowers mixed with smoke is like charred perfume.

Shayna whimpers in my arms as she takes in the scene around us, and I feel for her. I'm sure this place is like a second home after all the years she's worked here. I think Mallory even mentioned that Shayna was supposed to be taking the shop over soon. Watching her future go up in smoke can't be easy.

I cradle her closer, telling myself it's just to protect her as much as possible from the smoke. But when Shayna burrows her face into my chest, it feels like more than that. A thought I immediately shove down. This is Mallory's friend I'm thinking about.

When we finally make it out the front door, I take Shayna over to the ambulance, setting her gently on the stretcher. The EMTs place an oxygen mask over her mouth and nose and begin evaluating her body for burns.

I take off my mask and helmet and lean into my training, focusing on the patient I just saved rather than worrying about the fact that I know who is currently on the stretcher. "I have a twenty-four-year-old female suffering from smoke inhalation. She's alert and oriented." I think back to what happened on the plane. "But she has asthma."

I look to Shayna as she pulls her oxygen mask down. I bend down to pull it back up, but she places her free hand on mine to stop me.

"Thank you," she rasps. "For saving my life."

"Just doing my job." I place the oxygen mask back over her nose and mouth. "I know it's hard for you, but try not to talk. And keep this on, okay?"

Shayna shoots me a glare, but I can see a small playful smile on her lips under the mask.

"Porter. Give me a status update," Captain Dalton says over the radio.

I turn away from Shayna and press the button on the side of my radio. "I've evacuated the civilian from the building, sir."

"Copy that," he booms back. "Barnes. Fisher. Status on the fire?"

"We have it eighty percent contained, Captain," Barnes's soft but sure voice comes through. I'm only on my first week at the station, and she's already become someone I respect immensely—not just because of her position as a lieutenant, but because of the way she leads with confidence and kindness.

"Is the building…" Shayna pauses to cough. I turn around, ready to chastise her for not keeping the oxygen mask on. "…going to make it?"

I shoot her a look, and she places it back on her face. "They have most of the fire contained, but it'll be up to a building inspector to see if the structure is safe."

Her shoulders rise and fall in a sigh, making her cough again. I close the distance between us and place a hand on her shoulder. "I'm sure you have a lot of questions, and there will be time to get answers later. For now, I need you to focus on breathing into this mask." I tap it gently with my pointer finger. "Just breathe, Shay."

An EMT walks up. "Your numbers aren't quite where we'd like for them to be, likely because of your asthma. We're going to take you to the hospital for further evaluation."

Shayna shoots her a thumbs-up. My heart begins pounding in my chest, an unfamiliar rhythm. I examine her. Watching each breath she takes fog the mask slowly settles my own fear. She's breathing. Even if her oxygen stats aren't great, she's breathing.

"Porter, I want you to back up Barnes and Fisher."

"Copy, Captain," I say, shooting one last glance back at Shayna. She waves as they load her into the ambulance. I lift my gloved hand before putting my helmet and mask back on and jogging toward the building. I grab a spare hose and run into the flower shop. After quickly making my way back to my crew, I join them in spraying water onto the fire.

Once we have the fire fully contained, I survey the damage. I don't need a building inspector to know that this is bad news for Shayna. Because, from the looks of things, this building won't be ready to reopen anytime soon.

———— ♡ ♡ ♡ ————

"You missed a spot, probie." Gordon snickers as he drops crumbs from his crumbly granola bar onto the cement floor I just finished sweeping.

It took me a total of about five minutes to realize he's the self-declared leader—and also the sole member—of the hazing committee, even though he's also an unranked fire-fighter like me. The rest of the crew rolls their eyes, but I don't make a sound as I sweep up the mess he made before hanging the broom back in its spot.

I'd never want to be friends with someone who *enjoys* eating that poor, crumbly excuse for a granola bar, anyway.

"Knock it off, Gordon." Fisher offers me a sympathetic smile as he walks past.

I understand I'm new to this station, but I already have nine years of firefighting experience under my belt. So, while I'm technically the rookie at this station, I appreciate that everyone isn't bent on hazing the "new" guy.

"We've all been through the hazing. It's just a little team bonding." Gordon appears behind me, clapping me on the shoulder. "Right, probie?"

"Mm," I mumble.

I don't agree with what Gordon's been doing all week. I've never actively participated in hazing a probie, but I also know how much keeping the peace with your crew matters. Because when I'm at work, they're my family—sometimes a dysfunctional one, but a family nonetheless. You have to rely on your brothers and sisters to have your back. If I have to put up with a little bit of hazing, so be it.

"Porter," Captain calls from outside his office on the second floor, overlooking the vehicle bay. "I want you to go to the hospital and do a wellness check on the civilian you pulled out of the fire."

My stomach drops like I'm rappelling off the side of the cliff with no traction. I get a handle on whatever emotion is making me feel like I'm in freefall enough to respond. "Copy that, Cap." I turn to Fisher, adjusting the collar of my short-sleeved navy duty shirt. "Are wellness checks a thing you do often?"

Fisher nods. "When things are slower at the station. It's good for community morale."

"Right," I grunt. "I'll see y'all later, then." I rub the back of my neck. After grabbing my wallet and car keys from my locker, I head to my truck and take the long way to the hospital. I park in the visitor lot and make my way into the emergency room. The woman working the help desk's smile grows flirtatious when she sees the Louisville Fire Department logo on my shirt.

"I'm looking for Shayna Monroe's room. She was brought in after a fire." I slide my hands into my pockets and rock on my heels.

"Happy to help a public servant like you."

It takes all my willpower to not cringe at her seductive tone.

Rather than telling me where to go, she gets up and escorts me to Shayna's room, touching my arm way too much for my liking along the way. I don't think this kind of private tour is usually her job, and I can think of at least five HIPAA violations for leaving her desk with the computer still open. But I ignore them all as my stomach swirls with worry. Both for Shayna's well-being and the thought of potentially seeing her family and being asked a bunch of questions.

"Here you are." The woman wraps her hand around my forearm. "If you need anything—and I do mean *any-thing*—please stop by my desk on your way out."

I'll take things I will not be doing for $1000, Alex. Maybe a little *Jeopardy* humor will make her words feel less…gross.

"Thanks." I extricate my arm from her grasp and clumsily back into the door, making her giggle. I turn around faster than I've ever moved in my life and knock on the door. The second I hear someone say "come in," I practically jump into the room, closing the door behind me to create a barricade in case that woman thought my thanking her was an invitation.

When I look back, I find seven pairs of eyes fixed on me. "This is a fire violation."

"Good thing I have a firefighter for a brother who can protect us." Mallory comes over, pulling me into a hug. "Thank you for saving Shay," she whispers in my ear.

Mr. and Mrs. Monroe and Shayna's little sister, Reagan, join us, wrapping their arms around me in a group hug. My shoulders stiffen, but I accept it because I know this is their way of showing gratitude.

"We can never repay you for saving our girl." Tears brim in Mr. Monroe's eyes. His wife nods along, tears falling steadily down her cheeks.

Before I know it, Kelsey and Alyssa have joined in on the hug fest. I've become a human tissue for snot and tears at this point. I don't like hugs. I don't even really like being touched. I'm a reserved person. I have been ever since I was a child. It led to me being called every name in the book. Grumpy. Standoffish. Rude. Prickly. Bearish. Unfriendly. You name it, I've heard it.

Shayna is probably the one person who has never seen me as any of those things. She sees me for who I am—an introverted, reserved, stoic man who is scared of saying the wrong thing, so I just never say anything at all. At least, that's what she told me back when we were in high school—before I left her and my family behind to escape to Seattle where I could live my curmudgeon life in solitude.

I thought I would stay there forever and live my life in blissful solitude. But then there was Jillian. And I started to think life would be better lived with someone else by my side…until she left and reminded me exactly why a solitary life is all I'm cut out for.

I run a hand through my hair, refusing to waste another second thinking about *her* when I have a civilian wellness check to complete. I look over everyone's heads at the hospital bed in the center of the room. Shayna looks better than she did a few hours ago. She offers me a smile and a weak wave. I'm happy to see that she's okay, but the way she's looking at me has me feeling uneasy.

There's admiration in her eyes. Like I'm some prince charming who saved her from a tower. Though, I suppose I did just save her life. But I was only doing my job.

Mrs. Monroe releases her hold on me, triggering a domino effect as everyone steps back, finally granting me my personal space. "It was nice of you to come check on her," she says.

"The station sent me." I don't miss Shayna's wince at my words, making me feel like a jerk. I didn't realize how rude that would sound until it was already coming out of my mouth. It seems I always say the wrong thing, one of the reasons I try to say as little as possible. "How're you doing?" I ask Shayna.

The smile she gives me this time looks forced. "The nebulizer treatment they gave me did the trick."

"Glad to hear it." I fold my arms across my chest and look down at my boots. "I should get back to the station. Captain just wanted to make sure you were doing all right." I move toward the door.

"Connor, what about the shop?" The shakiness in Shayna's usually optimistic voice stops me in my tracks.

"The initial inspection usually happens within two days. They'll inform the owner and insurance company of their findings."

"You've seen situations like this before, though, right?" I turn back and watch Shayna anxiously wring her hands in her lap. "Do you have any idea how soon we'll be able to reopen?"

I run a hand through my beard, the coarse texture grounding me. "I can't say." When my gaze meets hers again, I wish I hadn't looked up. Because seeing the light in her eyes dim is as painful as a second-degree burn. "Sorry. I wish I had more information for you."

"It's not your fault." Her words are high-pitched and squeaky, like she's choked up and can barely get them out.

I hang my head, feeling like I made this day ten times worse for her than it already was. This is exactly why I'm better off not saying anything at all.

CHAPTER SIX
SHAYNA

TODAY'S THE DAY I should be taking over ownership of Shirley's Florist. Instead, I'm sitting next to Shirley on her stiff paisley couch, which she likely hasn't replaced since the '90s, in her excessively warm apartment—seriously, it feels like a sauna in here—waiting to hear whatever news she called me over to share.

"I heard back from the fire inspector yesterday." Her eyes fall to the teacup in her hands. "The structural integrity of the building was compromised."

That doesn't sound good.

"What does that mean?" I ask.

With a shaky hand, Shirley places her teacup on the coffee table before leaning over and taking my hands in hers. "It will cost more to repair the building than it's worth."

"No." I shake my head in disbelief. "I was there. It didn't seem that bad." Not that I was really looking around much when I had my head buried in Connor's chest as he carried me to safety… "Do—" I clear the emotion from my throat. "Do they know what caused it?"

"They said it was an electrical fire, likely caused by out-dated outlets." Shirley shrugs, looking more frail than usual, as if this situation has taken its toll on her.

I hang my head. "I should've done more."

"There's nothing you could've done, sweetie." She pats my hand.

As someone who loves to fix things, I hate that there's nothing I can do. That I'm letting Shirley, and myself, down. My little sister, Reagan, would tell me to let it be, that this is how things were meant to happen. To follow whatever path life takes me on.

But what am I supposed to do when the path I'm going down isn't leading where I hoped? In fact, it's leading in the exact opposite direction of everything I've spent years working toward.

I shake my head. I'm being selfish. It's an absolute honor that Shirley was going to entrust the business she built to me. She's the one who lost everything. I'll just have to find another flower shop to work at until I've saved up enough to open one of my own. Or maybe this is a sign from the universe that I'm not meant to run my own business.

"Are you still able to retire?" I ask.

"Of course, dear. Thank goodness for good insurance." Shirley offers me a sad smile. "I'm sad that you won't be able to carry on with the flower shop." She lets go of my hands, reaches for an envelope on the side table, and hands it to me. "But you've become family, and I want to give you what I can."

I look from the envelope to her.

"Well, what are you waiting for?" She tilts her head, making her gray bob sway. "Go on. Open it."

I slide my thumb under the seal and carefully open it before pulling out a check. The number written on it makes my eyes go wide. "Shirley, did you accidentally add extra zeros?"

"Consider it your severance package. I want you to use it to set up your future career. Buy your own shop." Her eyes light up. "Better yet, buy one of those flower trucks you're always looking at on Tickity Tock and The Gram."

I bite the inside of my bottom lip, holding back a laugh. I'm honestly impressed she was that close to the app names with her severe lack of social media knowledge. I mean, I had to fight the woman to add a *landline*.

She's not wrong, though. I've scrolled through posts and videos of mobile flower trucks for countless hours.

"I don't know." I hug my middle. I've always thought it was a cute idea…for someone else. I never thought about any other possibility when I was set to take over Shirley's Florist. "I'm sure those trucks are expensive."

Shirley taps the check. "This will more than cover it. I had one of the ladies' grandkids look it up at book club the other day." She leans back into the couch. "And, some positive news, the greenhouse is still functional since it's not attached to the shop, so you can still grow flowers there and connect with the local growers we usually source the rest from."

"You're serious?"

"As serious as a heart attack."

I've never liked that saying; it sounds morbid. But with the resolute expression on Shirley's face, I can tell she means it.

"You think I could run my own flower truck?" My voice is barely above a whisper, afraid that speaking it aloud will suddenly allow me to dream.

"I don't think so." She shakes her head, reaching over and grasping my hand in her wrinkled one. Despite her age, she still has quite the grip. "I *know* so. You can do anything you put your mind to, Shayna Monroe."

My eyes well with tears, humbled that she thinks so highly of me. That she believes in me, maybe even more than I believe in myself.

"Thank you." I lean forward and pull Shirley into a hug. "I wouldn't be where I am without you."

"The feeling's mutual, dear." She squeezes me tight. "You let me know when your new venture is open for business so I can be your first customer."

I pull back and smile when I see the warmth and pride in her eyes. "Deal."

♡ ♡ ♡

"Have y'all ever thought about how lucky we are to be alive at the time when the Jonas Brothers are touring again?" I pop a piece of popcorn into my mouth. "My middle school self is thriving."

"Okay, I completely agree with you." Kelsey shoots me a look that tells me there's a *but* coming. "But I'm guessing that's not what you called an emergency roommate meeting mid-week for."

"What if I just wanted to talk to my besties?" I tease, giving them my best doe-eyes and innocent smile.

"I should be offended that you're teasing about our friendship, but I'll let it slide." Mallory crosses her legs up under her and grabs the pink chunky-knit blanket from the back of the couch, spreading it across her lap.

Alyssa runs her hand over her already smooth blonde waves. "I gave up my evening Pilates class for this tea, so spill it, sister." She attempts to shoot me a stern look but fails, her eyes crinkling at the corners and her lips tilting up into a small smile.

"Yes, tell us," Kelsey agrees.

"Before we die," Mallory adds.

Alyssa shoves her shoulder. "You can't say that when she could have died in the flower shop fire."

A passing image of smoke slowly filling the back room of the flower shop flashes in my mind. I shake my head, forcing away the memory. That experience was terrifying, but I refuse to dwell on it. I won't lie, there have been a few nights I've tossed and turned more than slept, but I'm choosing not to let one scary moment steal my joy. Life is too short to be anything but positive.

"Yeah, *could have.*" Mallory emphasizes the words with a sassy tilt of her head. She fiercely loves the people in her circle and would do anything for them, but I think the only way she can deal with the thought of me being stuck in a burning building is with humor.

I smile good-naturedly. If that's what she needs, I'll gladly play along. Isn't that the true definition of a friend—putting someone else's needs above your own? The same can be said for romantic relationships, but I can't think about that. Because if I start thinking about dating, my mind instantly goes to Connor Porter. And I cannot have thoughts about how attractive he is when I'm sitting across from his sister.

"Ditto, what they all said," Tess says, snapping me back to reality. "Well, maybe except the dying part."

Tess joined our friend group only a few months ago when her younger brother, Tyler, started dating Kelsey. Even though we've only known her for a short time, she fits right in as if she's been right by our sides since middle school. She's a piece of the puzzle we didn't know we were missing. Not to mention the fact that her daughter, Evie, is the sweetest little girl that's become our honorary niece.

Mallory waves her hand in front of me. "Hello? Earth to Shayna."

"Fine," I concede. "I had my meeting with Shirley today, and the structural integrity of the shop is compromised from the fire."

They all share a worried look, and I understand their hesitation. My friends know how excited I was to become a flower shop owner.

"What does that mean for Shirley's retirement?" Alyssa dances around the question I'm sure she really wants to ask—what does it mean for my future career?

"She's still going to retire." I wring my hands in my lap. "But now there's no building or business for her to leave to me."

"Oh, Shay." Kelsey reaches over and grasps my hand as the rest of our friends get up from their usual spots.

Tears fill my eyes as the girls I love like sisters pull me in for a group hug. As they hold me in the silence, I feel safe enough to let out everything I've been holding in. The tears begin to pour down my cheeks as I'm surrounded by their support.

When I finally pull back, Tess dabs under her eyes, a true empath. "I'm so sorry."

Alyssa frowns. "We know how much that shop meant to you."

"Thanks." They return to their seats as I wipe my face, feeling lighter than I have all week. "I really needed that." I let out a watery laugh as Kelsey's golden retriever, Winston, runs over and jumps up, placing his front paws on my lap like he needs to be part of the action, too. I scratch his head, and he licks my hand before jumping back down and sitting in front of Kelsey.

"Is no one else going to ask the obvious question?" Mallory looks around and sighs when no one says anything. She turns to me, her eyes softer than usual. Maybe it's from the fact that she's now dating the famous actor, Griffin Reynolds. Love has a way of softening a person. But I also think she's always had a soft spot for me, the yin to her yang. We're complete opposites, but I think that's what makes us such wonderful friends. She encourages me to stand up for myself and would defend me to the grave, while I help her have a more positive outlook on life.

Mallory's voice is gentle and more careful as she asks, "What are you going to do now?"

I shrug. "Shirley has this crazy idea."

"We love crazy ideas." Kelsey wraps her arms around Winston. He looks up at me and tilts his head, making his ears flop. We've always said he has the craziest personality of any dog, but in this moment, I'm half convinced he understands us and is saying that he agrees.

"I fake-dated a celebrity—I don't think it gets much crazier than that," Mallory agrees.

"That you're now completely in love with," Alyssa adds, smoothing her hands on her workout leggings.

Mallory chucks a pillow at her. "It was still crazy."

Alyssa catches the pillow midair and places it on her lap. "Yeah, it was kind of crazy."

"But y'all encouraged me to do it, and look where I am now." Mallory takes down her curly brown hair from its messy bun just to flip her head over and pull it up into another one. "So maybe Shirley's idea isn't really out there."

"We'll be the judges of that," Kelsey says.

I tell them everything—from how Shirley said that I'd still be able to use the greenhouse to the generous check she gave me as a severance package, ending with her suggestion about the mobile business. When I'm done, I take a deep breath. "I mean, it's ridiculous, right? I can't just buy a flower truck."

Mallory furrows her brow. "Why not?"

"I never thought about anything other than becoming the owner of Shirley's Florist. I mean, I've worked there since my senior year in high school."

"It's what you know," Tess says.

I nod. "I'm happy there. It's comfortable."

Mallory opens and closes her mouth a few times before saying, "No, it's safe."

My eyes shoot to hers. "What do you mean?"

"Not in a bad way—it's just who you are." Mallory places her elbow on the armrest and lets her chin fall into her palm. "You like stability. You're the kind of girl that has a backup plan for a backup plan."

"I do plan a lot for the future, but losing the business to a fire wasn't a possibility I ever thought of." I let out a dry laugh. "So, what does that mean for me? The girl who always has a plan that's now planless."

Kelsey tucks one foot up under her lap and turns to face me. "Let me ask you this: Is there any other reason you have for not buying a flower truck aside from the fact that you planned on running the flower shop?"

I close my eyes and really think about her question. "I guess the thought of something I'm unfamiliar with is terrifying."

"The unknown," Tess says.

Alyssa wraps her arms around the pillow on her lap. "I don't think anyone likes their future being uncertain."

"But you have this gift from Shirley to set you down whatever path you want." Kelsey nudges my thigh with her knee. "And you've sent us lots of videos of those cute flower trucks."

Mallory blows out a low whistle. "So many videos." She shoots me a meaningful look. "I think you should take a chance on yourself, Shay."

Alyssa nods. "I know the thought of a new path is scary, but if that's what you want, you won't be doing it alone."

"You have us," Tess agrees.

"Forevermore," Kelsey says, our version of a promise. One that means I love you and that we're friends—*family*—forever.

The more I sit with the idea, the more it feels like the perfect next step. A mobile flower truck owner. I never even thought of it as a possibility, but listening to everything my friends are saying, it just feels…right.

The unknown of having a moving business is still scary. But with support like this—I look around the room at my best friends—I know I can do anything.

"I think that's what I want," I say, struggling to believe that this is happening. "I can't imagine a life where I'm not working with flowers."

"They're more than just flowers to you," Alyssa points out.

Truer words have never been spoken. To some, flowers are just something you put in a vase and enjoy looking at on occasion. But they're so much more than that.

Flowers mean being around for people's weddings, birthdays, and milestones.

Flowers say what words often can't. *I'm thinking about you. You're loved. I notice everything you do, and I appreciate you.*

Flowers are the reason someone has a smile on their face. To put it simply, flowers are a token of love and magic.

And if I can start my own business where I get to drive around and sell bouquets to different people and play a small part in that…well, I can't think of a better purpose.

I nod with finality. "I'm going to do it. I'm going to open my own mobile flower truck."

Before I know it, everyone is on their feet, and I'm wrapped in another warm blend of hugs, giggles, and happy tears.

These are the nights I live for. Solid moments of girlhood where we talk about our dreams and share our lives. Even though a few of us have fallen in love—and some of us, namely *me*, are trying to ignore their complicated feelings—we always make time for each other. I don't know what I did to get so lucky to call these friends mine, but I wouldn't trade our friendship, our *sisterhood*, for the world.

Once we're all sitting again, Mallory asks, "So, this is really happening?"

I nod. "Once I find the right truck and figure out the business side of things."

Alyssa grabs her phone off the coffee table. "I'll text Austin and see if he can reach out to his agent about some local lawyers. They might be able to help you with the business side of things."

"I'm not sure I'll be able to afford the kind of lawyers Austin would use." I purse my lips.

Alyssa's best guy friend, Austin Bradford, is the starting shortstop for the Louisville Mustangs. I don't think I could afford a normal lawyer, let alone one recommended by an MLB player or his agent. He probably makes more money in one contract than I'll make in my entire life.

"Is there a certain kind of truck you want?" Tess grabs her phone out of her purse. "We can help you look for one."

"Agreed." Kelsey and Mallory pull out their devices, and the three of them look at me expectantly as if they're prepared to type at record speed in a race to see who can find me a flower truck first.

"I've always liked the look of converted Volkswagen Buses," I say. "It has a vintage feel while still being cute and approachable."

Kelsey glances up at me. "Any specific year or color?"

"No, but one that's already been renovated to sell things would be ideal." I don't even want to think about how much work that would take or, namely, how much those changes would cost.

Alyssa finishes texting Austin and jumps in to help as we all scour the internet for any renovated Volkswagen Buses for sale. Most of the ones we find are tens of thousands out of my price range. I'm about to give up for the night when Mallory tilts her head.

"Okay, it needs some TLC, but this one is in your price range. Plus, it's only an hour drive away." She turns her phone, showing me a 1972 VW Transporter.

It needs some serious work, but I can see the vision. A new plan for my future flashes in my mind. I'm selling flowers at a market. The rust is gone, and a fresh coat of paint coats the truck. The back of the vehicle is filled with specially made wood stands and galvanized metal vases holding bouquets for sale. And a canopy covers the top, finishing off the vintage look.

"It's perfect." My eyes probably look like ones from those old cartoons, with hearts shooting out. My friends look at me like I've lost my sanity. "Or at least, it will be once I get it fixed up." I laugh. "Do any of you know someone who's good at fixing and building things? And also knows a good automobile painting place?"

"I think it's called car restoration," Mallory teases. "But I know just the person to help."

"Don't tell me Griffin details cars and builds things in his spare time." Tess wraps her arms around her middle. "That man needs to leave some talent for the rest of us."

"No, not Griffin. Although he is good with—"

Alyssa holds up a hand. "You can spare us the intimate details."

"Get your mind out of the gutter." Mallory smirks, feigning innocence. "I was going to say, he's good at all the little details. He's such a romantic." She looks back at me. "The actual solution for all your problems is Connor."

My stomach drops.

"He has multiple days a week off when he's not on shift at the fire station." Mallory smiles widely, like she just handed me the solution to all my problems on a silver platter. I'm not sure she'd be looking at me like that if she knew the kind of thoughts I've been having for her brother since the fire. Really, since the plane ride. Okay, actually, since I met him in sixth grade.

I swallow hard, thinking of his calloused, strong hands cupping my face on the plane and how effortlessly he lifted me with them in the flower shop. I think I'm in need of a good fire hose to the face to wash them away, and even that may not be enough.

Mallory starts typing on her phone again, and I panic-vomit out a bunch of words. "He just moved back, and I already inconvenienced him by having to save my life." I wipe my brow, not wanting to show how much the thought of working alongside Connor makes me sweat. "I'm sure there's someone else who can—"

"I already texted him. It's settled."

Wonderful. I duck my chin and press my lips into a firm line.

"Do you have any ideas for a business name?" Tess asks. I've never been more grateful for a change in topic in my life.

Picking a name before I've officially bought the flower truck feels a little premature, but it also feels invigorating. It makes it feel *real*.

I say the first thing that pops into my mind. "Sunshine Blooms." It feels right. True to the light I believe flowers bring to people's lives.

"I'm really going to do this," I whisper to myself, in awe that this is all happening.

"Yeah, you are," my friends echo back. The way they have such unwavering confidence in me has me overflowing with joy and feeling brave.

I pull my phone back out and click the link Mallory sent me to the run-down VW Transporter. Before I can second-guess myself, I select the button to make an offer.

CHAPTER SEVEN
CONNOR

I STARE AT THE text I received from Mallory last night. I haven't responded yet because I know better than to argue with the force that is my sister. But I have some serious concerns about her message, starting with the fact that I have no clue what she's roped me into.

> Hi, Con Con! Just a little FYI that I signed you up to help Shayna with something.

I heave a sigh and type out a response.

It's Mallory's planning period at school, so I see the three dots signaling that she's typing back almost immediately.

I clench my free hand into a small fist, trying to ignore the fact that sounds like a *Dateline* episode waiting to
happen. *Not my problem.* It goes against all my protective
instincts, but she's an adult and can make that decision on
her own.

Already covered that, Einstein. What did you volunteer me for?

MALLORY

I think it's better if you see it with your own eyes.

Fine.

MALLORY

You're the best brother ever—love you!

I run a hand over my beard. The scruffy feel of it usually grounds me, but right now, it has me feeling self-conscious about seeing Shayna. I know she already saw me like this—twice. And she stared at my lips. I push that thought far from my mind. But I let myself go a little while living out in Seattle. I mean, I still worked out every day to keep my body in shape for my job, but I stopped caring about other things like shaving or cutting my hair.

Before I can think twice about it, I shoot another text off to my sister.

Isn't Alyssa a hairdresser?

MALLORY

Yes! Are you finally going to remove that monstrosity you call a beard from your face?

I roll my eyes. Can't a guy just need a haircut?

ME

Thought it was time I part ways with my rugged look.

MALLORY

Rugged is saying you look like Noah from *The Notebook* after the breakup. I would say you look more like a recluse emerging from a cave after five years.

ME

Don't know what any of that means.

MALLORY

Is it impossible for you to ever put the word "I" at the beginning of a text?

ME

Why use more words than necessary?

MALLORY

Maybe so you don't actually sound like a caveman, too?

ME

Are you going to answer my question or not?

MALLORY

I already did. YES, Alyssa is a hair stylist.

ME

She free today?

woman face-palming emoji

I'll text her, but only because a haircut will make Mom happy. I'm pretty sure she thinks you're going to live in solitude forever.

I'm just speaking the truth. It's what family does.

And also elementary schoolers.

I have this one kid in my class, Aiden, who can totally tell you the truth about your caveman ways if you need a rude awakening.

I'll take that as a maybe.

Ooh, Alyssa had a last-minute cancellation. She can squeeze you in at one.

ME

Where?

MALLORY

Belleza Salon.

ME

A chick place?

MALLORY

Do you want the appointment or not?

ME

I'll take it.

MALLORY

Wow, ladies and gentlemen, he can form a complete sentence!!!

MALLORY

Alyssa has you marked down for one. You better get going so you're not late to help Shayna.

"Don't remind me," I mumble. Hopefully whatever she needs help with will be a quick, one-time thing.

MALLORY

I've gotta go, my students are coming back from art class.

ME

Sounds good.

MALLORY

No "thank you"?! We'll have to continue rectifying your caveman ways another
day. A sister's work is never done.

I lock my phone screen and slide it into my pocket as I get up from my couch. I grab my wallet and keys from the kitchen countertop before heading to my truck.

The things Mallory says have gotten more ridiculous ever since she went and fell in love with an actor. The sister I grew up with would never reference a romance movie in a text message. But Griffin seems to make her happy, so I'm choosing to accept this new version of her, even if I don't understand all the mushy things.

I spend the drive to the barbershop—I refuse to say I'm going to get a haircut at a *salon*—psyching myself up. I'm sure Alyssa will try to talk to me the entire time, which will exceed the limit of my social battery today.

The barber I used to go to was great. He would ask me if I wanted my usual, I would nod, and then he'd get to work. No awkward small talk. But he moved away while I was in Seattle, hence my current predicament.

I park and head inside, where I'm hit with a strong scent of girly shampoo and enough hairspray to light this building on fire with a single match. All the eyes in the building turn to me, all very female and apprehensive, seeing as I'm the only man in the shop. Unless you count the little boy who is running around holding a fistful of cut hair that I hope is his mother's.

I shove my hands into my jeans pockets, wanting to look as nonthreatening as possible. Although, I'm not sure it says *I promise I'm not a creep.*

I'm pretty positive I hear a woman gasp in horror as she turns away from me, pulling the baby on her lap closer. Maybe my sister was right about me looking like a caveman. I'll never admit that to her, though.

"Hey, Connor." Alyssa walks out of the back of the salon and waves me over.

Finally. I rush toward her and sit in the chair at her station. She drapes a black cape around me, buttoning it at the back of my neck.

"It's great to see you." Alyssa smiles at me in the reflection of the mirror. "Mallory said you had a hair emergency?"

I frown. Of course, she did. "Not an emergency. Just need my hair cut and beard trimmed."

"Well, that'll be"—she runs her fingers through my hair, but they get stuck in the back—"easy." The inflection in her voice makes it sound more like a question, and I don't blame her. I'm not sure I even own a brush. If I do, it's somewhere long forgotten in a box from the move. "How much do you want cut off?"

"Like the way I used to wear it. Shorter. Easier to maintain, but still long enough up top—"

"To run your fingers through," she finishes my thought. "You always used to do that, even back when we were kids."

I nod. Alyssa carefully untangles her fingers and grabs a spray bottle, holding it up like it's the answer to all her problems. She spritzes water all over my hair until I see little rivulets dropping down the front of the cape.

"How's your new job? I haven't seen you since you moved back." Alyssa runs a comb through my hair, tugging harder to get it through the worst knots, while I do my best not to wince. "Well, except at the hospital." She blows out a long breath. "It's crazy you already saved a life in your first week back, and it's even crazier that it was someone you knew."

Alyssa is nice and all, but having one of my sister's best friends cut my hair and ask me questions while I'm stuck in this chair isn't my idea of fun. More like forced torture while wearing a cape. Her weapons of choice: hair shears, electric clippers, and an onslaught of questions.

"Good," I mutter.

She reaches for the hair shears with a laugh. "I see you're still a man of few words." When I don't respond, she continues. "I'm sure your mom is thrilled to have you back."

I nod when she's not making a cut. "That's an understatement."

Alyssa continues to snip away, clumps of my blond hair falling to the black floor. "If you don't mind me asking, what made you move home?"

I'm quiet for so long that I'm sure she thinks I'm ignoring her. In reality, I don't know the full answer to her question. It's partly because I was tired of having everything Jillian said to me when she ended things dredged back up whenever I ran into her in town. Also, my dad would call me just about every week, reminding me to call my mom because she was worrying about me. Flying home during the holidays was also more expensive than I'd estimated, and definitely not a tradition I'd be able to uphold on a firefighter's salary. While I liked the peace and quiet whenever I wasn't on shift, I never felt settled in Seattle. Even if my family can be a bit much at times, I know their overeager involvement in my life is out of love, and I missed them. I missed *home*.

"I, um…" I let out a slow exhale, mulling over my answer. Trying to figure out how to not bungle my words.

"It's okay." She places her hand on my shoulder, giving it a gentle squeeze. "You don't have to tell me. Just know that everyone is happy to have you back."

She stays blessedly quiet the rest of the time. Maybe she doesn't know what to say, or she sensed my need for silence, but either way, I appreciate it.

"Okay, take a look and let me know what you think." Alyssa spins my chair around, and I look in the mirror, seeing a younger version of myself. She left my hair long enough for me to run my fingers through, but short enough that it's no longer tickling the back of my neck. It looks really good, honestly—better than my barber ever cut it.

I clear my throat. "Looks great. Thanks."

"Great, I'll just get it styled, and then we can figure out"—she gestures to my beard—"this whole situation."

After she's finished styling my freshly cut hair, Alyssa holds up her electric trimmer as she moves in front of me with a smile. "Now, time to clean up this beard."

CHAPTER EIGHT

SHAYNA

I reread the email, a permanent smile fixed on my face.

Congratulations! Your offer on the converted 1972 VW Transporter has been accepted.

My jaw dropped the first time I read it. I'm still in awe, even though I practically have the entire email memorized at this point from the countless times I've read it.

I still haven't figured out how I'm going to *get* said soon-to-be flower truck. I need someone to drive me and tow it back so it can get a much-needed makeover and tune-up, but I like to be the person helping others, not the one asking for assistance.

It probably has something to do with my undiagnosed eldest-daughter issues. The revelation hit me when I listened to track five—if you know, you know—on the newest Taylor Swift album, and the tears started flowing as if the song had tapped into something deep in my soul. I have never felt more seen in my life. The fact that I always feel pressure for everything to be perfect. My intense need to watch out for my little sister. The way I struggle to say no. *Boundaries?* What are those?

But I'm an optimist above all else, so I think being the eldest daughter also made me more of an empathetic and responsible adult. See? I'm just an independent and caring person. Take that, boundaries.

I shake my head. It's time to stop rereading this email and figure out how to make a balloon-animal monkey.

Yeah, that whole boundaries thing means I'm horrible at saying no. Even when a friend of a friend asks if I know how to make monkey balloon animals for her son's zoo-themed birthday party. To be clear, I one hundred percent do *not* know how to make a monkey out of a long, thin balloon. But I've never been one to back away from a challenge…or say no, is more like it.

I take a fortifying sip of my favorite drink, an iced strawberry matcha, then thumb back over to the instructional video I've already watched five times. With a glance at all my failed monkeys on the kitchen table that look more fitting for a horror-themed party than a zoo one, I sigh and press play again. Sixth time is a charm, right?

Okay, maybe not.

I'm thirteen balloons in—fourteen, if you count the one that exploded when I overfilled it—and am no closer to anything resembling a monkey.

I lock my phone screen and grab the long balloon I just blew up with a pump.

"You are a master balloon-animal maker. You've got this," I whisper to myself. Maybe some false confidence will instill me with whatever skills I'm clearly lacking.

"What are you doing?"

The masculine voice behind me makes my arms jerk, practically throwing the balloon in the air. The only reason I'm able to maintain some semblance of calm is that I immediately recognize the voice as if it's the chorus to my old favorite song.

"You can't just sneak up on a girl." I whip around and move my hands behind my back, hiding my sad excuse for a balloon-animal monkey. My eyes drink in Connor Porter standing in my living room in a long-sleeved tee with the LFD Station 13 logo on it as if he's the last swig of lemonade on a hot summer day. He has no business looking that good in a plain T-shirt. And I can't help but notice how his fresh haircut and shave have him looking just like he did in high school. Connor is a creature of habit, but once you find a look that works that well for you, I suppose there's no use changing it up. My heart does a little pitter-patter in my chest. Obviously, I'm doing a great job at tamping down this crush.

"What was that?" he asks.

"Nothing."

He would think I'm so weird if he saw what I was doing. Definitely not the impression I want to make on the man I've been crushing on since before I even hit puberty.

Connor takes a step closer.

I move back, ramming my hip bone into the kitchen table. "Oh, petunias."

His brows furrow. "What?"

I stare at him blankly.

"Why did you say petunias?"

"It's a new thing I'm trying out—saying the names of flowers instead of cursing."

"That's oddly specific, but fitting."

I smile. "I thought so."

He closes the remaining distance between us, wraps his arm around me, and grasps my hand. The feeling of his skin on mine again takes my breath away. Except this time, it's not because of anxiety from a plane ride or being stuck in a burning building. It's only *him*.

I'm powerless against his strength as he pulls my hand back in front of me and the poorly made balloon animal along with it. Connor peers down and tilts his head, probably trying to puzzle together what the heck I'm holding.

He continues to stare, and a blush blossoms on my cheeks. I haven't told my family or even my best friends about all the crazy requests I've said yes to because of my inability to feel like I'm disappointing people. Now my longtime crush is seeing it with his very eyes.

Connor finally drags his gaze up and looks over his shoulder at the sea of failed monkeys on the kitchen table behind me. I've had a lot of embarrassing moments in my life, but I think this one officially takes the cake.

He opens his mouth and shuts it. I don't blame him. I have no words to explain the scene behind me. After a painful stretch of silence, Connor finally puts me out of my misery. "Are you joining the circus, flower?"

I'm so focused on my deep-seated mortification that I almost miss what he said. My eyes dart up to his, searching. "Did you just call me flower?"

He makes a weird sound between a cough and a sputter. "Uh, no."

I raise my eyebrow as if to say *Really?*

"I said, 'Are you joining the circus forever?'"

He most certainly did *not* say that. But if he wants to pretend, I'll play along.

"No, I'm not joining the circus, Eeyore."

Connor's lips don't even twitch, ever a firm line. Maybe it's a trick in the lighting, but his eyes do look softer, like there's a hint of humor there.

"Would you rather be called Blaze?" I shoot him a teasing smile. "Ooh, what about Sparky?"

"No." He pinches the bridge of his nose. "No firefighter nicknames."

"We could just go with Grumpy."

"As in, one of the seven dwarves?" I nod, and he sighs. "No."

"Nicknames are bestowed upon you." My brows furrow. "You can't say no."

Connor shrugs. "I just did."

I drop the balloon I'm holding in the pile on the table and place my hands on my hips, knowing better than to get into a battle of wills with Connor Porter. "What are you even doing here?"

"Helping you."

"With what?"

He crosses his arms, making the material of his shirt stretch taut across his chest and biceps. "That's what I'm here to find out. My sister wouldn't tell me."

"How did you even get in?" I purse my lips. "I'm the only one home."

"Mallory told me to let myself in." He hitches a thumb over his shoulder, toward the front door. "You know, you really should keep that locked. It's dangerous."

"The only person who has ever let themselves in is you. So are you saying you're a dangerous person?" I pull my phone out of my floral-print jeans. "Should I call the police?"

"You're safe with me."

Goosebumps erupt on my skin like they do every time I listen to "Long Live." But this time, it's because of the protectiveness in his tone and the thought of how safe I felt next to him on the plane and in his arms when he carried me out of a literal burning building.

When I realize I've been staring at him, I clear my throat. "Oh, good. I've already called 911 one too many times this month."

His jaw ticks, and I have to avert my gaze. There's something about a protective man that's just so attractive.

"Too soon?" Joking about the situation is the only way I seem to stay calm. Connor has seen me in a state of panic two times too many in the last fortnight.

I reach forward and brush my fingers on his freshly shaven, chiseled jawline before I can stop myself. "I can't believe you shaved your beard."

He flinches like my fingers are shards of glass. I move to step back out of instinct, ramming my hip into the table again. Yep, definitely going to have a bruise there in the morning. "Candytufts," I hiss.

I swear, Connor's lips twitch. It is now my new personal life goal to make Connor Porter smile. Better yet, to make Connor Porter laugh.

"Gesundheit," he says.

I swat his arm. "It's a shrub."

"My sentiments remain the same."

I choose to ignore his comment because, again, I'm not about to get into a battle of wills with the most stubborn, strongheaded person I know. "Why'd you shave it?"

"There was a mishap at the haircut place."

"A mishap?" I grab the edge of the table with my hands and push myself up, sitting on the edge of it. "This sounds like a story I need to hear."

He grunts. "It's not that good. Just a kid running around with a fistful of hair who decided playing tag with Alyssa right as she was trimming my beard was a wonderful idea."

I laugh. "At least it wasn't while she was cutting your hair."

"Yeah." Connor runs a hand through his hair, slightly curled at the end of the strands. "I'm just glad she has a barber certification, otherwise I would've had to leave with a giant patch of my beard missing."

I tilt my head. "Well, it looks good." I keep my hands to myself this time, not wanting a repeat flinch. My fragile little heart can only take so much rejection from him.

"Thanks." He points to the pile of balloon animals. "Are you going to tell me what that's about?"

"I'll tell you as long as you promise to not think I'm crazy." He shrugs, and I think that's as good a guarantee as I'm going to get. "Well, I learned how to face paint for Reagan's friend's little sister's birthday party last year, and apparently my mediocre skills were a big hit, because one of the moms reached out, asking if I knew how to make balloon-animal monkeys. You see, her son is having a zoo-themed party, and I guess she thought that subpar face-painting skills would translate over to balloon animal making skills." I gesture to the failed monkeys. "Obviously, that wasn't the case."

"Why'd you say yes?"

"To what?"

"To all of that."

"I couldn't say no." I wrap my arms around my middle, feeling sick at the thought of letting someone down.

"Why not?" He shoves his hand in his front pockets, looking the picture of nonchalant, as if there's nothing hard about saying no to people when they ask something of you.

I blink. "How would I even do that?"

"Do what?" The lines on his forehead deepen as he frowns.

"Let someone down. Tell them no."

"Easy. You just say no."

"That's not easy." I shake my head. "Just like asking for help isn't easy either."

"We can talk about how you can say no later." Connor's shoulders rise and fall as he blows out a long breath. "For now, we'll focus on asking for help. I'm already here—just tell me what you need."

"It's not that simple." I wring my hands together.

"Just hit me with it."

I let the words fly out of my mouth in one breath without questioning them, scared that if I think about them too much I'll never ask. "I need someone with a tow hitch to help me go pick up a flower truck that I bought, but it's an hour drive away."

"That's not so bad," he says, but I continue.

"The truck is a little *rough*, so I also need someone to help me figure out what parts might need replacing without getting seriously upcharged by the people at a shop." I lean closer to him and whisper, "You know, like when I go in for an oil change and leave with a new air filter and blinker fluid."

He stares at me blankly, like he doesn't have a clue in the world what language I'm speaking. Wonderful. If I continue sharing everything I need help with right now, maybe it'll make it easier for me to ask someone to actually help later on. Because there's no way I'm asking Connor to spend hours every week with me. That sounds like a recipe for a broken heart.

"Anyway, I want to make sure she runs smoothly, and she needs a serious facelift, if you know what I mean." I nudge his arm with my shoulder like we're co-conspirators. "A good paint job and logo should fix her right up. And then there's the whole matter of getting a new canopy to cover the back of the truck and buying some wood stands for the galvanized metal vases that will hold the flowers and bouquets I'm selling. All of which I need someone to help me shop for. It's a whole ordeal. Oh, and did I mention that my goal is to have the flower truck ready to open so that my first event can be at the Dogwood Festival in April?"

I smile sweetly, but I'm sure my eyes look a bit crazed. I know it sounds like a big ask.

There's another long stretch of silence before Connor says, "Why do you keep calling your truck a 'she'?"

"After everything I just said, *that's* your question?" He offers the barest dip of his chin. "I'm naming the business Sunshine Blooms, so it's not like the truck can have a masculine name."

"You name your vehicles?"

I shoot him a look. "You don't?" Let's just say, if we were in a staring contest where the goal is to show no emotion, Connor would win, hands down. "Scratch that. For a minute, I forgot who I'm talking to."

He rolls his shirt sleeve up and glances at his watch. "How late is the place where you bought the truck open?"

"Five. Why?"

Connor slides his sleeve back down and shoves his hand back in his front pocket. "If we leave soon, we should be able to make it in plenty of time."

"Oh." I shake my head vehemently. "I wasn't asking you to take me to pick it up."

"How many other people do you know that have a tow hitch?"

None. Zero. Zilch. Nada.

"I'm sure I know someone." My voice comes out an octave higher, making me sound more unsure than the confident woman I'd rather come across as to him.

"I'm already here, and my truck is out front."

"I guess you could just drive me to pick her up, if you really don't mind." I drop my gaze and rock on my feet. "I can figure out the rest, though."

"I'm pretty good with my hands," Connor says, and my eyes immediately move to his pockets. He clears his throat. "Er, handy." He rubs the back of his neck. "I can build things."

"You really don't have to—"

"Mallory already volunteered me," he interrupts. "I don't mind helping on my days off. On one condition."

I raise an eyebrow. He's not one to ask much of people, so this has to be good.

"You let me help you learn how to say no."

"I know *how* to say no."

"That doesn't mean you're good at setting boundaries. You can't tell me you're actually enjoying trying to make those?" He gestures to the failed monkey balloon animals.

I purse my lips. No. I hate it. It makes my hands smell like latex for the rest of the day, no matter how many times I wash them. And tying the little knots hurts my fingers worse than the occasional thorn prick I get when working with flowers.

"That's what I thought." He crosses his arms, and I ignore the way the cotton material of his shirt pulls tight across his chest this time. "Do you even know what you like to do? Or do you just do whatever someone asks of you?"

His question feels like a gut punch. Emotion rises in my throat as tears sting my eyes, but I fight to shove it down. "I'm not sure," I admit, my voice shaky.

"I'll help you with your flower truck if you let me help you learn how to set boundaries. Learn what you like."

My eyes drop to his lips. There's one thing I know I'd like for sure: the feeling of Connor's mouth on mine.

"Do we have a deal?"

"What are you getting out of this?" The arrangement all sounds a little one-sided.

"I like projects." Connor shrugs. "Plus, it will keep me busy, which will give me a reason to tell my mom why I can't go out with all the single daughters of her friends or a lady at church or her grocer. Basically, no dates. Really, you'd be doing me a favor, but it's up to you."

The thought of him not having the time to go on dates with another woman would definitely be an added bonus. I look at him for a long moment before waving my hand and heading up the creaky stairs in our Victorian home to my bedroom. "Come on. If you're going to offer to help me, you may as well have all the information."

CHAPTER NINE
CONNOR

I HAVE NO IDEA where Shayna is leading me or what kind of information she thinks I need to know before deciding if I'm going to help her with her flower-truck renovations and learning how to set boundaries.

But I do know that I'm a complete idiot.

With each step up the creaky stairs, I overanalyze everything I said in our conversation downstairs.

Why on earth did I call her *flower*? I don't give people nicknames, let alone cute ones. I'm not even going to think about the fact that I willingly touched her. Again.

I knew walking into this house with the sole purpose of helping Shayna was a stupid idea. I should've told Mallory I was too busy unpacking and trying to get settled with my job and being back in Louisville. Neither of which is true, but I think they at least sound like valid excuses.

Shayna opens a door at the top of the hallway and leads me into what I'm immediately able to identify as her bedroom. *Why is she taking me in here?* I scream the question in my mind, but I try not to let my panic outwardly show.

I do my best to keep my eyes fixed on her and not look around. Being in her room feels like an invasion of privacy, even though she's the one who brought me up here. I take a deep breath and immediately regret it when I'm hit with the sweet, floral scent of her perfume. I shove my hands in my front pockets and rock on my feet. "Why are we up here?"

"You'll see." Shayna opens her closet door and kneels before moving a giant box out of the way. She slides out the slightly smaller box that was hiding behind it. She remains kneeling on the ground and looks at me warily as she gestures to the box. "Go ahead."

I bend over and open the box. I'm not scared of much—it's part of the job—but I have no clue what I'm getting into when I pull the first item out. "What is this?" I pinch the large bundle of itchy yellow fabric between my thumb and pointer finger, holding it in front of me.

"A ball gown. I dressed up as Belle from *Beauty and the Beast* for a musical, even though I can't sing, because the ladies at Sunrise Springs—the assisted living facility where Kelsey works—insisted I play the part. Obviously, I couldn't disappoint the vivacious elderly women."

Right. Of course she couldn't. "And that right there is your problem." I drop the dress back into the pile.

"At least most of them are hard of hearing, so their ears were saved from the travesty that was my singing."

I feel my lips twitch, but I repress the smile. What is it with this woman and the strong emotions she pulls from me? Ones that no one else does. I'm just going to chalk it up to the fact that Shayna doesn't do anything halfway. She's always all in. All joy. Exuberance. And she's trying to rub it off on me, but I made the mistake of letting someone in before—of thinking about a bright future with someone else—only for everything to come crashing down. I won't let that happen again.

"What else is in there?" I gesture to the box, feeling like it's a magician's hat, where you never know what they're going to pull out next. Or maybe more like Mary Poppins's bag.

Shayna reaches deeper into the box and pulls out a large plastic bag filled with different sizes of paintbrushes and paints. "Face-painting supplies for the birthday party I told you about." She sets it aside and grabs another bag with various-sized tubes. "These are makeup products I bought from old friends who sell products online, and I couldn't say no, even though I'll never stray from my trusted makeup brands." She shoots me a pointed look. "And by friends, I mean people who suddenly decided to reach out to me years after we've graduated high school, even though we hadn't talked since then."

I run a hand along my chin, still not used to the smooth feel of my skin. "Why don't you just say no? Better yet, don't respond."

She gasps in horror. "I could *never*."

"We'll work on it," I grumble. "Dare I ask what else is in there?"

Shayna continues to pull out a plethora of random items ranging from perfume samples to knockoff sunglasses sold by a mall vendor that she wasn't able to walk past without feeling pressured to buy something.

Once we've finally gone through the whole box, she sighs. "Then there's all the balloon animal–making supplies you already saw in the kitchen." She glances back at the full box. "I'm not sure how I'm going to fit it in here, but I'll figure it out."

I don't understand why she would say yes to so many things she clearly doesn't like or want to do. "Why keep it all?"

Shayna blows out a long breath. "I guess I could sell or donate some of it. But what if someone needs me to face paint at another party or play Belle again? I wouldn't want to buy *another* princess dress."

It sounds like I have my work cut out for me.

Shayna looks up at me from her kneeling position with wide eyes. I see both trepidation and hope lingering in her irises. "Now that you have all the information on how much of a lost cause I am, do you still want to help?"

If anyone should be scared, it's me. I'm the one who will likely say something stupid and make my sister mad because I hurt one of her best friends' feelings. But if it will keep me busy and save me from having to go on a date with my mother's church friend's great-niece, I'm game. "Sure."

"You don't sound super confident."

I grunt. "I said I'll help." There are a lot of things that I'm not, but I do try to be a man of my word.

"All right, then." She stands and moves to slide the box back into the closet.

I stop her with a hand to her lower back. There I go, touching her again. "Don't put that away," I manage to get out, yanking my hand back as if I'd touched a hot stove.

She turns to face me, a slight flush on her cheeks. "Why not?"

"We're going to donate everything in that box on our way out."

Shayna's eyes widen as she shakes her head. "What if I need something again?"

"If you can tell me one thing in that box that you've used more than once, I'll let you keep it."

She rolls her bottom lip into her mouth until she finally lets out a resigned sigh. "Fine, we can donate it."

I raise an eyebrow. "Including the…what did you say they were downstairs?" It was impossible to tell what kind of animal they were when all they looked like were mangled snakes.

"Monkeys." She winces. "We can throw out my attempts. But I still need the balloons and pump for the party."

I shoot her a look.

She lifts her arms into the air before letting them fall dramatically back to her side. "I already said yes—I can't back out now. I like to follow through on my commitments."

"When's the party?"

"In two months."

"Perfect, that gives them plenty of time to find an *actual* balloon artist to come to their party." I bend down, lift the box, and head back downstairs. I hear Shayna's light steps following closely behind me. "We can work on a text message for you to send them while on the way to pick up your flower truck."

"But—" she starts.

"No buts." I have to stay firm if I'm actually going to help. "If you want to learn how to set some boundaries and say no, we're starting today."

"Fine." She sniffles.

I don't look back. I've never been good with tears. "Grab anything you need and meet me at my truck." I open the front door and step out onto the porch before yelling back over my shoulder, "And make sure you lock the door behind you."

I press my lips together. I don't know why I said that. I swear, Shayna has some kind of magical power to get me to open up. Whenever I'm around her, it's like I have a word disease, where I can't seem to control what comes out of my mouth, and I'm not sure there's a cure.

If she responds, I don't hear her, because I shut the door behind me and head to my truck. I throw the box into the back seat before leaning against the passenger door. While I'm waiting for Shayna, I think through the checklist of work she said the truck needs. If I remember correctly, one of my high school baseball teammates now owns a local body shop. I open the social media app that I haven't checked since high school and search for his username.

I find a link to a business page. When I click on it, all of the posts are pictures of newly painted cars. They look nice, so I click the phone number up top and press call.

After two rings, a familiar voice answers on the other end. "Pat's Auto Body, this is Pat speaking. How can I help you?"

"Hey, Pat. You may not remember me, but this is Connor Por—"

"Connor Porter! How are you, man? It's been, what, nine years?"

I rub the back of my neck. "Something like that."

"Well, it's great to hear from you. Are you back from Seattle?"

"Moved back about a week ago."

"Great, you'll have to come play a pickup game with me and the guys. We play at the park on the first Saturday of every month. I'm sure everyone would love to see you."

I grunt, unsure what to say to the random invite. This is why I don't make phone calls often. I open my mouth to try to formulate some kind of response, but Pat blessedly ends my small talk misery. "Anyway, what can I do for you, man?"

I clear my throat. "I have a friend who's opening a flower-truck business, but the truck needs a tune-up, some external work, and a fresh coat of paint. Problem is, it all needs to be done by next month."

"Well, you're in luck, because we're located right next to a mechanic shop. I can contact one of the guys over there and get her truck in for the tune-up, then move it over to my shop for all the body work. What color does your friend want it painted?"

"I'll have to ask her."

"Oh, it's a she, huh? I never thought I'd see the day when Connor Porter was caught up on a girl," he teases. "Remember how you always used to roll your eyes at the guys on the team who had girlfriends coming to their games? The only girls who came to cheer for you were your mom, sister, and Shayna Monroe." He blows out a low breath. "She was beautiful, even in high school. I wonder what she's up to now. Do you know?"

I grit my teeth and hope my words come out sounding less tense than I feel. "That's the friend I'm helping."

"Oh, sorry, man. Didn't realize she was your girl. Good for you. I always wondered if she had a thing for you."

My brow furrows. I don't know what's happening or why he thinks we're dating when I've only referred to Shayna as my friend. That's even pushing it. Acquaintance-slash-friend-of-my-sister is more like it. And why would he think she had a thing for me?

My mind is swirling with questions when Pat's voice comes back through the speaker. "Just ask Shayna what color she'd like it painted, and consider it done. I'll get everything covered as a gift to an old friend. Consider it an early wedding present."

My eyes bug out. *Wedding present?* It's like we're both having an entirely different conversation.

"Drop the truck off whenever you can, and I'll get the job expedited for you, no problem."

"Uh, thanks?"

"Just promise you'll come to our pickup game next month, and it's a done deal."

I take a deep breath and run a hand through my hair. "As long as I'm not on shift at the station."

"Works for me. Later, man. Tell the missus hi for me."

The line clicks, and I grab the handle of the passenger door to keep from falling over. How did we go from friends to fiancés to an old married couple within the stretch of two minutes?

Shayna chooses this exact moment to emerge from the house. The wind blows her short hair back, making it look like a slow-motion montage in a movie or like a model walking down a runway. Objectively, I can see why Pat said she was beautiful. She's always had a certain aura of joy about her that draws people in. But right now, on the way to pick up the truck to open her dream business, she shines brighter than the sun. I don't know what words are even bigger than joy. Maybe exuberant. Glowing. Vivacious. Sparkling.

All the complete opposite of any words that have ever been used to describe me.

Get your head in the game, Porter.

I can't let Pat's words get to me, because while Shayna might be beautiful, this is nothing more than a friend helping out another friend.

I open the passenger door for her.

"Thanks." Shayna raises her strawberry matcha toward me and hops in with ease.

I dip my head in a nod and ensure she's situated before shutting the door and jogging around to the driver's side.

I step up into the cab of my truck. As my butt hits the driver's seat, I'm hit with a wave of nostalgia, remembering the smell of Mallory, Shayna, Alyssa, and Kelsey's perfumes that would leave a weird aroma in here for days whenever I'd drive them around in high school.

But right now, all I smell is Shayna's perfume. By itself, it's intoxicating. A perfect mixture of florals that's pleasant, but not overwhelming.

I clench my jaw, furious at myself for letting Pat's words get to my head.

"I'll navigate," Shayna announces. She places her drink in the cup holder, then reaches down, grabs my car cable, and plugs it into her phone. Soon enough, the navigation directions blare through the speakers. "I can't believe you still have Sulley."

I feel the lines on my forehead crease. "Sulley?"

"Yeah." She runs her hand along the dash. "I can't believe he's still running."

"Sulley?" I repeat. "*He?*"

"Well, you never named your truck, and you drove us around so much in high school that I named him for you."

"You named *my* truck?" I blink.

"We already went over this." She rolls down the window and rests her elbow there, letting in the cool spring breeze.

"Why did you name him—*it*—Sulley?"

"He's blue and can come across a little grumpy and standoffish, but he's soft in the end. It just took the right person coming along."

"The right person?"

"Boo."

"What?" I ask, utterly confused by this conversation. It's not Halloween, and there's not a ghost in sight. "Is that supposed to be a knock-knock joke?"

"Boo was the girl who came along and helped him soften, made him care." She leans over and pats my arm. My whole body tenses. I think my shoulders might become a permanent part of my neck around her. "I just wanted you to know I've never seen you as a grumpy, standoffish monster."

I nod slowly. "Good to know."

Without missing a beat, she says, "Who were you talking to on the phone before I came outside?"

"Pat."

"Pat Young? From high school?"

My lips press into a thin line. Of course, she'd remember him. Maybe he had it all wrong, and *he* was the guy she was crushing on. "Yeah."

"What's he up to nowadays?"

"He owns a local body shop." She doesn't say anything, so I continue. "He said that there's a mechanic next door that can do any needed work, and then he'll paint the exterior of the truck. Pat's willing to do the work for free and expedite it so it's ready for your event. He just needs to know what color you want it painted."

She's uncharacteristically quiet. I glance over at her when we reach a stop sign and see tears on her cheeks.

Crap, did I overstep by trying to help?

"I'm sorry. I didn't mean to upset you—I thought I was helping."

Shayna shakes her head and uses the sleeve of her blazer to wipe her cheeks. "These are happy tears. I can't believe you did all that for me." She leans over and wraps her arms around me in a hug. "Thank you, Connor."

"You're welcome." I swallow hard, trying not to think about the fact that her arms are around me. "So, uh, what color do you want the truck?"

Shayna opens her mouth and shuts it again before shrugging. "I don't know."

"Well, what's your favorite color?"

She shrugs again. "I work around such a variety of beautiful colors with all the different blooms that it feels unfair to discriminate against any of them."

If that isn't the most Shayna thing I've ever heard, I don't know what is. Shayna has always been the girl who thinks about everyone around her. Always made sure everyone was included at school. Worried about other people's needs and preferences above her own. Like how she couldn't care less about any sports but still came to almost all of my baseball games in high school with Mallory and my mom just to support me, even in the pouring rain.

It makes me wonder if there's anyone who shows up for her in the same capacity she does for everyone else.

I shake my head. I'm doing what I can to offer my assistance, and the rest isn't up to me. "Okay then, what color brings you the most joy?"

Shayna grabs her drink and takes a sip. "Huh." She tilts her head, making her straight dark-brown hair swing with the movement. "I never thought about it like that." She only has to think for a second before saying, "Yellow."

"I'll let Pat know when we see him."

"Wow." She wiggles on the bench seat. "We haven't even picked up the truck yet, and you've already figured out so much of my checklist. I didn't even know where to start. Thank you."

I grip the steering wheel harder, forcing myself not to look over at her beaming smile and ignoring the strange mix of emotions swirling within me. While I'm normally most comfortable in silence, I feel the need for a change in conversation. I'm thinking of things I could say when I remember what she mentioned earlier about not being able to say no to mechanics. "By the way, you know blinker fluid isn't real, right?"

"It's not?" She groans. "Thank goodness you're here."

CHAPTER TEN

SHAYNA

"Well, she's…" I purse my lips, trying to think of something nice to say about the vehicle before me.

"Something," Connor finishes for me.

The truck is definitely rustier than the sale pictures indicated, and there are some dents that weren't mentioned either. I guess this is why they say you shouldn't make an expensive purchase sight unseen.

"Stinking Roger," I mumble.

Connor makes a noise in his throat that sounds like a mix between a chuckle and a cough. Like he wants to laugh, but his body won't let him. "Who is Roger, and what did he do to you?"

"It's another flower name." I sigh. "But wouldn't it be fitting if the last owner's name was actually Roger?"

"Sure." He says it more like a question than a statement.

The uncertainty in his tone makes my lips quiver. "Do you think it's fixable?" I hate the shakiness in my voice.

His hand twitches at his side as if he's considering reaching out to comfort me but thinks better of it. "Anything is fixable."

I turn to him, my eyes glassy. "You think so?"

Connor's face remains stoic, but he nods. "You texted that mom on the way here and let her know you weren't going to be able to make fifty monkey balloon animals at her son's party."

He's right. I felt sick to my stomach for the entire twelve minutes and thirty-seven seconds I waited for her response. But I did it. She didn't even seem mad that I backed out, just that she understood and thanked me for letting her know so far in advance. I still feel awful about it, but I guess saying no wasn't as horrible as I anticipated.

"If you can start making changes after years of never saying no, don't you think the car experts can get it running perfectly and make the truck look good as new?"

"You're right." I stand taller.

"Do you want a picture with it?"

It's kind of him to offer, but I'm not sure anyone should ever see the level of disaster that is this truck before we fix it up. Although, maybe the before-and-after pictures could make for some good marketing videos. "Sure. Why not?" I pose in front of the truck with my arms up in the air and smile wide, trying to convince myself that I'm excited when right now we still have a long way to go.

Connor pulls out his phone, snaps a few pictures, pockets his device, then unhooks a measuring tape from his belt loop and moves toward the vehicle.

"What're you doing?" I ask, turning to face the truck again. I attempt to withhold my grimace at the dirt and grime caking it.

"What does it look like?" He hops up onto the bed of the truck like he's some kind of spider monkey or an Olympic jumper. "I'm measuring."

"Thanks for that stunning revelation, Captain Obvious," I deadpan. "I mean, why do you need to measure the truck bed?"

Connor analyzes the measuring tape with his tongue sticking out slightly in concentration. It might be the most adorable thing I've ever seen. He pulls out a pencil and a small notepad from his pocket and scribbles down a few numbers. I love a man who comes prepared.

"So I know how much material we'll need to buy." He glances up at me. "You said you wanted wood stands, right?"

My heart melts that he was listening when I spilled all my thoughts out to him. He's making this whole forget-ting-about-my-feelings-for-him thing really difficult.

I suck in a long breath and slowly exhale. "Right, but what kind of material are you talking about buying? I figured I would get premade stands."

"Building 'em will be cheaper." Connor runs a hand through his hair.

I shake my head. "You don't need to build them for me. You're already giving me your entire afternoon; I didn't expect you to—"

"This is your business, Shayna." He jumps down from the truck, landing beside me with ease. "Don't you want it to look professional?" Obviously, he already knows the answer, but I nod anyway. "And a deal's a deal. I'm here to help."

"You really don't mind? Do you even know how to build something like that?" I place my hands on my hips with a self-deprecating laugh. "I, for one, know that you can't become an expert at everything from YouTube videos."

"I know—I threw exhibit A into the trash at your house."

I gasp. "Did you just make a *joke*?"

His face remains stoic as he says, "I think I did."

I pull out my phone and open the calendar app.

He leans over and furrows his brow when he sees what I'm doing. "Why are you typing 'Connor made a joke' in your calendar?"

"I'm marking the date to remember this momentous occasion." He shakes his head at my antics. "But seriously, you didn't answer my question."

Connor sighs. "I think I can figure out how to build a few stands. As I said, I like projects."

"If you're sure you'll have the time for it."

"I'll make it happen." The certainty in his tone doesn't leave room for further discussion. "Do you want the stands stained, painted, or natural?"

"Probably stained or natural," I say. "I'd want to compare a piece of the wood with the galvanized metal vases once I buy those to see what looks best."

Connor nods. "I have some ideas, but we can take a look at the hardware store. There are lots of different types of wood, so I'm sure we can find something that fits your vision. In the meantime"—he jumps back up onto the bed of the truck—"may as well figure out the dimensions for the canopy, too." He points to the stained and tattered thing I'm hesitant to call a canopy currently covering the back. "I'm assuming you're going to want this disposed of?"

I wrinkle my nose. "Definitely."

After taking a few more measurements, Connor rejoins me on the ground. "Ready to get it dropped off at the mechanic shop and pick out a paint color?"

"Her," I correct.

He stares at me, stone-faced.

"I'm ready to get *her* dropped off."

He rolls his eyes. "It's an inanimate object."

I lean forward and pat the car I've decided I'll name Daffodil. "You're hurting her feelings." My hand comes back coated in dirt, and I discreetly try to wipe it off on a tissue from my flower-shaped purse.

Connor doesn't notice, though, since he's already halfway back to his truck. "Doesn't have feelings," he calls over his shoulder.

I shake my head as he backs his truck up to attach the flower truck to the hitch. Maybe spending more time with Connor is a good thing. If I see just how different we are, it could potentially act as a deterrent. Yeah, maybe by the end of this, I'll finally be rid of this crush on Connor Porter.

♡ ♡ ♡

After we've dropped Daffodil off at the mechanic shop, we walk next door to Pat's Auto Body. The little bell on the top of the door rings as we step inside.

Pat pops up from behind his desk with a wide grin. "Connor, long time no see, my man." He goes in for a typical bro hug, but stops mid-motion when Connor only extends his hand. It results in an awkward handshake with Pat partially clapping Connor's shoulder. My cheeks burn with secondhand embarrassment.

He turns to me with open arms. "Shayna, you haven't aged a day."

I wrap my arms around him, giving him a quick squeeze. "Nice to see you, Pat."

"It's better to see you." He flashes me a wide smile.

I feel Connor's eyes on us. When I pull back, he's looking at Pat with enough fire to burn a forest.

Pat clicks his tongue as he looks back and forth between us with a grin. "You know, I wasn't sure how you two would work, but now that I'm looking at you together, I totally see it."

My brows knit together. It feels like I jumped in mid-conversation. I have no clue what Pat's talking about. I look to Connor for some clarity, but with the steely look on his face, I don't think I'm going to get an answer. It looks like he wishes he could wring Pat's neck. I'm not exactly sure why, but seeing him all protective is insanely attractive. I add that to my mental list of things I need to forget about Connor Porter.

1. The way his strong, calloused hands felt on my face.

2. How he was able to bring me down from a panicked state and make me feel safe.

3. The way he effortlessly lifted and carried me to safety out of a burning building.

4. The feeling of his strong, muscular arms wrapped around my body.

5. How irrationally hot he looks when he gets protective over me.

I could be making it all up in my head. I mean, he was volun*told* by his sister to help me with this project rather than being a willing volunteer. And he probably feels protective of me in a familial sense. Or maybe I'm reading him all wrong and this glare-filled look is his new resting state. It's not like I've been around him much in the past nine years since he graduated high school and left his family—and me—behind without a glance back.

Meanwhile, I've been the silly younger girl still pining after him. The hopeless romantic in me won't settle for less than someone who makes me feel that fairytale, swept-off-my-feet, knight-in-shining-armor kind of love.

I've given other men a real, fair shot, but no one has ever made me feel like Connor does. Not after one date, and not even after ten. I know it's not fair to hold men to a standard, but even though Connor's not perfect, he's made me feel all those things. So, how could I possibly accept less when I know there's so much more out there?

"Like I said, we're not together," Connor grumbles. "Just helping out my sister's friend."

Oof. There it is, the dose of reality I needed to remind me why I created my mental list of all the things I need to forget about him.

My sister's friend.

Not even *his* friend. That's all I am to him. He's helping me out as a favor to Mallory. Nothing more. I wish his words would burn my crush to ash, but my optimism seems to be clinging on for dear life, refusing to let me give up hope.

"Oh, yeah. We're *so* not together." I let out an awkward laugh, acting like the very idea of us being together is ridiculous.

Pat raises his eyebrows before flashing me a flirtatious smile. "In that case, what're you doing Friday night?"

I feel Connor's eyes on me, but I refuse to look up at him. What should he care if I go on a date with someone else? I'm just his sister's friend.

But I don't think Pat is the kind of man I'm looking for. I've always had a thing for more reserved guys—okay, really just Connor. But definitely not guys who look like they have asked out their fair share of women and know exactly what to say to get a woman to say yes. Unfortunately for him, charm isn't on Pat's side this time.

"Sorry, Friday nights are for the girls," I say.

Connor shifts next to me, but I still don't look his way.

Pat's smile doesn't dim, confidence oozing from him despite the fact that I tried to let him down gently. "Another time, then." I force a smile as Pat retreats to his desk. "I know the truck will be with the mechanic for a bit, but have you decided on a color?"

Before I can open my mouth to respond, Connor answers for me. "Yellow."

Pat looks up from the color swatches in his hand to Connor. After a moment, he dips his head in a subtle nod. "Sure thing." He selects a few of the cards and walks back to us. "Do any of these stand out?"

One shade immediately catches my eye among the swatches. Sunshine Yellow. It's as if it was created for my new business, Sunshine Blooms.

"You're welcome to take them if you want more time to decide." Pat tilts his head with a smirk, making a dimple appear. "Maybe when you bring them back, I could take you on that date."

Connor's hands ball into fists at his sides. I wrap my hand around his arm, in case he's thinking about doing something crazy, like punching Pat, and gesture with the other one to the color. "No need. I know what I want."

Pat blows out a low whistle. "Are you sure you want a color that…bright?"

"She said that's what she wants." Connor practically growls the words.

"It's perfect." I clap my hands, trying to rid this space of whatever weird tension is in the air.

"All right." Pat puts the sunshine swatch on top before glancing up at me. "I'll keep you updated." Connor clears his throat, and Pat says, "Or you?"

"Run all communication through me." Connor's tone leaves no room for discussion. "I'll make sure any important news gets relayed to Shayna."

The way he's taking care of me would make me go weak in the knees, but I lock those babies and remind my silly, hopeful heart that he's only doing it for Mallory.

Pat offers him a tight smile. "All right, I'll be in touch. Y'all have a good day, and Connor, you better be at our next pickup game. A deal's a deal."

Connor escorts me out of the building with a hand to my lower back.

It's not him being possessive. Don't read into it, Shayna. I repeat those sentences to myself like they're my new mantra until Connor finally removes his hand once we're outside. Maybe spending more time with him isn't the cure for a crush after all.

CHAPTER ELEVEN
SHAYNA

I wasn't lying to Pat when I said that Fridays were reserved for the girls. It's our sacred time that no boyfriend is able to touch because it's for the Long Live Girlies.

It's wild to think that we were all single just a year ago, and now both Kelsey and Mallory have fallen in love faster than it takes for poppies to grow from seed to bloom. I couldn't be more thrilled for them and the wonderful men they've found who love them in a way I've only ever dreamed of. But at least I have my fellow single ladies, Alyssa and Tess, to keep me company until we find our own happily-ever-afters.

I walk into our living room in a pale-blue matching set covered in a dainty floral print and smile when I see my friends in their own version of pajamas. Mallory's wearing a dusty rose sweats set. Kelsey's in one of Tyler's sweatshirts that's so long it covers her shorts completely, making it look like that's the only thing she's wearing. Alyssa looks picture perfect in her ribbed pajama set covered in a pink bow pattern. And Tess is the image of comfort in her leggings-and-oversized-shirt combo. We're all different, but I think that's what makes us work well together.

I take a seat on the couch between Alyssa and Kelsey, while Tess and Mallory curl up in the armchairs.

"It's finally happies and crappies time." Alyssa tucks one of her long legs up under her.

Our weekly check-in is usually my favorite time of the week. But tonight, I'm anxious at the thought of opening up. The girls already know about the flower shop incident, but I don't want to talk about Connor. And I certainly don't want to tell my friends that my flower truck is in such bad shape. I'm an optimist, but even I am having a hard time putting a positive spin on this week's events.

"I'll go first," Tess volunteers, giving me the time I need to figure out what I'm going to share. "My crappy was being called in by Evie's teacher because she continues to stand up and dance in the middle of lessons."

I giggle at the mental image of her five-year-old daughter learning phonics while doing a plié.

"But my happy is that Evie loves dance so much that she can't help but practice her skills at all waking hours."

"I can't wait for her spring performance." Kelsey will be Evie's aunt one day when she marries Tyler. He hasn't proposed yet, but it's only a matter of time with how attached at the hip they are.

"We *all* can't wait," I amend. After we attended Evie's fall recital when Tess was out of the country, little Evie became an honorary Long Live Girlie.

"She can't stop talking about how her cheering section is going to be the biggest out of everyone in her dance class." Tess shakes her head, but a smile pulls at her lips. "I keep telling her there aren't cheerleaders for dance, but y'all know how stubborn she gets when she has her mind set on something."

"I'll bring the pom-poms," Mallory says, making us all laugh since she's more of a rough-edged girl than the cheerleader type.

Once it's quiet again, I nudge Alyssa's knee. "You go."

"All right, my happy is that I only have to wait a few more weeks for the first Mustangs game of the season."

The rest of us exchange knowing glances. We've been waiting for her and Austin to get together since they met. They're absolutely perfect for each other, even if they're both too blind to see it.

She lets out an exasperated sigh. "Because I want to support my friend and I love ballpark popcorn. Y'all need to stop trying to make 'us' a thing. It's like the word *fetch*—it's not going to happen."

I appreciate the *Mean Girls* reference, but it doesn't make me believe her. Anyone with eyes can see their chemistry and connection, but we all know better than to push it at this point.

Alyssa continues talking, obviously wanting to move past the topic. "My crappy is that I got a wedding invitation in the mail this week from my cousin."

I grimace with her. We all know who she's talking about without her even having to say the dreaded name—Bianca Cartwright. Although, I guess she's the soon-to-be Bianca Vanderbilt. She's always been the worst. If we're still talking about *Mean Girls*, she is, without a doubt, a Regina George. The kind of girl some people wish they could be and others fear. But to me, she's just the horrible person who made fun of us growing up and then stole Alyssa's college boyfriend. And now she's marrying him.

"I can't believe Bradley is actually marrying that"—Mallory glances at me as if she's choosing her next word carefully—"witch."

"Does your family expect you to go?" Tess asks. Even though she hasn't been part of our friend group for long, she's been to enough girls' nights to get the down low on all of our dating histories.

"My parents would understand if I didn't, but I think I need to. I don't want Bianca and Bradley to feel like they've won, like their being together still affects me." She rolls her eyes. "I was over it a long time ago, and honestly, I think they deserve each other."

"Scum deserves to be with scum," Mallory deadpans.

I reach over and squeeze Alyssa's hand. "You're a gem who deserves to be treated as such."

Everyone else nods in agreement, and Alyssa smiles. "Y'all really know how to boost a girl's confidence."

"You know what else would boost your confidence?" Kelsey asks. "Showing up to their wedding with Austin." Alyssa shoots her a look, and she holds her hands up. "Can't people go to weddings as friends?"

"It's not a bad idea," Tess murmurs.

"I like it." I smile, knowing it could be the perfect opportunity for them to get close in a romantic environment.

"It's still months until the wedding." Alyssa's expression softens. "But I'll consider it."

I think that's the best we can hope for in this situation.

"Who wants to go next?" Alyssa looks around before her eyes settle on me.

I beat her to the chase, wanting to avoid talking about myself and the past week working with Connor for as long as possible. "You're up, Mal."

She lights up instantly. "My happy is obviously that I'm about to visit Griffin in LA for spring break. And my crappy is that I still have to wait another thirteen hours for my flight to go see him." Her crossed leg bounces in anticipation. I never thought one of my friends would date a celebrity, let alone the man dubbed Hollywood's Hottest New Actor, but I couldn't imagine a better match for Mallory. The way Griffin pursues her is like something straight out of a rom-com. Knowing Mallory had given up on love after their missed connection, only to find it again three years later, fills me with hope.

I smile at her. "We're thrilled for you."

"How do you feel about getting to visit a movie set?" Tess asks.

"I won't get to visit the set until summer, when they start filming. He's still doing extensive physical training right now." Mallory shrugs. "But I don't mind watching him train, especially if there's a sword involved." She lets out a dreamy sigh. "I'm dating a hot, sword-wielding, morally gray villain. I'm living every romantasy lover's dream." She looks to me for confirmation. "Did I say all that right? I'm still trying to understand all the trope things."

I place my hand over my heart. "That was perfect. I feel like a proud mom."

"Good, I'll impress Griffin when I see him in"—she glances at her phone screen—"twelve hours and fifty-eight minutes." Mallory lets out a long breath. "Do y'all think I'm going to stick out like a sore thumb in LA?"

"I think Griffin will make you feel right at home." Kelsey wiggles her eyebrows, causing another round of laughter.

"We'll miss you, but I know you're going to have the best time." Alyssa smiles.

"You're right. I love y'all, but I can't wait to see my man." Mallory sits on her hands, as if to force herself to sit still and not jump on an early flight.

"Is it bad that I wouldn't be surprised if you hopped on the plane tomorrow and didn't come back?" Kelsey says.

"Don't tempt me with a good time." Mallory smirks. I know she's just teasing, since she's not the kind of girl to leave her friends and family—let alone her students—behind without any explanation or notice. But love does tend to make people do crazy things.

"I think it's your turn now." Mallory gives me a pointed look.

I take a deep breath, knowing I can't avoid talking forever. "My crappy was obviously the fire in the flower shop, but my happy is that it led to me buying Daffodil."

"Oh, that name is perfect," Alyssa coos. "Is she going to be yellow?"

"As if she could be another color with that name." I wink.

"That's the perfect color to match your bright, joyful personality." Tess beams at me, and happy tears threaten to fill my eyes at the compliment.

"Did you take any pictures when you picked her up?" Kelsey asks.

Alyssa quickly turns, and her long hair nearly whacks me in the face. "I didn't realize you already drove to get her. We need to see pics."

I have the picture Connor texted me—the one he took of me with the truck—but I can't find the courage to show my besties. "I think she would be better seen in person for the first time."

After she's back from the mechanic and body shop.

"Fine." Alyssa leans back into the couch cushion with a sigh. "When are you hoping to have it done by?"

I haven't told my friends my plans, not when it feels like a far-off dream. I've been scared to share it out of fear that it won't come true, like telling someone what you wished for when you saw a shooting star or before blowing out your birthday candles. But then there's the fact that I spilled my guts, including all my dreams for this flower truck business, to Connor. I think that, deep down, I know I can trust him. Also, with how reserved he is, I know it's not likely he'll blab everything I tell him to anyone. He's the kind of person that could know everyone's secrets and take them to the grave.

But what are best friends for if not to be your secret keepers and the ones to not only encourage you to chase your dreams but help you actually achieve them?

"I'm hoping to have the flower truck ready to open so that my first event can be at the Dogwood Festival in April." I play with the ends of my hair. "I know it's a lofty goal. I mean, it's not even a registered business yet, and who knows how long all the work will take in the shop. So, it's probably not even plausible, but the event organizer told me they had a spot open up, and I—"

"Shay." Kelsey reaches over and squeezes my forearm. "It's not a lofty goal."

"It's not?" My lip trembles as tears cloud my vision.

"Not when you have us by your side." Alyssa pulls me in for a side hug.

"Tell me who I need to strong arm into a rush order, and I'll do it," Mallory says. "Better yet, I'll have Griffin do it. What good is it having a celebrity boyfriend if he can't help my friends with his fancy name?"

I laugh and wipe the tears from my eyes.

"I don't have a fancy boyfriend to offer up, but Evie and I are happy to help however we can." Tess offers me a reassuring smile.

"Count me and Tyler in, too," Kelsey chimes in.

"And don't worry about the business side of things," Alyssa says. "There's a strong possibility Austin has the perfect birthday present in store for you later this month."

Tears gather in my eyes again. I don't know why I ever considered not sharing my fears with them. These girls are my village. The people I want around me not only to celebrate my wins but to pick me up and help me carry on when life gets hard. If it wasn't already obvious before, it is now. My people will do anything for me. They'll take on my burdens as their own and help me find a way to do what otherwise seems impossible. I couldn't be more grateful.

"I love y'all. Thank you."

Kelsey smiles. "We're always here to help, Shay. All you have to do is ask." She makes asking for help sound as simple as talking about my favorite flowers. I wish it felt that way. That I didn't overthink things every time I asked for a small favor. That I didn't feel the need to do everything on my own.

But at least I'm taking baby steps.

"Speaking of all the truck stuff, is Connor being helpful? He can be a real pain, but I can use my powers of persuasion on him if he's not helping you." By the way Mallory's eyes light up, I'm guessing she's thinking of some very colorful ways to force her brother to help.

I don't want to be an unknowing accomplice in whatever she's planning, and Connor has already helped me plenty. "He's been great." I swallow nervously. "He got everything sorted for me with the mechanic and body shops with no complaints, and even got them to do a rush order. But I'll let you know if he ever needs any nudging."

"Really?" Mallory raises an eyebrow. "Who does Connor know that would do a rush order for him? It's not like he has an abundance of friends."

I do my best not to wince. The thought of Connor living a solitary life with no friends makes my heart hurt for him. "Pat."

"His old baseball teammate?" Mallory wrinkles her nose. "I didn't know they kept in touch enough to ask him for a favor."

I never thought about it that way. I wonder what all Connor is doing—what he's sacrificing—just to help me. It's not like I'm going to let it get to my head. He made it very clear that there's nothing going on between us at the body shop. But then why did he have a reaction to Pat asking me out, almost as if he was, dare I say, jealous?

"It didn't really seem like they'd talked since high school," I admit.

Mallory looks at me as if I just told her that I hate flowers. "Then why would Connor reach out to him? Getting him to call or text me back is like pulling teeth."

"You were the one who volunteered him to help me." I shrug. "Maybe your powers of persuasion were already at work."

Mallory doesn't look convinced, but she doesn't push the topic further.

"What are you going to do while you wait to get the truck back?" Tess asks. "Do you need any help?"

I send her a grateful smile. "Connor and I are going to the hardware store on Sunday to pick out the wood and vases for the back of the truck. I don't think I need any help yet, but I'll let you know if I do."

Tess nods. "You've got it."

I press my cheek to my shoulder with an awkward smile, feeling uncomfortable having the attention on me for so long. I turn to Kelsey. "You're up, girl."

"My happy was watching Darla convince this month's guest dance instructor at Sunrise Springs to teach her a hip-hop dance after they were finished learning the foxtrot." She laughs. "I'll never forget the looks of horror on the other residents' faces as they watched her."

Tess rubs her eyes. "No details, please. I don't need the mental image of my great-aunt pop, lock, and dropping stuck in my head."

"Tyler said the same thing." Kelsey grins. "I don't think I have a crappy. That made my whole week."

"She better not try to teach her new moves to Evie." Tess shakes her head. "Can your next instructor just teach them the art of slow dancing?"

My heart thumps rapidly in my chest as the memory of when I learned how to slow dance floods my mind in flashes. A dark kitchen. The glow of the refrigerator light. Strong hands on my waist. And Connor Porter's smile aimed at me. Suddenly, I remember it all too well.

CHAPTER TWELVE
SHAYNA

TEN YEARS AGO

I wait until I'm positive my friends are asleep before tiptoeing out of Mallory's bedroom. My steps are slow and careful down the stairs and through the living room as I head toward the kitchen.

Until the girls fell asleep, they couldn't stop talking about our first homecoming dance. Now that we're finally freshmen, our school dances will probably look a little different than the awkward middle school dances where most boys and girls danced on opposite ends of the room to songs like "Cupid Shuffle" or "Cotton Eye Joe."

While Kelsey, Mallory, and Alyssa are all excited at the prospect of being asked to slow dance, I'm terrified. I don't know where to put my hands or how to move to the rhythm. What if a boy asks me to dance and then laughs at how bad I am? And since we all go to different high schools, I won't have my besties there to dance with me or cheer me up if everything comes crashing down. I'll be like one of those girls in the movies who runs to the bathroom and locks herself in a stall to cry until her parents finally come to pick her up.

I sigh. It's times like this that I wish I could be more like my friends. That I wouldn't care as much about what other people think. Just enjoy each moment as it comes. While I like to think of myself as a positive person, the only thing I'm positive about at this moment is that I have no idea how to slow dance with a boy.

Hence why I'm wide-awake right now while my friends are all fast asleep.

I round the corner into the kitchen, hoping a little one-in-the-morning snack will help me fall asleep, when I see the shadow of another figure behind the open fridge door, lit only by the glow of the refrigerator light. I gasp and fling a hand to my chest.

A head pops up from behind the door, but with the way they're backlit, all I can make out is a male figure. "Shayna?"

My heart pounds in my chest, but now for an entirely different reason. "Connor, you scared me."

He closes the fridge door, cloaking us both in only the faint glow of streetlamps and the moonlight streaming through the blinds on the window over the sink. He steps closer, allowing me to see his messy hair, wrinkled baseball tee, and sweatpants slung low over his waist like he haphazardly threw them on. It appears he spent some time tossing and turning in bed, unable to sleep, before getting the same idea as me.

"What're you doing up?" Connor asks.

"I could ask you the same thing."

He raises a bottle of water. "I was thirsty."

"Oh. Me, too," I say, not wanting to admit why I actually came down here.

Connor passes the bottle to me. "Here."

I take it from him, and my fingers graze his in the process. My body shivers involuntarily. I hope he thinks it's from the chill of the water bottle rather than his touch. "Thanks."

Connor opens the fridge and grabs another water for himself. When he turns and sees I'm still standing there, his brow furrows. "You good?"

I really should mumble an excuse about being tired and run back upstairs. But I don't.

The words are tumbling out of my mouth before I have a chance to stop them. "I don't know how to slow dance."

The furrow lines between his brows deepen. "So, *not* good?"

I shake my head and will myself not to cry. Connor's expression softens. My trembling bottom lip probably gave me away. The little sellout.

"Can I ask why you're thinking about slow dancing after"—he glances at the clock on the microwave—"one in the morning on a random Friday night?"

"Homecoming is a few weeks away."

Connor dips his chin in understanding. "And your friends are excited for their dances, but you're not." He closes the fridge and leans against it. He has no business looking that good this late at night, his hair all mussed like he's run his hands through it a hundred times. It certainly doesn't help my unrequited crush.

"Yeah." My voice is barely above a whisper. I should be embarrassed about everything I just told Connor. He's been my crush for three whole years. That's like a lifetime in teenage years, where most girls change their crush as often as they change their favorite emoji. But me? I'm stuck on Connor like the strongest superglue.

I don't know if I'm baring my soul to him because he makes me feel comfortable or if this is something I'm going to wake up in the morning and majorly regret, but for tonight, I choose to lean into it. "Do you know how?"

He stares at me, expression blank.

"To slow dance?"

He shrugs. "It's not rocket science."

My shoulders fall, and I feel myself shrinking in. This is exactly what I was worried about—a boy making fun of me for being terrible at dancing.

"Do you want…" Connor swallows. I watch his throat bob. It's almost like the rest of his sentence is stuck there until he finally rasps, "…me to teach you?"

Yes. A million times, yes.

I shrug, feigning nonchalance. "If you're not busy." He gestures around the dark kitchen, and I giggle. "Right, it's the middle of the night. Why would you be busy?" My arms wave around, feeling disconnected from my body. I have no clue what I'm doing, but I probably look like a wacky waving inflatable-arm-flailing tube man.

He opens the fridge again, stopping me from my mental spiral.

"What're you doing?" I ask.

"We need some kind of light so we don't trip in the dark, and I don't think either of us wants the bright overhead ones on at this hour."

"Smart thinking." I set my water bottle down on the counter and clasp my hands together in front of me. "So, how do I do this?"

Connor puts his water bottle back in the fridge and extends his hand. When I place mine in his palm, he gently pulls me closer. "There are two ways." His voice is low and slightly raspy, evidence of his lack of sleep after a week of waking up early for school. He places his hand at the dip of my waist.

Thank goodness I wore my cute pajamas tonight: floral-print bottoms paired with a thin pale-blue long-sleeved shirt. Where his fingers land, grazing my top, has me feeling the warmth of his palm through my shirt. The weight is comforting. Steady.

"One option is for the boy to place one hand on your hip like this and hold your hand in his." He wiggles my right hand, which he's already holding. "You'll place your free hand on his shoulder or the back of his neck—depends on how close you want to get."

If Connor were mine, I'd tangle my fingers in the hair at the nape of his neck. But in this case, shoulder it is. I move my free hand there, trying to apply a gentle amount of pressure. Acting like this is totally normal when it's anything but.

"Is this right?"

He nods. "Now you just sway to the beat of the song."

"But there's no music playing." I look up at him.

Connor removes his hand from my waist, sliding it into his pocket. He pulls out his phone and scrolls for a minute before the familiar beat of "Thinking Out Loud" by Ed Sheeran starts to play softly. He sets his phone on the counter and rests his hand back on my waist.

We begin swaying back and forth to the song, and my nerves begin to settle. "This isn't so bad. What's the other way?"

Connor lets go of my hand and grasps my waist. "The boy will have both hands on your waist or lower back, and you'll place both on his shoulders or around his neck. You'll see this version more at high school dances. The other is a little more old-fashioned."

I clasp my hands behind his neck, and my mouth goes as dry as sandpaper. It's immediately obvious why this is the

position high school students prefer—it puts you exception-
ally close to your dance partner. Our bodies are practically
touching, so close I could lean forward the slightest bit and
rest my head on his chest.

In Connor's strong, steady hands, I lose track of the song,
completely lost in him. I don't notice he's stopped moving
until it's too late, and my foot lands on top of his. He winces.

"I'm so sorry." I jump back.

"It's fine. You did good."

"Until I stepped on your foot," I mumble.

"At least you weren't in heels." He grabs a water bottle
from the fridge before shutting the door, leaving us in the
dark. Connor steps toward the counter and stops the song,
sliding his phone back in his pocket.

"You're right. That would definitely be worse." I pick up
the bottle he handed me earlier and drop my gaze to my
feet. "Thanks for helping me. I didn't want to look like an
idiot at the dance if I end up going."

"You haven't bought a ticket?"

"I did. I just wish the Long Live Girlies all went to the
same school. I'd feel more confident going to a dance with
them." I sigh, keeping my gaze on my fuzzy floral socks.
"What am I supposed to do if none of the boys ask me to
dance?"

Connor steps closer and awkwardly pats my back like I'm
a baby he's trying to console. "Any boy would be lucky to
dance with you, Shayna. Don't let anyone ever make you
believe otherwise."

I peer up at him and melt at how earnest but gentle his
expression is. Without second-guessing myself, I fling my
arms around his neck, pulling him into a hug. The water
bottle he's holding is crushed in between us, but I don't
care. I squeeze him tight. "Thanks, Connor."

I can feel the hesitation slowly leave his body as his shoulders loosen up. He wraps an arm around me, giving me a gentle squeeze, and I'm completely enveloped in all things Connor. His strong arms. The fresh scent of his soap from his shower mixed with the woodsy scent of his deodorant. The way his hands offer me warmth and reassurance.

I slowly pull back and look up at him. And that's when I see it. Connor Porter is smiling. I repeat, Connor Porter is *smiling*. The smile on his face looks slightly unnatural, but I think that's what makes it look even more beautiful. The boy who never cracks a smile despite the many jokes we've told him over the last three years. The boy whose mom complains that he never smiles in family photos. He's standing here, smiling…*at me*.

"Good night, Shayna." Connor's mouth returns to its typical neutral state, but the smile is still evident in his eyes.

When he leaves the room, I hold my water bottle to the back of my neck, in need of a good cool down.

If it wasn't certain before, it is now: I'm never getting over this crush.

CHAPTER THIRTEEN
CONNOR

I gesture to the large selection of lumber. "Here are your options."

Shayna's eyes go wide as she looks up at the towering shelves. "Um, do you have any favorites? I've only heard of common kinds, like oak and pine. And I've heard of redwood trees, but I'm not even sure if they make wood out of those."

Looks like we're basically starting from ground zero. I move closer to the shelves. "For a project like this, I'd suggest cedar or maple." I point each of them out on the shelves, running my hands along the grains. "They're both pretty water-resistant and look nice on their own, but they take well to stain if that's the route you decide to go."

She takes a sip of her strawberry matcha and looks back and forth between them like it's the hardest choice to make, rather than just simply selecting a species of wood.

"Just pick the one you think will look the best paired with flowers," I say.

"It feels like a big decision." Shayna places her free hand on her hip. "Which one do you think I should get?"

"Are you forgetting our deal?"

"No." She shakes her head. "You said I had to learn how to say no and set boundaries, not make a big decision about the shelves that will be on my flower truck for years to come."

"Part of saying no to people was also about discovering what you enjoy." I shove my hands in my pockets. "You need to figure out what you like—what you want for yourself—not because someone else asks it of you or suggests it."

Her expression grows determined. "You're right." She peruses the options once more before pointing at the cedar. "That one. It's really pretty."

"Cedar it is." I pile the correct number of planks into our cart, based on the measurements we took of the back of her truck.

Before I can push the cart to the next section, Shayna steps in front of it. "I have to ask one more time. Are you sure you don't mind building the shelves? I can always hire someone."

"I've got it."

She hesitates. "I know you work long shifts. I really don't want you to have to watch tutorial videos on your days off."

I blow out a long breath. This wasn't information I was planning on sharing with her—with anyone—but if it will make her not feel bad about me working on this project, then I know I need to tell her. "I don't need to watch any videos."

She steps around the cart, closer to me, puzzled. "How do you know how to build tiered shelving?"

"There were a lot of rainy days in Seattle, so I decided to pick up a hobby other than fishing."

"Woodworking?" she asks, and I nod. "What have you built?"

What *haven't* I built is the real question. I've tried my hand at just about everything: rocking chairs, dressers, coffee tables, and benches. But, oddly enough, my favorite things I've made are vases. I enjoy taking wood and crafting it into unique shapes and designs and adding a glass interior to hold flowers. I've never sold anything I've made—I'm still an amateur woodworker, after all—but creating something new with my own two hands has been a great escape for me.

"Just…things," I grunt, hoping she'll leave the subject alone.

"Oh, come on. You can tell me." She looks up at me expectantly.

"It's nothing special."

"I find that hard to believe." I see her smile out of my periphery as I push the cart forward. "You're not the kind of man to do anything halfway."

Her words strike a chord in me. I'm a hard worker, but I've always struggled with doubting myself. Doubting every word that comes out of my mouth. Doubting that I'll ever be enough for anyone. Doubting if I'm really meant to climb the career ladder at the station. Doubting why anyone would ever buy mediocre wood projects from a nobody when they can get something similar from a professional.

"Mallory didn't say anything about special wood pieces after your family helped you unpack." Shayna takes quick steps to keep stride with me.

"The movers I used brought my truck, furniture, and my boxes first. The final truck has all of my tools and wood pieces."

"When is this load coming?"

"Tomorrow," I mutter.

"Mal didn't mention helping you unpack again."

"That's because she doesn't know," I say, wishing she would quit digging.

Shayna stops walking in the middle of the main aisle. I sigh and turn around, ready for whatever verbal lashing I'm about to get.

"Were you ever going to tell anyone?"

"Wasn't planning on it."

She closes the distance between us and grabs my arm. My brows knit together when my initial reaction isn't to pull my arm away. I don't have much time to think about it, though, because she continues talking.

"Why are you so insistent on keeping everyone at arm's length?"

"I'm not," I argue.

Shayna doesn't back down. "Then why doesn't your family know about this huge hobby of yours? One so big you have a separate moving truck bringing all the things you've made."

I rub the back of my neck. "I don't know."

"If you're not against it, then how would you feel about a small entourage showing up at your house tomorrow to help?"

I walked right into that. "I—"

"Great, it's settled, then. What time are the movers coming?"

"Eight, but—"

She waves her hand. "Say no more. We've got you covered." She pulls out her phone, probably sending out a group text to assemble her *small entourage*.

I give the cart one good push to get it rolling again and head across the store to where I know they stock vases, occasionally glancing over my shoulder to make sure

Shayna's still following and didn't run into anything while texting and walking. It can be just as dangerous as texting and driving.

During one of my shifts in Seattle, our station was called to a scene where a civilian had walked right into a coned-off section of the road and fallen into an open manhole. How does one walk into a construction zone that's clearly marked? By texting while crossing the road.

Thankfully, Shayna reaches the vase aisle unscathed, though there were a few close calls involving some displays. She slides her phone back into her purse and takes another large sip of her matcha before looking up at the vases. "How did you find them so fast?"

I shrug. "I come here fairly often."

"And you just remember where everything is?"

"Most things."

She fans her face. "There's something so hot about a man who knows his way around a hardware store."

My mouth falls open in shock, and I can't help it—I laugh. This time, it doesn't sound dead. It's alive, echoing throughout the store.

Shayna's eyes go wide as her cheeks turn bright pink. "Please tell me I didn't just say that out loud."

"I would, but then I'd be lying."

"Sweet pea," she hisses, as if it's a curse, making me laugh again. She swats my arm. "Would you stop laughing? Can't you see that I'm mortified?" Shayna shakes her head as she attempts to move around me. "I'm going to go find a dark corner to hide in."

I grab her wrist, stopping her. She looks up at me, a deep blush still evident on her cheeks. Her eyes dart between me and the open aisle over my shoulder, like she's deciding if she has enough room to escape. When she looks up at me again with vulnerability clear in her gaze, I'm hit with a feeling deep in my gut.

I place my free hand on my stomach, wondering what's going on in there. Maybe the chicken sandwich I had for lunch isn't sitting well. Shayna worries her bottom lip and my eyes track the motion. There's that feeling again in the pit of my abdomen.

No. It's not possible. I don't get *butterflies*. But it feels like hundreds of them are taking flight, trying to lead me to her. This can't be happening. Women need more than what I can offer. It's like my ex told me—I'm just a boring, eternal homebody who can't even hold a simple conversation. Shayna deserves more than that. She's sunshine in human form and needs a man who can make her shine brighter, not dull her.

There's no way I can be attracted to Shayna. Scratch that, there's no way I can be attracted to one of my sister's best friends. There has to be some kind of unspoken sibling code about that.

"Sorry," I say, my voice gentle. "I shouldn't have laughed."

"I don't blame you. That was so embarrassing." She peers up at me through her lashes, only a faint blush remaining on her cheeks. "And I like your laugh."

I don't have a response to that. It's usually hard for me to remember the last time I laughed, yet I can recall two distinct times in the past few weeks that I've laughed because of something Shayna said.

"Don't be embarrassed." I let go of her wrist, wanting to break this weird connection between us. "Consider it forgotten."

She presses her lips into a thin line, leaving me to wonder if that wasn't the reaction she wanted. But this—*we*—can't be anything more. "Right. Thanks." Shayna moves farther down the aisle, perusing the galvanized vase options.

I stay by the cart and wait for her, processing everything that just occurred. While Shayna needs to figure out what she wants, it looks like I need to brainstorm some ways to keep myself from thinking that *she's* what I want.

♡ ♡ ♡

I'm refilling my coffee mug the next morning when I hear voices outside. I glance at the time on the microwave. 7:54. The movers shouldn't be here for six more minutes, so that can only mean one thing: Shayna's arrived with her entourage.

I finish topping off my coffee, knowing I'll need the extra boost of caffeine today, before I slide on my shoes and head out front. But no amount of caffeine could have prepared me for the scene before me. When Shayna said she'd have a small entourage ready to help, I was thinking two or three people. Not seven adults on my postage stamp of a front lawn.

There's Shayna, of course, along with Kelsey and Alyssa. I'm pretty sure the brunette talking to them is named Tess, if I remember correctly from the winter trivia night my sister held at her house a few months ago. Then there's Kelsey's boyfriend, Tyler, and both of my parents. Thank goodness Mallory is visiting Griffin; they'd probably be overflowing onto the street, otherwise.

My mom spots me first as I step onto the small square of a front porch. "Connor," she chides as she squeezes around the group to get to me. "Why didn't you tell us you had more stuff to move in? We gladly would've helped." Her eyes glimmer with hurt that leaves me feeling like a horrible son. "Thank goodness Shayna called us."

It's no use. No matter how much I try to do things on my own, to not hurt those around me, I always end up saying or doing something that inevitably leads to disappointing the people I care most about. "Sorry, Mom. I didn't want to make you come back out for another load."

"We want to be here for you." She steps closer.

I'm not a hugger, but I can tell this is something she needs. I open my arms, careful to balance my mug so I don't burn her, and my mom pulls me into a tight embrace. I let her hold on for as long as she needs, even though physical contact makes me uncomfortable the second it starts. When she loosens her hold, I step back and take a sip of my coffee.

"I'll try to remember that," I say.

She smiles and gestures to the group on my lawn. "Go ahead and greet your guests."

I hadn't planned on it. Talking to large groups, even when they're comprised of people I know, always makes my body tense up and my palms clammy.

"Right." I step onto the grass and everyone turns to me. I swallow hard. It's just friends and family. They won't care what I say. I take a deep breath, then open my mouth, hoping something resembling a coherent sentence will come out. "Thanks for coming to help. Really appreciate you all taking time out of your week to be here. I—" When I spot the moving truck rolling down the street, I sigh in relief. "I think the movers are pulling up now."

Everyone turns to face the road, and I use the distraction to wipe away the fresh beads of sweat that have formed on my forehead. I know there's no need to be this nervous, but I can't help it. As someone who tries to keep the majority of my life private, it feels scary knowing people are about to see the projects that feel oddly personal.

Once the moving truck is parked in front of my house, they hop out and open the back, revealing the large variety of projects I made over the last few years.

"Con, what is all this?" My mom stares at the contents of the truck in awe.

"Some wood projects."

"You made all this?" she asks, and I reluctantly nod.

"They're amazing." Tess shoots me an impressed look.

Shayna sidles up next to me and squeezes my arm. "Connor, I know you said you picked this up as a hobby, but I didn't expect this."

Alyssa's jaw drops. "How can I buy some of your pieces?"

"I don't sell them." I look at my feet, kicking a random rock on the road.

"Why not?" Kelsey balks, sounding exactly like I'd expect my sister to if she were here.

"They're not professional."

"Not professional?" This time, it's my dad who sounds personally affronted.

My mom looks from my projects to me. "You're kidding, right? I'd be lucky to feature any of these items in my house and tell every single visitor exactly where it came from."

"Because I'm your son."

She shakes her head. "No, because pieces like this deserve to be seen."

I've never been good at accepting compliments. It's awkward to have people tell you how amazing or talented or handsome you are. Especially because I think people often expect a compliment in return. But I'd get all anxious and probably say something ridiculous like *I like your face.*

The guy I've been in contact with throughout this cross-country move reaches out and shakes my hand. "Where do you want us to put everything?"

"The shed out back."

"Copy that." He and the other mover start unloading the truck.

My unpacking crew turns to me.

"How can we help?" my mom asks.

"Maybe figuring out how to organize all my projects once they're unloaded. Some of them require two people to lift."

"You heard the man," Kelsey says, and everyone moves to the back of the house.

"Did you not have to work today?" I ask everyone as we walk, surprised so many people would show up on a Wednesday morning.

"I moved a few clients around," Alyssa says.

"My PA is covering my appointments for the morning," Tyler pitches in.

Tess pulls her long brown hair back into a ponytail. "I was already taking the day off to run errands, so this just became my first stop of the day."

They all step into the shed while I stand outside, stunned that they would show up at the last minute for me. I've had a lot of teammates over the course of my life, between sports and my job at the station, but I've never had many friends. I know my parents would drop anything to help me, but the fact that my sister's friends are willing to show up when I don't feel like I've done anything to deserve it leaves me feeling unusually emotional.

Shayna pops her head out of the shed. "Are you coming?"

I nod and follow her inside, where I find everyone looking around the space.

"Connie, I can't believe you have such a knack for wood-working." I've always hated my mom's nickname for me, but she's the woman who birthed me, so I suck it up. She turns to me, teary-eyed. "This is amazing."

I glance around the space, trying to take in the room with fresh eyes. All of my project lumber is shelved on the walls in neat rows. One side of the room is bare, ready to be filled with the pieces the movers are about to bring in, while I have a giant table that will hold my different saws and woodworking tools on the other side. My current project, a custom coatrack to go next to my front door, is out on the table, waiting to be sanded one more time before I stain it.

"It's not much." I mean, I did buy this house primarily for the large shed, knowing I could use it as a project space, but it's nothing compared to the massive workshops some people have.

"Not much? This is more than a hobby, son." My dad claps me on the shoulder.

Everyone makes small remarks of agreement. I rock awkwardly on my heels, not knowing how to accept all their praise. Thankfully, the mover comes in, carrying one of my larger benches. I direct them to the corner of the unused area.

While everyone else seems distracted by the projects coming in, Shayna approaches me. "You're seriously talented, Connor."

I shrug. "It's just a hobby."

"It's not *just* anything." Shayna turns and places her hands on both of my shoulders, forcing me to look at her. "It's art."

There's a sincerity in her words and gaze that makes me feel proud of my work. Like it's not just something she's saying to puff me up, but because she actually means it.

"I think I need to add an amendment to our deal."

"What's that?" I ask.

"We're going to work on your confidence. No more doubting yourself." She gestures around the shed. "Not when you're this talented."

It's my biggest weakness: self-doubt. I'm not sure it's something that can magically be fixed over the span of a few weeks. My insecurity doesn't only apply to my wood projects; it overflows into nearly every aspect of my life. My job. My inability to choose the right words whenever I'm talking to people. My now nonexistent dating life. How am I supposed to be confident when the only person I've ever dated brought up every aspect of who I am and smashed it to smithereens?

I frown. "I thought we already had a deal?"

"That was before I realized you can't take a compliment and don't believe in your art."

I press my lips into a firm line. She's not going to let this go, which means I only have one option here. "I guess you have yourself a new deal."

Shayna smiles. "You won't regret it."

She's wrong—because I already do.

CHAPTER FOURTEEN
CONNOR

"Porter, you've got a visitor." Fisher leans closer and wiggles his eyebrows. "Of the *female* variety."

I put down the laundry I was folding and leave our locker area, following Fisher to the station's lobby. My eyes widen in surprise when I see Shayna standing there in a floral sweater tucked into a black skirt. "What're you doing here?"

She hands me a box bearing the logo of a local mom-and-pop donut shop. The sweet smell of sugary dough hits me, making my mouth water. "I wanted to drop these off for your crew as a thank you for saving me the other day."

"You didn't have to do that. We were just doing our job."

"I know, but my mama always taught me to show my gratitude through baked goods. And since no one would want to eat anything I've baked, I figured donuts would do."

A faint memory pops to the forefront of my mind of a time when she made cookies and brought them to one of her Friday night sleepovers with Mallory. We quickly learned that her snickerdoodles contained an obscene amount of cinnamon since she didn't know the difference between teaspoons and tablespoons.

Shayna must see the wheels turning in my brain because she rubs her forehead. "Please tell me you're not thinking of my snickerdoodle snafu." I shrug and she sighs. "I've learned my lesson. Baking: bad. Buying sweets from bakeries: good."

I lift the box slightly. "The crew will appreciate these. Thanks."

"Are you coming Friday?"

I quirk a brow, unsure what she's referring to.

Her cheeks flush pink. "You know, Alyssa's and my birthday party?"

Oh, right. Now that she mentions it, I remember getting an invitation via text from Mallory. The second I saw the word *party*, I closed out of the message and didn't think twice about it until now.

No.

The word sits on the edge of my tongue, but before I can say it, Shayna says, "It would mean a lot to me if you did."

How am I supposed to say no now? Especially after I told her to start sharing what she wants. I dip my chin. "I'll be there." Guess I need to go shopping for two birthday presents when I get off my shift. *After* I do an internet search for birthday-present ideas for women in their mid-twenties.

"Great." She beams. "Well, I'll let you get back to work. I just wanted to drop those off." She gestures to the box of donuts I'm still holding.

"Thanks." I place the box on the counter and lead her out to the engine bay, since the exit through there is closer to the parking lot.

"See you Friday." Shayna waves goodbye and smiles at the rest of my crew, who seem to have miraculously appeared in the two minutes we were in the station and are now pretending to do random jobs that don't need doing.

It's a good thing firefighters aren't tested on their subtlety, because my crew would fail. Miserably. Fisher's broom isn't even touching the cement. He's literally sweeping the air.

"Who was that?" Malone tosses me the rag she was rubbing the already spotless engine with before pulling her long hair up into a bun.

"The woman I saved in the flower shop fire," I say, figuring it's best to include as little detail as possible.

Fisher lets out a wolf whistle. "Did she want to come see you in action again?"

"No," I grunt. "She was dropping off donuts as a thank-you."

"I can think of some other ways she probably wants to thank you." Fisher takes the rag from my hands and winds it up before using it to slap me on the butt.

I roll my eyes. "It's not like that with Shayna."

"Oh, she has a name." Malone and Fisher share a conspiratorial smile.

"Sounds like you've got yourself a badge bunny." Gordon leans against the fire pole, wearing a smirk.

"A what?"

"Badge bunny," Gordon repeats. I stare at him blankly, waiting for further explanation. "You know, a woman who loves a man in uniform." Gordon gestures to the door Shayna just walked through. "You saved her from that fire, and now she's showing back up because she's attracted to the man who saved her. We've all been there, probie. But if you get tired of her flirting with you, feel free to send her my way. She is smoking hot." He steps forward and gives me a hardy clap on the back. I have to dig the heels of my boots in to avoid being pushed over, but there's no way I'm letting this guy feel like he won—and I'm definitely not letting him talk about Shayna that way.

"Be careful how you talk about my sister's friend." My tone remains calm, but the threat in my words hangs in the air.

Gordon raises a brow like he's amused that he struck a nerve. "So there's a history there?"

I'd love to wipe the smirk off his face, but that's not the kind of impression I'd like to make on my station in my first few weeks here.

"I think we've had enough fun for today." Lieutenant Moreno steps out from behind the engine. I never even saw him. The man is stealthy. "Back to work, Gordon. The oven needs cleaning after you burnt that pizza yesterday."

"We had to leave for a call," he mumbles.

Moreno crosses his arms over his broad chest. "And you left the oven on."

"Yes, Lieutenant." Gordon leaves the bay like a dog with his tail between his legs.

Moreno looks to me. "You good, Porter?"

I nod. "Yes, sir."

He nods back and walks away as quickly as he arrived. It didn't take long for me to realize that he's a man of few words, just like me. It makes me relate to him more and gives me a sliver of hope that someone like me who doesn't talk much and chooses their words carefully could thrive in a higher position at the station.

"This is delicious." Fisher smiles through his mouthful of donut.

"Gross," I mutter before moving past him to grab a donut for myself. Anything sweet doesn't last long at this station.

The box is already mostly empty when I get to it. I move to grab the last fritter, but Gordon snatches it before I can.

"You snooze, you lose, probie." He winks before heading toward the kitchen.

I grab a glazed donut. It's a poor replacement for the fritter, but it'll have to do. I eat it in a few bites and head back to the locker room. I look at the mound of laundry I need to finish folding and realize there's a small baggie sitting on top. I pick it up and am hit with a sweet apple-cinnamon scent. An apple fritter. I read the flower-shaped yellow Post-it note stuck to it.

I wanted to make sure you got your favorite! Thanks again. Xoxo, Shay

I always requested a fritter when my mom picked up donuts for Mallory and her friends whenever they slept over. But I can't believe Shayna remembered that. I also have no clue how she got back here. Maybe she asked someone on the crew to put it in the back for me.

I put it in my locker to eat later since I already had a glazed donut, then attempt to fold a shirt, but my mind keeps going back to Shayna. It's not just her personality that's infectious—it's her. Everything about her makes me want to be around her. Her encouraging spirit. Her kind heart. Her ambition. The way she can make me laugh and feel more alive than I've ever been. Not to mention the fact that she's beautiful.

It's more than that, though. I'm beginning to realize that she means something to me. But I'm not built for a relationship. Jillian's words replay in my mind like an annoying fly I can never seem to swat away.

I groan, wringing the shirt in my hands that I seem incapable of folding. I need to get Shayna out of my mind. I throw the mangled shirt back onto the clean pile and head to our in-station gym. There's nothing a hard workout can't fix.

CHAPTER FIFTEEN
SHAYNA

"Happy birthday, dear Alyssa and Shayna. Happy birthday to you," all of our friends and family sing in unison. I'm not the kind of girl who loves being the center of attention, but I love any opportunity to be surrounded by loved ones, so if that means dealing with everyone staring at me while they sing completely off-key, I'm here for it.

I close my eyes and make the same wish that I've made every year since I turned twelve: that Connor Porter will fall madly in love with me or that I'll finally find a man who makes me feel more for him than I ever have for Connor. One of these years it's bound to come true.

I squeeze Alyssa's hand, and we lean forward and blow out the candles on our cake. With our birthdays only a week apart, we've celebrated them together ever since we became best friends in middle school. It's made the day even more magical getting to share the celebration with her, and one of our favorite parts is picking out a new cake flavor each year. With this being the fourteenth year we've celebrated together, we've already had a variety of flavors like white chocolate raspberry, triple chocolate, Funfetti, and lemon blueberry. We've even had our fair share of ice cream cakes in our teenage years, but this time we decided on a berry Chantilly cake. It feels like a more sophisticated choice as we enter our twenty-fifth year.

While everyone claps, I seek out Connor in the crowd. My eyes instantly spot him. He's my opposite in nearly every way, but just like two ends of a magnet, I'm drawn to him. It doesn't matter if we're in a crowded room or the only two there. It's like there's an invisible string that connects us, and I feel this gentle tug toward him every time he's around. This undeniable feeling of connection that ties him to me.

If only he saw it—felt it—too.

But, hey, maybe this will finally be the year my birthday wish comes true. Either I'll get over Connor once and for all, or he'll open his eyes and truly see me. This is the year of me chasing my dreams. While it would be amazing to have a man who loves me more than anything else in the world right by my side through it all, I'm still grateful to have friends and family who love and support me.

Kelsey grabs a knife and begins cutting the cake. She worked at a bakery for one of her many previous side jobs. She only lasted a month there, but she insists on cutting cakes at every event since she knows how the pros do it. And she does cut a pretty and even slice.

"Here you go, birthday girls." She hands me and Alyssa plates and plastic forks.

We each scoop up a forkful and clink them together. "Cheers to twenty-five." I take a bite, and it's heavenly. The cake itself is light and, mixed with the sweet frosting and the berry jam, it's the perfect harmony of flavors.

"Y'all have to try this," I say around my mouthful. Every-one starts grabbing plates while I plop down on the couch, ready to go to town on this cake. There might even need to be seconds involved. It's my birthday, after all—I can eat two slices of cake if I want to.

Connor approaches me right as I take another bite. "Is this seat taken?" I shake my head, and he sits beside me. He keeps glancing between me and his plate like there's something he wants to say but is debating it.

I finish chewing, then say, "Whatever it is you're thinking, you can just say it."

"You have frosting on your lip."

Well, that's embarrassing. I rub at my mouth with the back of my hand. "Did I get it?"

He shakes his head and reaches toward me. "May I?"

The thought of his hands on my face—on my lips—has me speechless, so I nod out of fear that I'll say something ridiculous if I attempt to formulate a sentence right now.

He inches toward my face in what feels like slow motion. When his large hand cups my jaw and cheek, I can't help but imagine that he's grabbing my face for an entirely different reason. I lean into his touch as my eyes flutter shut. He gently wipes his thumb across the corner of my mouth, and my lips part out of instinct.

Connor sucks in a sharp breath and yanks his hand away. "Got it," he mumbles.

I open my eyes, wondering if he's feeling the same way I am. That quick little inhale has to mean that I make him feel something. Or I've simply reached a whole new level of delusion.

His face is as red as a fire truck, and Connor looks anywhere but at me. Maybe I'm not *entirely* delusional.

"Thanks." I shovel another bite of cake into my mouth, trying to make this situation feel normal again. I gesture to his slice. "You'd better eat that before I do."

The color on his cheeks begins to fade as he shakes his head at my antics. Connor shoots me a wide-eyed look as he raises his fork and takes a bite. I can't help but stare at him as he licks a little bit of rogue frosting from his lips. I've never once wished to be Chantilly frosting…at least, not until today.

He nods thoughtfully. "You're right. This is good."

Kelsey sits down on my other side with a slice of cake three times the size of mine. I look from it to her, and she grins. "I built up an appetite cutting all that cake." She takes a giant bite and hums. "Definitely worth it."

"That's what I just said." Connor takes another bite, and I can't help but smile. It feels so right having him here.

Kelsey leans around me to look at him. "I don't think I've ever heard you willingly string so many words together."

He shrugs but doesn't respond.

She looks at me with a raised eyebrow that seems to ask *What was that about?*

I shake my head. I don't know what to tell her. I know everyone seems to say that Connor is this quiet, grumpy guy who doesn't say much, but he's never seemed to have that issue around me. Yes, he's a little reserved, but we've had plenty of conversations, especially recently.

"Present time." Tess appears from the kitchen with two gift bags in tow. Everyone gathers in the living room as I finish off my slice.

By the time I've opened the majority of my gifts, I'm feeling extremely thankful for this community of people I have around me. They know and love me so well, as evidenced by all my flower-themed gifts. My mom always told me that if you tell people you like something, you'd better be prepared to get gifts revolving around it for the rest of your life.

I guess it's a good thing that flowers are my life, because I'll never get tired of people thinking of me when they see anything involving them. Everything from my clothes to my decor is always floral focused, and I'm here for it.

My lap and the floor in front of me are covered in things like a new dainty floral-print throw blanket, a check to buy more flowers from my suppliers and wrapping materials for the bouquets I'll sell on the truck, and a hot-pink floral midi skirt Alyssa found at a boutique. Spending time with my favorite people is enough of a gift in itself, but I can't wait to put all these new items to use.

"I have a little something for you." Austin crosses the room and hands me an envelope.

"Thanks." I open the card and read the note inside.

Happy birthday, Shayna. I hope this year as a new business owner is the best one yet. Hopefully your birthday present, a meeting with the best local small business lawyer I could find, will help you get ready to launch. Everything is fully covered, so all you have to worry about is showing up and letting them do the rest. I can't wait to see the finished truck. -Austin

Alyssa already told me that Austin had a birthday present that would help with the business side of things, but I thought he was going to connect me with someone, not pay for all the expenses that come with registering my business.

"Austin, this is too much." I mean, I know he's a famous MLB player, but it feels like a big gift for me to accept from a friend of a friend.

"Nonsense." He hands me a business card so fancy it only has a name and phone number. "All you have to do is call her office to set up a meeting time that works for you."

I'm trying to learn how to accept help that's offered to me, so instead of arguing with Austin, I hop up from the couch and give him a quick hug. "Thank you so much."

"I'm happy I could help." Austin reaches into his jacket pocket, pulls out another envelope, and hands it to Alyssa. "Happy birthday, Lyss."

Her smile is shy as she carefully rips the envelope open. She reads the card, and her jaw drops. "Shut up. You did not."

"I know it's not Taylor Swift, but since she's not touring right now, I thought this was the next best thing."

Alyssa squeals and flings herself into Austin's arms. "Thank you. This is literally the best present ever."

"What is it?" I ask.

"He's taking me to see the Jonas Brothers with Jesse McCartney as their opener."

"Oh my word, talk about nostalgia." I grab her arm and bounce excitedly in place with her.

Austin pulls four more tickets from his pocket. "Then it's a good thing you're going, too." He hands me, Kelsey, and Tess a ticket, and the extra to Alyssa. "This one's for Mallory. I figured a private box to dance with your best friends would be more fun than just going with me."

Alyssa hugs him again. If she wouldn't kill me, I'd yell, "Just kiss already!"

"You're coming, too, right?" Alyssa asks him.

"I'd never pass up the chance to see the Jonas Brothers. They're my favorite boy band."

Tyler blows out a low whistle. "You're a braver man than me. Come give me a visit if your eardrums can't handle the decibel that will be reached in that box with all the Long Live Girlies."

"Hey." Kelsey pouts.

He leans over and kisses the frown right off her face. "I love you, Anderson. But you scream-singing at a concert with your friends is something I'm not sure I ever want to experience."

She sighs. "That's fair."

"Remind me to bring my earplugs." Tess laughs. "I will sing and dance my heart out with y'all, but your girl's got older ears that will ring for days."

"Oh, you're only what?" Alyssa purses her lips like she's doing the math in her head. "Seven years older than us?"

"And I feel it more every day." Tess rubs her lower back. "But that could also just be from trying to keep up with Evie."

"What do you mean by 'keep up with me'?" Evie pops her head out of the kitchen where she's eating her second slice of cake.

Tess shakes her head, wearing a soft smile. "You have fast little legs and lots of energy that I don't have anymore."

"Yeah, that's because you're old," Evie deadpans, eliciting a lot of snickers from everyone in the living room. "It's another reason I need you to find me a daddy. Clock's ticking, Mom."

Tess covers her laughter with her hand. She turns to us, shaking her head in bemusement. "Where does she come up with these things? I'd better go over there before she starts concocting a plan with Uncle Ty."

I glance back at Evie to see that Tyler is now kneeling next to her chair as she whispers animatedly in his ear. "You'd better hurry."

"Yep." Tess moves across the room with the kind of speed only a mom possesses.

Connor clears his throat next to me. "Happy birthday, Shayna." He hands me a box wrapped with floral paper and entirely too much tape. The fact that he thought to buy me a gift and spent the time wrapping it himself sends my heart racing before I've even opened it.

I offer him a shy smile as I rip off the wrapping paper. It takes a little more arm strength to tear through the loads of tape, but I finally manage to remove it all and slide the lid off the box. I can't hold back my gasp when I see what's inside—a yellow shirt that says Sunshine Blooms. It's a beautiful font, and the o's are even shaped as flowers.

I look at him with happy tears pooling in my eyes.

"I hope it fits. I asked Mallory for your size."

"Where did you get the design?" I ask, running my fingers over the letters.

"I had a designer create it. Once you get your real logo, I can have another shirt made."

"Can *this* be my real logo?" I hug the shirt to my chest.

He raises an eyebrow. "Seriously?"

"Yes, it's perfect."

Connor rubs the back of his neck, looking adorably shy. "I can send you the files if you really like it."

"This was so thoughtful." I lean over and throw my arms around his neck. "You're the best. Thank you." He's as stiff as a statue at first, but after a moment, he seems to settle into the hug. His strong arms wrap around me as he returns the embrace.

Everything about this hug feels infinitely different than the one I shared with Austin minutes ago. Being completely enveloped in Connor has my pulse skyrocketing. Every breath I take in brings another whiff of the woodsy deodorant he's used since high school. With my head against his broad chest, I can hear the steady thud of his heart and feel the ridges of all the muscles he works hard for in all his training sessions.

"I'm here," Mallory shouts as she walks through the front door. "Sorry I'm late."

Even though I don't want our hug to end, I pull back.

She drops her luggage in the doorway and runs to where Alyssa and I are sitting, pulling us into a group hug. "Happy birthday, friends."

We thank her and squeeze her back. It's a good thing Mallory is back from her trip to LA to serve as a hefty dose of reality.

Over her shoulder, I make eye contact with Connor. His gaze is unreadable. I can see the walls that seemed to come down when he hugged me rebuild themselves brick by brick.

I bite my bottom lip and grip the shirt he made me more tightly in my hand. I need to grow up and stop wishing on birthday candles and shooting stars. To stop thinking this is anything more than Connor helping out his sister's friend because she asked him to.

But after spending so much quality time with Connor lately, this doesn't feel like a childhood crush anymore. It feels like the real deal. So moving on is going to be a whole lot easier said than done.

CHAPTER SIXTEEN

CONNOR

THANK GOODNESS MALLORY WALKED in and saved me from my embrace with Shayna.

Okay, that's a lie.

Thank goodness Mallory walked in and saved me from *myself*. From the weird mixture of emotions that started rising to the surface like small green flower buds popping through the dirt at the first sign of spring.

I don't know who I am anymore—who Shayna is making me become. She has me speaking in flower talk and thinking about things like her floral perfume and questioning what I really want.

I clench my hands—which are still trembling from hugging Shayna—into fists, trying to get a grip on myself. After my sister is finished greeting her friends, she falls onto the couch beside me and nudges me with her elbow. "Griffin says hi."

Everyone falls back into conversation around us, laughter filling the room. This kind of environment has always been overstimulating for me and makes me retreat into myself even more. I turn to my sister. Since she's family, I usually feel a little less awkward around her than most people, but being in a party environment leaves my palms sweaty and my mind racing. I move my gaze around the room and instantly spot Shayna. My shoulders fall as the tension leaves my body.

I turn my attention back to Mallory. "Good trip?" I keep things short and sweet to leave no room for error.

I expect her to roll her eyes at my briefness, but my sister has a far-off look about her, like her mind is still in LA with her movie-star boyfriend. "It was amazing. Being with Griff in person reiterated everything I feel about him. He's the one for me."

I search out Shayna in the room again and ask, "How do you know he's the one?"

Mallory stares at me, probably trying to figure out if I'm an imposter. "Who are you and what have you done with my brother?"

Yep, I called that. I shrug. "Just curious how people know things like that."

She raises an eyebrow. "For any particular reason?"

I think she's trying to call my bluff. But I don't know if there's anything to even bluff about. I avoid emotions like they cause third-degree burns. That makes it a little more difficult to understand the cacophony of things stirring inside me lately. But talking about my feelings…that thought feels like walking into a burning building without my turnouts.

I frown. "Just making conversation."

She stares blankly. "I repeat, who are you and what have you done with my brother?"

I let out an exasperated sigh. "I won't ask any more questions."

"No, no. I'm just shocked you're trying to hold a conversation." Mallory takes off her jacket and drapes it across the end of the chaise. "You really want to know why I think Griffin's the one?"

I gesture for her to continue.

"All right, let me start by saying I don't think it's a one-size-fits-all kind of thing. There's not some magic formula that adds up to let you know you found the one."

I hold in a sigh. A concrete formula sure would make it a lot easier to understand.

"But for me, I knew he was the one when I pictured myself old and wrinkled and sitting on the back porch, looking out at a yard of my kids and grandkids running around and laughing while I sip on a Dr Pepper. I can't imagine anyone else but Griffin at my side." Mallory smiles softly. "For some people, it happens right when they see the other person—love at first sight. For others, it's more of a slow burn that grows over time. And, to speak in your woodworking terms, sometimes love slaps you like a two-by-four to the head you never saw coming."

Before I can fully soak in her words, Shayna sits beside Mallory, pulling her in for a side hug. "I missed you so much."

"I was only gone for a week." Mallory's entire demeanor softens. Shayna seems to have that effect on most people. "But I missed y'all, too." My sister blows out a shaky breath, offering a rare display of emotion. "Why does the love of my life have to live all the way across the country from everyone else I love?"

"It won't be forever. That boy loves you too much to be gone for long." I'm pretty sure I see tears glimmering in Shayna's eyes. I wonder what it would feel like to love and care for others so strongly that it brought tears to my eyes seeing them hurting. She looks up and makes eye contact with me. It feels like her gaze sees right through me, like

I'm transparent and she can read my every thought. Shayna offers me a smile. "Sorry, did I interrupt y'all?"

I shake my head. "Not at all." I push off the couch and stand. "I'm going to head out. I have an early morning at the station tomorrow."

Shayna gets up and wraps her arms around me. "Thanks for coming, and for my shirt."

I gingerly pat her back, not ready to encounter the effects of a full-on Shayna hug again. I've had enough feelings and talk about emotions for the day. I pull away and fold my arms in front of my chest. I ignore the fact that Shayna's eyes immediately drag along my forearms and up my biceps. "If I have downtime at the station tomorrow, I'm going to work on the design for your shelves. I'll text you if I have any questions."

She blinks rapidly and nods. "Sure, sounds good. Thanks, Connor."

I raise my hand in a small two-finger wave and make my way through the crowd of people until I find Alyssa. The thought of showing up to their joint birthday party with only a gift for Shayna felt weird, so I got Alyssa a Sephora gift card thanks to a random Reddit thread for female gift ideas. Once I give it to her, I head outside and take quick steps toward Sulley.

I inhale deeply and slowly let out a breath through my nose as I put my key in the ignition. After starting the truck, I grip the steering wheel until my knuckles turn white. I don't know when I started thinking of my truck as Sulley, the name Shayna gave it, but I guess it's just that Shayna effect again.

Now that we've picked the materials I need from the hardware store, I should have a little bit of time to myself to work on the shelves for her flower truck. Time where I don't have to see her. Be in her orbit.

I don't know what exactly it is about Shayna that has made me feel some type of way lately, but I think some time apart will be good.

"Porter, I need to speak to you." Captain Dalton disappears into his office.

"It was nice knowing ya." Gordon winks at me.

I grimace and attempt to shake off whatever *that* was as I head to Cap's office. I can't think of a reason he'd have to fire me less than a month into me being here. But what if he's decided that I'm not a good fit for the crew? Or maybe he thinks I'm too quiet or standoffish to work with.

I take a deep breath as I reach his office. I think of Shayna telling me to be more confident, so I push down the doubt filling my mind and stand taller as I knock on the glass door. Captain waves his fingers, motioning me into the room without looking up. The lack of eye contact doesn't bode well for me. I take cautious steps into the room and stand before his desk.

"I'm aware you haven't even been here for a month."

That start doesn't sound promising. I drop my gaze to my boots, clasp my hands behind my back, and steel myself as I wait to hear the fate of my job.

"But I have a favor to ask of you."

I lift my head to look at him. Captain's hands are steepled atop a pile of paperwork. I've never been good at reading other people, but the expression he's wearing is obviously tentative.

"I've heard around the station that you're single. Is that correct?"

My brow furrows. I don't know what being single has to do with my job, but since it's Captain asking, I nod. "Yes, sir."

"Have you heard of the LFD's annual community fundraising event?"

"Can't say I'm aware of the specifics, sir."

"The firefighter's calendar brings in the most money for the LFD every year."

I swallow hard, silently pleading for him to not ask me to pose shirtless for a calendar.

"But our big event is the firefighter auction."

"I've heard the crew mention that."

"Good. Well, firefighters from a variety of stations are selected to be bid on. The highest bidder wins a date with that firefighter"—he spreads his arms wide like he's telling me I won the lottery—"and you've been selected as a last-minute addition to represent Station 13."

My cheeks puff up, and I blow out a long breath. "Why would the LFD choose me? I just started."

"When a firefighter saves a local woman during his first week on the job, it's bound to catch the attention of the higher-ups."

I press my lips into a hard line. "I'm guessing I don't have a choice in this, sir?"

Captain offers me a reassuring smile. "Just remember, it's for the kids. Think of how many extra Christmas gifts they'll be able to provide for the community later this year because of your generosity."

It's not like I could exactly tell my captain no, but when he brings up the kids, it's impossible to turn him down. Even though the last thing I want is to be a date auctioned off to the highest bidder. A shiver wracks my body at the thought of some of the women who come to events like this with the sole purpose of sinking their claws into a firefighter.

"Isn't it soon?" I don't know if I want it to be soon to get it over with or far in the distant future so I can avoid thinking about it for a while.

"This Saturday morning. The dates will take place directly after the event." Captain Dalton rounds his desk and claps me on the shoulder. "Thanks for being a good sport about this. Good luck, Porter."

I'm definitely going to need it.

CHAPTER SEVENTEEN

SHAYNA

I need your help.

Ask away!

I would say you failed for saying yes without knowing what I need help with, but I'm desperate.

I know you wouldn't ask for help unless you really needed it. What's up?

I have to fill out a questionnaire.

I'm not really seeing the issue…

It's asking me questions about myself and what I look for in a date.

> Still not seeing the problem…

I don't like talking about myself. Also, how am I supposed to know what my best qualities are?

> Ah, so you reached out because I'm supposed to help you build your confidence. Or you just want me to tell you how amazing you are?

I didn't mean it like that.

The three little dots appear and disappear repeatedly. I can picture the frustration on Connor's face as he tries to figure out how to explain his request, so I decide to put him out of his misery before his face becomes stuck in a permanent frown.

> Relax, I'm messing with you.

> Be there in ten!

I pull up to Connor's house. As I put the car in park, my stomach swirls at the realization that I don't know what Connor's questionnaire is even for. Or why the form needs information on the kind of woman he wants to date. It's going to kill me if I have to hear him describe qualities I don't possess. Maybe this wasn't such a smart idea.

I'm about to grab my phone and text him that something came up to save my heart a world of pain when Connor steps out onto his front porch and waves. He must've heard me drive up.

"Bugleweed," I mutter. There's no turning back now. I reposition my headband and smooth my hands along my ribbed floral long-sleeved shirt before stepping out of the car and closing the distance between us.

He leaves one hand in his pocket but spreads his other arm wide as I near him. I wrap my arms around him, accepting his hug. Only, he doesn't squeeze me. I pull my head back, and that's when I realize that he was gesturing for me to come inside, not opening his arms for a welcome hug. Splendid. Wonderful. Fan-freaking-tastic.

Connor awkwardly pats my back while I hold onto him like a barnacle.

Just call me a stage-six clinger.

I clear my throat and step back, moving inside his house with a speed I didn't know I possessed while avoiding eye contact. Connor's footsteps sound behind me, and I hear him shut the front door as I take a seat on his couch next to his open laptop.

My panic dissipates a little when I see the internet search he has pulled up: *How to make myself sound more confident than I feel.*

If someone who looks like a man sculpted to perfection by none other than Michelangelo himself can struggle with confidence, then it makes me feel less alone with my inner battles.

Connor takes the seat beside me, grabs his laptop, and exits out of the tab. The next web page pops up. From the brief glance I'm able to get, it appears to be whatever he wants help filling out.

The swirling sensation in my stomach returns. "You never did tell me what this questionnaire was for."

He drops his face into his hands. "It's embarrassing."

Can't be as embarrassing as me thinking he was opening his arms to hug me when he was only gesturing for me to go inside.

"Try me."

Connor runs his hands through his hair. My eyes track his movement, appreciating the way his muscles bulge against his cotton shirt. "I'm going to be one of the bachelors in the annual LFD charity auction."

A laugh bursts out of my lips at the ridiculous thought of Connor on a stage and being bid on for dates. But when I see the grim look on his face, I sober. "Wait, you're serious?"

"Unfortunately."

I grab the laptop from him. He attempts to take it back, but I hold a hand out to stop him as I read over the questions. They don't seem too outlandish. The questionnaire covers everything from the highest level of schooling he's completed and what words his loved ones would use to describe him to asking him to share his ideal date and what he looks for in a partner.

"So, you need me to help you answer these so you can get the best date there." I pick at the yellow polish on my nails, trying to look nonchalant. "Anyone specific you have in mind?"

He shakes his head. "I just don't want to look like an idiot up there, and that's exactly what will happen if I answer these questions myself."

I reach out to comfort him but think better of it since he seems to still pull away whenever I touch him. I pin my hand under my thigh, putting it in leg jail. "You're selling yourself short."

"No." His voice is firm. "I think you have too much confidence in me."

"There's no such thing. Come on, I'll show you." I gesture with my free hand to the laptop, ready for him to shoot a question my way.

"All right." Connor clears his throat. "Highest level of schooling."

I tilt my head. "You could put 'High school graduate. No further schooling was necessary when I found my passion: fighting fires for my community.'"

He glances at me but continues typing. "This is why I need you."

Connor needs me. My traitorous heart raps in my chest. No, he needs my help getting a date with another woman. The hope welling inside me bursts like a bubble hitting concrete.

"Words my family and friends would use to describe me?"

"Give me a few minutes for that one." I pull out my phone and type out a group text to Mallory and her mom.

Annoying. Grumpy. Hermit.

Veronica Mallory Porter, I raised you better than that.

Ooh, I got the full name. That must mean I'm really in trouble.

And to think I was going to make chicken and dumplings for family dinner this weekend since it's your favorite.

I guess I'll just have to make Connor's favorite.

NOOO.

You know how much I hate chili.

Whoever thought ground beef belongs in soup deserves jail time.

Don't be so dramatic, dear.

Also, chili isn't soup.

As entertaining as this is, I really do need some words to describe Connor!

Okay, I'll play nice as long as Mom agrees to still make chicken and dumplings.

Deal.

GIF of a man saying 'get in my belly'

Connor is pragmatic.

Courageous. He's always been my brave boy.

He's diligent and meticulous. I mean, have you seen his house and shed? In high school, I moved the lamp on his nightstand a few centimeters to see how long it would take him to notice, and he noticed IMMEDIATELY.

He's hardworking and reliable. I don't think he's ever shown up late in his life.

As much as I love to rag on him, Connor's loyal, too.

The most loyal kind of man you'll ever meet.

These are all great, thank you both so much!

Dare I ask what you need all these adjectives for?

Let's just say it involves a fundraiser.

OH MY GOSH!!! Please tell me he's going to be in the firefighter auction.

Ding, ding, ding. We have a winner!

I don't know that I like the idea of women bidding on my son like he's a piece of meat.

But I suppose since it's for charity…

I just looked it up and sent you the location, day, and time, Mom. We're so there.

I'm not sure he'll like having people he
knows there…

Which is exactly why I HAVE to go. I'm never letting him live this down.

He won't even know we're there.

Speak for yourself, mamacita.

I bite my bottom lip. I hope Connor won't be mad that his family found out because of me. I look up and find him watching me intently.

"Good news: I got some adjectives to describe you from your mom and sister."

"And the bad news?" he asks.

I look down and continue picking at my nail polish. "Your mom and sister figured out why I was asking and are planning on attending the auction."

He sighs. "It's not your fault. Let's just hope I don't make a complete fool of myself. I'm sure Station 13 will be there, too."

"Sounds like you'll have quite the audience."

"That's what I'm afraid of," he grumbles.

"You're going to do great."

Connor shakes his head. "I'm out of my wheelhouse here."

"I have confidence in you." I knock my knee against his. "And your family does, too." I read off the adjectives his family used to describe him as Connor types them into the questionnaire.

"Thanks," he murmurs, but his shoulders are slumped. The way he doubts himself breaks my heart. I wish he could see himself the way I do.

In an effort to cheer him up, I say, "You're also someone who is willing to help others at the drop of a hat without expecting anything in return."

Connor stops typing. "I mean, I did make you agree that you'd learn to set boundaries and figure out what you like in exchange for helping you with your flower truck."

"But that was still your way of helping me."

"Even though you didn't ask for it?"

I nod. "Because you saw a need I had and decided to step in without needing to be asked."

"I think you're right." Connor's eyes soften. "Having you around is good for my confidence."

You know what would be good for *my* confidence? A hot little make-out sesh with the man I've been dreaming of locking lips with since middle school.

I fan my face with my hand. *Not the time, Shay.* "Okay, what's next?"

"What is one thing you can't live without?" He raises his eyebrows and grumbles, "Solitude."

I purse my lips. "I'm not sure that's the kind of answer they're looking for."

"Even if it's the truth?"

"The ladies want to get to know the man they're trying to win a date with."

"Then they may as well learn up front that I like my peace and quiet."

I look around his living room, trying to find a better answer from the stuff he has lying around. "What about noise-cancelling headphones?"

"What about them?"

"As your answer to the question."

Connor's fingers hover over the keyboard. "You don't think that's too boring?"

"Not at all. It could mean a lot of things, like you enjoy listening to music or use them when working on projects."

"Or that I like peace and solitude."

I shake my head. "Okay, onto the next question. What are your favorite hobbies?" I grab his computer and pull it onto my lap. "This one's easy." I type *fishing, woodworking,* and *listening to country music* into the question box. He peers over my shoulder and nods his approval.

We go through a few of the simpler questions, then I shoot him a look and hold up my fist to my mouth as a fake microphone. "Connor Porter, are you ready to answer questions about what you look for in your dating life?"

His eyes twinkle with amusement as he looks at my fist, though his mouth remains a firm line, unfazed. "Let's get this over with."

"That's the spirit," I tease. "Just tell me the first thing that comes to your mind—it's easy peasy."

"If you say so," he mutters.

I poise my fingers over the keyboard, ready to type. "What do you look for in a partner?"

"Nothing."

I turn to look at him. "What do you mean, *nothing*?"

"I don't plan on getting married, so I don't really see the point in dating." He shrugs as if he didn't just drop the biggest bomb on my dreams of a future with him.

I clear my throat, willing myself to sound normal and not like I was just given devastating news that rocked me to my core. "Well then, hypothetically, what kind of woman would you picture yourself with?"

Connor crosses his knee and stares at the wall for so long, I'm positive he's not going to answer. I'm about to make something up when he finally opens his mouth. "Someone who appreciates my desire for peace and calm and isn't afraid to step in and be the social one at family gatherings or events. A woman who supports my hobbies, but also has passions of her own. Someone who doesn't want to change me. Someone who accepts me for who I am."

I'm drinking in every word like they're the final drops of a strawberry matcha.

Me, I want to scream. I'm the one you want. It's me. Okay, now I'm channeling my inner Elphaba, but it couldn't be truer. I've always accepted Connor just as he is. I love how much his presence calms me. And I love when I'm able to elicit a smile or laugh out of him. I just love being around him. How safe and grounded he makes me feel.

I start making a list in my head of reasons I need to calm down.

One: He's only listing hypothetical things.

Two: He literally just told me he never plans on getting married.

Actually, those are the only two reasons I need. If I can't have *all* of Connor Porter—the marriage, a dozen babies, the whole shebang—I don't want him at all. I would never be able to settle for dating scraps when I want so much more in the future. And if he doesn't plan on getting married, there can't be anything between us.

Doesn't mean I'll stop dreaming about his lips or the way his arms feel when they're around me…but this is the reality check I needed.

I type his answers into the questionnaire. "Perfect." The word comes out dull. Lifeless. But how else am I supposed to sound when every dream scenario I ever imagined, even if I knew they could never happen because he's off-limits and never showed interest in me, was just ripped from my grasp?

I rush through the next few questions, making up most of the answers for him when he can't think of anything. I read the final question out loud: "What is your ideal date?"

"Fishing, I guess. Or something where I can use my hands."

I can think of plenty of ways he can put his strong, calloused hands to good use.

Well, now I'm parched.

"Mm," I murmur, unable to string a coherent thought together. I type the words *an outdoor date, including a picnic and fishing* into the final question box and pass the laptop back to Connor for his approval.

His fingers brush mine as he takes the device from me, leaving a trail of fire in their wake that has me craving more of his touch. Where's a fire hose when you need one?

Connor reads over the answers while I try to mentally cool down. "Looks good to me." He nods. "Thank you. I couldn't have done this without you."

I jump up from the couch, ready to hightail it out of his house before I say or do something I'll regret. "Happy to help. Well, I've got lots of flower things to do, so I'll leave you to it."

He gets up and walks me to the door like the gentleman he is. Normally, I'd appreciate the chivalry, but right now

I'd much rather have a solid ten feet between us at all times to avoid doing anything stupid.

"Will I see you there?"

"Where?" I squeak.

"At the auction."

I whirl around to face him. "Why would I be there?"

Connor slides his hands into his jean pockets and leans against the wall, crossing his legs at the ankles. I bite back a groan. I know I'm supposed to be helping him with his confidence, but if this man knew the kind of effect a pose like that has on me, I think his ego would be bigger than the whole state of Texas.

"You, uh. It would be nice. Since you already said my family will be there and probably my crew, you know." He runs a hand through his hair. "What I mean is, you would be a nice distraction in the crowd."

Me? A distraction for Connor? Where do I sign on the dotted line? "I'll be there."

Something must be in the water at the fire stations that produces the most attractive men. Every bachelor that steps onto the stage is gorgeous, as evidenced by all the squealing women around me who are fanning themselves with their bidding paddles. The suspenders and turnout pants don't hurt, either. The only thing that would make it better is if they were shirtless.

Objectively, I can appreciate all the bachelors for their attractiveness and service to the community I've called home my entire life. But, in my not-at-all-biased opinion, there's only one man worth bidding on at this auction. I've told myself a million times since helping Connor fill out the questionnaire that I will *not* bid on a date with him.

We don't want the same things. I want a future filled with a husband who adores me, a whole baseball team of kids, and a house in the suburbs complete with a white picket fence. Yet as he steps out onto the stage looking adorably shy and as handsome as I've ever seen him, I know I'm going to be waving my paddle in the air like a madwoman.

Because regardless of Mallory standing next to me or the fact that Connor and I don't have the same future in mind, there's one truth that rings even louder in my brain: I don't want anyone else to have him.

CHAPTER EIGHTEEN
CONNOR

"You're up next." A woman with a headset who looks like she means business nudges me forward.

I peek around the curtain, and my mouth goes dry at the sight of the crowd of feral women around the stage. It feels like I'm a rare piece of meat about to walk into a den of hyenas.

I close the curtain before I'm spotted. Maybe there's still time to back out. Better yet, *run*. I turn to make my escape, but the woman shoots me a look that keeps me rooted in place. She'd make a wonderful bodyguard. No one would dare come near her with that intimidating glare.

Looks like I'm trapped.

The emcee's voice booms over the speakers. "All right, ladies, now you're in for a real treat. Our final bachelor is none other than our local hero from Station 13, Connor Porter."

"It's Raining Men" blares over the speakers, and I'm too stunned to move. I think I might be sick. I shake my hands out, trying to build up my confidence, when the woman in the headset practically shoves me through the curtain and onto the stage. A spotlight hits me, and I hold my hand up to shade my eyes from the harsh light.

Once I can see again, I glance over at my crew to find Gordon snickering behind his hand. Looks like he's to thank for this walk-out song. Shayna's standing near them in a yellow sundress that matches her bright personality. Knowing she's in the same room as me and feeling her positive presence radiating as she smiles at me helps ground me.

I take a deep breath. *Focus, Porter. Don't trip. And don't glare at the audience.* Not sure that would win me any dates. My crew would never let me hear the end of it if I didn't even get bid on.

I remember Captain's words. This is for charity, for the kids. I can do it for them.

My lips pull into a smile that feels more like a grimace as the emcee reads my intro. "Connor has been a firefighter for nine years and just moved back to his hometown of Louisville." He pauses as the crowd cheers. I don't really understand the sentiment of cheering for us living in the same city, but to each their own, I guess. "In his first week on the job at Station 13, he saved a local woman from a flower-shop fire."

Excited murmurs ripple through the crowd as I watch women ready their bidding paddles. I swallow hard and shift on my feet, hating all this attention on me, especially at the mention of me simply performing my job.

"When he's not at the station, Connor enjoys fishing, woodworking, and listening to country music, which is why he would never want to live without his noise-canceling headphones. His family and friends describe him as pragmatic, hardworking, loyal, and someone who is willing to help others at the drop of a hat. He's looking for someone who will be the social butterfly to his introverted spirit and is willing to accept him just as he is. Connor's ideal date involves outdoor activities like fishing and taking a lucky lady on a picnic. Don't miss out on the man who has been dubbed Mr. Hero Hottie."

I grit my teeth. Who is calling me Mr. Hero Hottie? It better be absolutely no one. My face feels as red as a fire engine.

"Let's start the bidding at fifty dollars."

I have to stop my eyes from bugging out. Who in their right mind would pay fifty dollars to go on a date with *me*?

A woman who looks to be in her late twenties, with her hair slicked back so tightly in a ponytail that it looks like it's pulling her forehead back with it, raises her paddle in the front row before shooting me a suggestive grin.

That answers my question. In a very unfortunate way, but an answer nonetheless.

I glance over at my crew and make eye contact with Fisher. He does a variety of flexes. My brow furrows. He's never been one for showboating before, but… Oh, now he's pointing at me. Fisher wants *me* to flex. He hasn't seemed to steer me wrong before, so I decide it's worth a shot.

Honestly, I'd do anything at this point to have anyone bid on me other than Ponytail. I'd even take the grandmother in the back who's eyeing me like I'd be the perfect man to do all the grunt work around her house. That actually might be my best-case scenario.

Before I can second-guess my actions, I ball up my fists and flex. The paddles go flying into the air.

"I have one hundred. Do I have one fifty?" The emcee points to another woman in the crowd. "One fifty—do I have two hundred?"

I slide a hand into my turnout pants and grab hold of my suspenders with the other. I hear a lady in the front row audibly sigh. Maybe Gordon was onto something with the whole "badge bunny" thing after all.

Women in the crowd start shouting out increasing bids faster than the emcee can keep up. I run a hand through my hair, not knowing what to do with all this attention on me. More paddles shoot into the air.

Seriously? What's special about ruffling my hair?

"All right, we are at seven hundred dollars. Do I hear seven fifty?"

Ponytail raises her paddle in the air and shoots me a flirtatious wink.

"Wonderful. This is officially our highest bid of the night." The emcee smiles widely. "Do I hear eight hundred?"

I know that the grandma tapped out at a few hundred dollars, but thankfully there's the woman who just bid seven hundred. My eyes search for her in the crowd. When I finally spot her, she looks at her phone and shakes her head with a sigh. I feel my stomach drop. No. I wasn't excited about the prospect of a date, but spending the entire afternoon dodging Ponytail's advances sounds even worse.

I attempt to smile again and make my pecs dance against the taut material of my T-shirt, a trick I learned I could do by chance a few years ago. I've never shown another soul that I can do that, but I'm pulling out all the stops, begging someone else—*anyone* else—to bid on me.

"Seven fifty going once. Seven fifty going twice."

I close my eyes, unable to bear looking at Ponytail's face when she realizes she gets to spend a whole afternoon with me.

"One thousand dollars."

I lift my head as gasps erupt across the room. I think one of them might have even been mine because I recognized that voice. I look at Shayna's raised paddle and feel the relief flooding my veins.

"Going once, twice." The emcee gestures to Shayna. "And the date goes to the woman in yellow for one thousand dollars."

Ponytail turns around, probably to shoot daggers at Shayna, but she doesn't seem to notice because her eyes are locked on mine. The spotlight is in my eyes and she's at the back of the crowd, so it's hard to tell how she's feeling. All I can see is my sister grabbing Shayna's arm, her mouth agape, before the woman with the headset comes back and leads me off the stage while the emcee talks over the speakers about how that was the biggest donation they've ever received for a single date.

I inhale a sharp breath. I forgot that Shayna just shelled out one grand. It better not have been money she was supposed to allocate for her business. I couldn't forgive myself if I set her back.

The lady in charge stops when we reach a large room where I see the other firefighter bachelors chatting with women I'm assuming are their dates. "Wait here."

I do as requested because I'm more than a little terrified of finding out how she'd react if I didn't listen to her.

I place my hands in my pockets and stare at my feet as I wait. A few minutes later, she returns with a smiling Shayna at her side. Warmth swells inside of me. I chalk it up to extreme gratitude that I get to spend the afternoon with her rather than the overeager woman. But there's a feeling deep inside trying to climb to the surface that I snuff out, scared it's an ember that's trying to grow into a flame I can't ignore.

I don't have a choice other than to ignore it. It's like I told myself before, Shayna deserves *more*. Someone who wants all the things she does. Not a reserved guy like me who values my solitude. I wouldn't be a good long-term partner. Or a good partner, period.

Headset lady speaks to me without looking up from her clipboard. Not sure what's so important on there at a charity event that she can't even bother to maintain eye contact, but who am I to judge when I'm usually the wallflower in any room I'm in? "Connor, this is Shayna, the woman who won a date with you."

I don't even have a chance to say thank you before she's already gone, buzzing about something else into her headset. I rock on the balls of my feet, hands still in my pockets, as I finally get a good look at Shayna. I'm not sure what I expected her demeanor to be, but I certainly didn't think I'd see a determined set in her gaze.

"Why did you bid on me?" I ask.

Shayna takes a step closer. She's so close, I could reach out and brush my knuckles along her perfectly pink cheeks. Not that I want to. "You told me to figure out what I like." She traces her fingers along my suspenders before gently snapping them against my pectoral muscle. I'm too stunned to move. "Truth is, I've always known what I want—I was just too scared to go for it."

My brain rushes to catch up. There's no way I heard her correctly. Or maybe Mallory put her up to this prank. I look down into Shayna's eyes, expecting to see a teasing glint, but there's nothing but a soft, earnest look in her gaze with a hint of vulnerability. No, I heard her loud and clear. This wasn't a joke or something I'm reading into.

Shayna wants *me*.

Correction: Shayna said she's *always* wanted me.

CHAPTER NINETEEN

SHAYNA

I'm Little Miss Think-Things-Through. Little Miss Hold-My-Cards-Close-To-My-Chest-So-I-Don't-Get-My-Heart-Broken.

So, there's absolutely zero explanation for what in the hydrangea just possessed me to declare my feelings. *To. His. Face.*

I have no clue what I was thinking. Mallory is literally a room away. What would she think if she walked in and saw my hands running across her brother's chest like he's a canvas I'm trying to fingerpaint on? Or worse, what if she heard me say that her brother is all I've ever wanted?

I yank my hands back, thinking of a play on one of the life lessons my mama taught me: If you don't have anything nice to say, keep it to yourself. In this case, it's more like: If the man is off-limits, keep your hands to yourself.

I hold onto the strap of my purse to busy my hands, so I don't have another rare boost of confidence that ends in me snapping Connor's suspenders against his pecs. But seriously, his chest should come with a warning label for how attractive it looks with his cotton T-shirt stretched across it.

Warning: May cause women of any age to swoon with its chiseled nature and impeccable ability to dance. Pun intended.

If my cheeks weren't flaming red before, there's no doubt they are now. I take a shaky breath. "Can we forget I said that?"

Connor blinks a few times as if he's coming out of a daze. "What?"

Maybe he never heard me in the first place. That would be the ideal situation here. "Please ignore what I said."

He runs a hand through his hair, leaving it looking mussed in a way that has me wanting to tangle my fingers in it.

No.

Bad Shayna.

No touchy.

If I have to start talking to myself like a dog or a toddler, so be it.

Connor's eyes are full of unanswered questions, but he nods like the gentleman he is. "If that's what you want."

I gulp at the reference in his comment.

Truth is, I've always known what I want.

Yep, he definitely heard me.

"Yeah." I nod vehemently. "That's exactly what I want."

He dips his chin, and sweet relief fills my lungs. I take what feels like a first deep breath after minutes underwater. "All right, then. Let's go."

"Go where?" I ask.

"On the date you spent a small fortune on."

"Right, of course." The date I won because I couldn't stand to see that woman in the front row go out with him. Then there's the fact that Connor looked absolutely terrified on that stage, though that didn't pacify all the ladies in the crowd after they saw him flex. Especially after he literally made his pecs dance on stage like he's freaking Terry Crews.

I follow him out to his truck and hop in the passenger seat after he opens the door for me.

Connor gets in the driver's seat and pulls out onto the road. I don't normally feel like I have to try and fill the silence when I'm around Connor, but today it hangs heavy in the air like an impenetrable fog.

"Are we going fishing?" I try to peek out the back window of his truck to look for poles in the bed.

"That was my initial plan, but are you up for a detour?"

Right. Of course he doesn't want to take me on his ideal date. I can't blame him after I just pulled a complete switcheroo. I'm probably giving him more whiplash than a wooden roller coaster. Maybe it's for the best, though. It's not as if he has romantic feelings for me, anyway.

"Sure." I will my voice not to crack, refusing to sound as hollow as I feel.

We're silent for the rest of the ride around the city, and I enjoy the opportunity to not talk and say something else embarrassing. When Connor finally pulls into a parking lot, I gasp.

"Why are we at the botanical gardens?"

"Because that's where we're going," Connor says, as if it's obvious.

But I don't understand why he'd take me to a place he knows I'd love. If his intent was to take his date fishing, what does it mean that he'd change his plans for me? I don't know if he's simply being kind…but my thundering heart is trying to tell me it means more.

I get out of the truck as soon as he puts it in park. When Connor rounds the vehicle, he holds his hand back over his shoulder, locking Sulley. Something about the casual way he does it is so attractive.

Good heavens, I'm in trouble. Every little thing he does has me feeling some type of way. Next thing I know, I'll probably think he looks hot while eating corn on the cob at his family's annual spring barbecue next weekend. Spoiler: It's literally impossible to look attractive while taking a giant bite out of a corn cob. Butter dripping down your chin and kernels stuck in your teeth isn't a good look on anyone, but I'd probably still find some way to find him insanely gorgeous.

Connor clears his throat. "Shayna?"

I smooth my hands across the front of my sundress. "Sorry, what was that?"

"Are you planning on standing there all afternoon?"

"And miss my thousand-dollar date?" I move past him, heading toward the entrance. "I think not."

He jogs to catch up with me. "You were the one standing by the truck like your shoes were glued there."

"I was letting you lock Sulley."

"You stood there for a solid two minutes after that."

I place my hands on my hips and turn to him with a huff. "Are you really going to force me to admit that I was captivated by your muscles?"

Connor has the audacity to look abashed. "I—I didn't." He runs a hand through his hair, his nervous tic. "I wouldn't—"

I pat his arm. "Just accept the compliment, Con." Since I've already gone and outed myself today, I may as well utilize it. "You know, if someone compliments you, you're usually supposed to say something nice back."

He pauses. "You always smell nice. Like a field of flowers or the first day of spring."

I'll have to thank Alyssa again for the perfume she bought me last year. "Thanks."

Connor looks over my shoulder, unable to meet my gaze as he says, "And you look beautiful today."

I place my hand on my chest. "Okay, if you keep complimenting me, I'm not going to be able to fit my head through the door." I smile up at him as a blush climbs my cheeks. *He just called me beautiful.* "But thank you."

As we head toward the entrance, my mind races. Connor not only took me to a place he knows I'd love, but now he's complimenting me. I mean, the compliments *were* prompted, but still, he said them.

Connor blows out a breath. "I can't believe you dropped a grand for this. You know I'd hang out with you for free."

"I know." I drop my gaze to my sandals as we walk through the parking lot. "But I wouldn't be a good friend if I let that other girl win a date with you."

"I appreciate that." He lets out a small sound that's almost a laugh. "I guess I just feel bad. You shouldn't be spending your money for your business on me."

I stop walking as we reach the sidewalk. When he realizes I'm no longer beside him, Connor turns back to face me.

"You've invested so much of your time in me and have saved me money with the favor you cashed in with Pat." I look at him earnestly, wanting him to believe me. "Let me do this for you."

Connor dips his chin. "If you're sure." I nod, and he opens the door for me. "Have you been here before?"

"Only like a dozen times since they've opened."

His shoulders droop. "We can go somewhere else."

"Are you kidding?" I step closer and squeeze his arm. "You'd better not make me leave. I've been here so many times because it's my happy place." Waterfront Botanical

Gardens had their grand opening a couple of years ago, and they still have multiple phases left of areas to fundraise for and complete. But it quickly became my favorite go-to spot to be among other people who love flowers and plants like I do.

Connor stands taller, like my words instilled him with confidence in his date selection. "Lead the way, then."

CHAPTER TWENTY
CONNOR

Watching Shayna walk around the gardens is like witnessing a kid meet their favorite characters at Disney World. She said that she's been here a dozen times, but you wouldn't know it from her starry-eyed wonder.

"Aren't these Helmer Triumph Tulips stunning?" Shayna gestures to the flowers in front of us.

"They're really bright," I say, looking at the yellow petals with a dark red pattern. "The red on them almost looks like flames."

She turns and smiles at me. "I was hoping you'd notice that."

"What do you see when you look at them?" I ask.

Shayna clasps her hands in front of her and analyzes them. "They remind me of a canvas painted with rich strokes of yellow and maroon. Just looking at it brings me joy, which is no surprise since yellow tulips represent happiness and hope in flower language."

"That's where each kind or color of flower can express a different sentiment, right?"

"Exactly." She beams at me.

I move down to the next flower. The sign reads: Red Double Tulips. "What about these?"

"I work with tulips a lot. They're a popular cut flower." I raise a brow, and she laughs before offering me further explanation. "They're long-lasting blooms that can be cut and placed in vases." She points to the tulips. "These ones can typically last about a week once they're cut."

My shoulders tense as I slide my hands into my pockets. I'm stupid for not realizing that cut flowers were literally just that. "I should've put the context clues together from the name."

Shayna loops her hand through my arm. "Not at all. You're not expected to know terms in the flower world, just like I would have no clue what half the words y'all use around the station mean."

The tension drains from my body. "How do you do that?"

"Do what?"

"Make me feel so at ease."

She squeezes my arm. "I was just speaking the truth."

I clear my throat and try to change the conversation. "Do red tulips mean something different than the yellow ones?"

Shayna blushes.

Crap. Do they mean something bad like violence and bloodshed?

"They represent deep, long-lasting love."

Oh.

We both stare at the tulips for a few minutes in silence. Naturally, I'd be the reason our conversation was brought to a halt.

Shayna opens her mouth, then shuts it before finally saying, "Can I ask you something?"

"I'm an open book," I deadpan.

"Obviously…*not.*" She laughs before leading me back to a bench. With her hand still looped through my arm, we end up sitting close enough that our thighs touch. I crane my neck to look down at her.

"Okay, so I know you mentioned you don't plan on getting married."

I gulp. Not sure I like where this is going.

"Is there a reason why?" She lets go of my arm and places her hands in her lap. "I mean, how do you know that's not what you want if you've never been in love before?"

I swallow hard. I hate talking about my feelings. Guess I expected to have this conversation at *some point* in my life. I just didn't know today was going to be that day. But I suppose if there's a good person to share everything with, it's Shayna.

"I thought I was in love once," I say.

She bites her bottom lip. "Who was she?"

"Her name was Jillian."

Shayna gasps and clutches my arm. "She died?"

I shake my head. "Sorry, that didn't come out right."

"Oh, good." She gives my arm one more squeeze before letting go. "No need to apologize. You don't have to tell the story perfectly. Just talk to me."

She makes it sound so easy. Talking. Sharing about emotions and feelings that make me queasy. But it's like she said, all I have to do is put one word in front of the other.

There's only one place to start the story, so I take a deep breath and begin.

"I met her when I was twenty-two. I had been living in Seattle for four years, and everything was going great. I was happy at the station, and that was around the time that I started my woodworking hobby. So, I spent my days off working on projects or fishing. It was a good life. A solid routine." My chest aches as I think back to when I first met Jillian. "On one of my days off, I went to the gym.

Jillian approached me and complimented my form while I was lifting weights." I run a hand through my hair. "No one had ever been that forward with me before. She kept talking to me while I was working out and gave me her number before I left."

"You didn't call her, did you?" Shayna tilts her head. I guess she knows me better than I thought.

"No. And she made sure to tell me exactly how that made her feel when she saw me at the gym again later that week."

She raises a brow. "Sounds like the kind of woman who knows what she wants and goes for it."

"She was." I let out a slow breath as I recall the events leading up to our first date. "Jillian told me we should grab smoothies and didn't let me take no for an answer. She carried the conversation, and I learned a lot about her. She had just graduated college and was starting her first job with a business firm in downtown Seattle, so she was still settling in. And she loved the fact that I was a firefighter."

"I mean, who doesn't?" Shayna laughs, but the sound doesn't carry its usual brightness. "How long did you date for?"

I narrow my eyes, trying to think back. "Eight months. I saw her about once a week, aside from the days I saw her at the gym. She would usually come to my house and we'd order takeout. She'd sit with me while I fished, or we'd watch a movie." I shrug. "I thought things were going well. She was smart and ambitious. Didn't require much of me. It was easy to fall for her."

"What went wrong?" Shayna asks.

"Turns out, while I was considering a future with her, Jillian was starting to resent me." I sigh. Shayna squeezes my knee, giving me the quiet strength I need to continue. "One time when she was over, I asked if she wanted to order pizza or Chinese, and she just snapped. She said a lot of awful things." I grind my teeth, hearing them again in my mind. "Words that have stuck with me."

"I'm here if you want to tell me. And it's okay if you don't want to share."

Embarrassment settles deep in my gut at the thought of telling her everything Jillian said. But this is Shayna. If I can tell one person everything without fear of judgment, it's her. Besides, it might be cathartic to let out the words I've kept buried inside for the past five years.

I close my eyes and blow out a long breath. "Jillian complained that I never took her out on real dates. She said I was the most boring person she'd ever met because all we did was stay around my house. She told me you can't call something a conversation when only one person is talking, and that she was exhausted from always having to think of things to say. She said I spent more time in my workshop than with her, making stupid stuff that wasn't doing anything but collecting dust. She was also mad that she had to initiate everything." I press my lips into a thin line.

Shayna looks the closest to fuming I've ever seen her. "Did she ever hint at any of this before?"

"No. It came out of nowhere."

She grimaces. "Then it sounds like you did the best you could with the information you had. You can't be expected to read your partner's mind."

I hang my head, and Shayna reaches over and grabs my hand. I tilt my head to look at her and see tears forming in her eyes. "What's wrong?"

"You don't believe everything she said, do you?" Her lips tremble.

I squeeze her hand before interlocking our fingers. I'm surprised by the way it immediately grounds me. Physical touch has been something I avoid as much as possible, but with Shayna, it seems like it's just another reminder that I'm safe with her.

"How could I not?" I shake my head. "It's why I never plan on dating again. Women obviously need a man more outgoing than me. Someone who can carry their own in a conversation." I look back at the plant, unable to bear seeing Shayna's expression as I say, "How could I trap someone in a future with me when I know I'll never be enough?"

Shayna turns on the bench, her knee pressing against my thigh. She takes my face in both her hands and stares deep into my eyes, making me feel everything I've tried to hold in. I take a deep breath, trying to rid my body of all the pesky emotions. "Listen to me, Con. You are *more* than enough."

Her words cut right to my core. I want to believe her, but it's hard to rid my mind of the lies I've accepted as truth for the past five years.

"Who cares what Jillian-Schmillian said. We always have room for growth, but you can't take all the harsh words of someone who obviously wasn't right for you to heart." She lowers her hands from my face and takes mine in hers. "She sounds emotionally immature. Like someone who had this idea of you in her mind as this buff, young firefighter when she met you at the gym, and never took the time to get to know the real you. It's not your fault that she wasn't mature enough to end things or share how she was feeling throughout the relationship, allowing this resentment to build that was all based on some false reality." She rubs her thumb along the back of my hand. "There's nothing wrong with you. It doesn't make you boring to have hobbies that are usually done alone. And if she couldn't appreciate how introverted you are, then she didn't deserve to see how great of a conversationalist you can be when you feel comfortable." She gestures between us. "I mean, look at us having a genuine, deep conversation. The right person will appreciate you for who you are. They won't want to change you into this extroverted person that takes them out all the time. They'll enjoy the balance you bring to their world and love all your qualities because each one is what makes you the Connor they know and love."

"Even if I started to look past everything Jillian said, I'm not sure a person like you described exists," I say.

Shayna's eyes are clear now as she smiles. "She does." The words come out soft but with a gentle strength behind them, like she has enough belief for both of us.

I move my gaze to my lap and clear my throat. "I think it'll take some time to retrain my brain—to believe that I'm enough."

"That's okay. There's not a specific timeline for healing. And if the right person happens to walk into your life, maybe that will be healing for you, too. Having a healthy relationship with someone who doesn't want to change a single thing about you." She knocks her knee against my leg. "Even when your beard gets so long you start looking like a caveman."

I let out a small self-deprecating chuckle and untangle my hand from hers. "I might have let myself go a little bit after the breakup when my confidence was at an all-time low."

She shoots me a look. "It's been five years, Con."

I hold my hands up in innocence. "Hey, at least I got a haircut when I moved back."

"See?" Shayna lightly pushes my arm. "You're growing already. Now we just have to keep working on that confidence."

"Thank you," I say—and I truly mean it. "I wasn't sure I'd ever be willing to talk about Jillian. But I'm glad it was with you."

She smiles at me. "Me, too." A small furrow appears between her eyebrows. "Wait, no one else knows about her? Not even your family?"

I shake my head. "I was waiting to tell my parents. You know my mom would've freaked out and caught the first flight to Seattle if I told her." I lean back and stretch, stiff from sitting too long on the wooden bench. "Mallory kept pestering me for details about my life when I was out there, so I finally told her I was casually seeing someone. She doesn't know the details, though, just that things ended badly and I wasn't interested in dating anymore."

"If my opinion counts for anything, I think you should tell them. I'm sure they'd want to be there for you, too." Shayna smooths her hands along her dress. "And if the adjectives your mom and sister sent to me when we were filling out your questionnaire are any indication, I'm sure they will tell you the same things I did and remind you of the truth—of who you actually are."

The thought of opening up again to anyone else anytime soon has me feeling like I'm about to break out in hives. "I'll think about it."

She stands and turns back to me. "You ready to keep moving?"

I push up from the bench. "Lead the way."

She walks for a little bit before coming to a stop in front of the evening primroses. Shayna beams as she turns to me. "These open in the late afternoon and close by morning.

Isn't that cool? We only get to see their beauty for such a short amount of time that it makes seeing it in bloom feel like a little piece of magic." She steps closer and sniffs them, closes her eyes, and wears a soft smile on her lips, the perfect picture of peace.

My heart skitters in my chest. I close my eyes, and when I open them again, it's as if I can't help but see Shayna in a new light. She's beautiful. More than all the flowers around us. More than any other woman I've ever seen. And it's not just because of her outward appearance—although there's no denying that—but who she is as a person. Caring. Empathetic. Considerate. The kind of woman who would sit on a bench and listen to a man's sordid romantic history on a date she paid a grand for. Someone who truly listens and offers sympathy while reminding you who you truly are.

I barely talk as we walk through the rest of the gardens. I listen to her point out all her favorite flowers and share what they represent. But I don't think she minds being the one to carry the conversation, and I genuinely enjoy listening to her talk about her passion.

I'm not sure there's anyone else like her. Someone who fully sees me for who I am and doesn't run. She actually seems to like me even more for it.

As we make our way back to my truck, I decide to test something out to see if touching her gives me the same kind of safe reaction when I held her hand or if it makes me bristle.

I brush my pinky against hers. My stomach fills with a fluttery feeling, and my hand begins to tingle with this warm sensation. I suck in a breath, suddenly feeling like I'm in a sauna as I'm hit with a realization.

I'm attracted to Shayna.

CHAPTER TWENTY-ONE
SHAYNA

My pulse skyrockets and my body stiffens. Who knew one small finger could have such a giant reaction? Not me. I guess I was never brushing pinkies with the right people before.

"I can see why you like that place so much." Connor sounds completely calm, as if touching my pinky didn't affect him. "It's peaceful."

I swallow, trying to regain composure. "More peaceful than fishing?"

"Since I'm usually fishing alone, with only the sounds of nature to keep me company, no." I glance up at him as a ghost of a smile appears on his lips. "But it's a close second."

"That's fair." I cross my arms, holding in my disappointment that our date is already over. "Thanks for bringing me here. If you could drop me back off at my car, that would be perfect."

"Oh, we're not done." Connor reaches around me and opens the car door. "Hop on in."

My heart flutters. *He doesn't want to end our time together.* "Where are we going?"

He shuts my door and jogs around the front of Sulley before sliding into the driver's seat. "A date's not complete without food."

A man who takes me to see flowers and then feeds me? Swoon. You can't have him, ladies—he's all mine.

My stomach growls, and I laugh. "I'll never say no to a late lunch. Where do you want to go?"

A blush creeps onto his cheeks. "I had something planned for whoever bid on me at the auction, if you trust me?" The uncertainty in his tone makes me feel like I've failed. Because after all the time I've spent with him recently, how could he not know that I trust him implicitly?

I turn in the seat to fully face him. "Of course I trust you. I've known you more than half my life, and you've never done anything to make me doubt you."

He dips his head in a brief nod, but the blush on his cheeks deepens. "I trust you, too." His knuckles turn white as he grips the steering wheel. "This sounds crazy, but I feel like I can be more of myself around you than with anyone else."

Happy tears threaten to spill from my eyes at the confession. He may not feel the same kind of romantic feelings I do, but knowing that I can be a safe place for him to be one hundred percent himself is a major win. "That's not crazy at all."

"Holding a conversation with anyone else is hard for me, even my family. I overthink every word, so I say as little as possible. When I'm with you, though"—Connor sighs, sounding relieved—"words just come easy."

I couldn't hold back the tears if I tried. They fall onto my cheeks, and he leans over and wipes them away with the pad of his thumb.

"Was it something I said?" His free hand balls into a fist. "I told you, I always say the wrong thing."

I shake my head and offer him a soft smile. "They're happy tears." Even if he doesn't see me in a romantic light, I feel *seen* by him. My inner little Shayna is proud that she never gave up on liking the reserved boy, because look at where we are now. "I'm honored that you feel like you can talk to me."

The lines around his eyes crinkle as his facial features soften. His usual frown is replaced by an almost smile. "I don't think there's anyone in the world quite like you."

"Is that a good thing?" I hold my breath like it's a wish that, if I let go of, won't come true.

Connor wipes the last of my tears away and nods. "Yes, flower."

I blow out a breath, and my lips tug into a wide grin. "I *knew* you called me flower before."

He casually shakes his head as he pulls back out on the road. "I don't know what you're talking about."

"Mm–hmm, sure," I say, my tone dripping with sarcasm. "What made you start calling me that?"

Connor's fingers rap against the steering wheel. "There's the obvious answer: because you love and work with flowers."

"And the not obvious one?" I don't want to push him too far, but I'm not sure when I'll get the opportunity to ask Connor questions like this again.

"When you started working as a florist, I learned about flower language. I always thought it was fitting for you because you represent so many things."

My heart warms that he would take the time to learn about what I do for work, even when he wasn't living in Louisville at the time. "Such as?" I'm not ashamed to admit that I'm totally digging for another compliment.

"You're beautiful and strong. You're loyal and spark warmth and joy through your positive spirit." He tilts his head, looking thoughtful. "There's more to you, but those are the first attributes that come to mind." I sniffle at his kind words. "Please don't cry again."

"I'm sorry. I can't help it." I let out a watery laugh. "Since we'll see each other more now that you've moved home, you'll have to get used to it."

"I'll try."

I smooth my hands across my dress. "Now I need to think of a better nickname for you than Eeyore."

He shrugs. "I like it when you call me Con."

"Con," I say, and his smile is so radiant, I might need sunglasses if I look at him for too long. The moment is ruined when my stomach audibly growls.

Connor laughs, another smile spreading across his face. He turns off into the lot of a local park and pulls into a parking spot. "Let's get you fed."

"Yes, please." I giggle and hop out of the passenger side, meeting him around the back of the truck. "Are there some food trucks here today?" I glance around but don't see any.

"I've already got the lunch part covered." Connor opens the tailgate and pulls out a picnic basket and a gray-and-white gingham blanket.

I blink. "You brought a picnic for your date?"

Connor shuts the tailgate and steps closer to me, entering my personal space. I don't care one bit. He leans down and his lips brush against my ear, making me shudder. "Yes, it's all for *you* now, flower."

My eyes well with tears again. If he keeps being this adorable, I'm going to need to start wearing waterproof mascara around him. That's it. I can't be the girl who holds things close to my chest to protect my heart anymore. It's time to be a little more subtle version of the girl I was today. It's time to up my flirting game with the man I've been falling for since I was a preteen. If the things Connor was saying to me are any indication, then I think, deep down, he may have feelings for me, too. If that's the case, we'll cross the bridge of asking for Mallory's blessing when we get to it.

But from here on out, I'm going to be Little Miss Go-After-What-I-Want. And that just so happens to be Connor Porter.

CHAPTER TWENTY-TWO
CONNOR

Shayna takes the blanket from my arms. After a small fight with the wind, she comes out victorious and spreads it out on the grass. She holds her arms up in the air just as her stomach growls. I rub a hand over my mouth to hide my smile at the juxtaposition of such a loud, angry sound emanating from the sweet woman before me.

We both take a seat, and I open the picnic basket. "We'd better get you fed before your stomach decides to start a rebellion." I pull out a box of assorted crackers and a pack of presliced cheeses. "According to the internet, charcuterie was a safe bet."

Her stomach growls again, and she places a hand over her middle. "I think that's its way of thanking you." Shayna laughs.

I pass her a paper plate and continue pulling out the food I packed: summer sausage, prosciutto, a jar of olives, red grapes, and almonds. She pops a piece of cheese in her mouth before she fills her plate.

I hand her a bottle of water. "Sorry, if I'd known you were the one who would win the date, I'd have brought you an iced strawberry matcha."

She smiles, then eats a cracker with cheese and prosciutto. "Someone pays attention."

I'm quiet, but it doesn't mean I'm not observant. If anything, I think it means I pay more attention to my surroundings. I've seen her with a matcha in hand nearly every time we've been together. Has she dated people in the past who weren't attentive?

The thought of her dating anyone else sends jealousy coursing through me. After the conversation we had in the gardens, I'm even more glad it's me that she's on a date with right now. It's time I push my fears aside—even just for today—and allow myself to believe who Shayna told me I am rather than all the lies I've believed. She thought I was worth it enough to drop a grand on this date. The least I can do is give myself permission to see if there's something here.

"And for dessert." I grab the last item and pull it out of the basket. "Chocolate."

Shayna takes the bar from me. "You really went all out."

"Again, I was just listening to the internet."

She pops a grape into her mouth as I begin piling food onto my plate now that she's made hers. "Well, I appreciate you."

My hand pauses mid-reach for the slices of cheese. I look into her eyes, my lips tilting up in a smile. It still feels unnatural when I do it, but it's becoming more of a common occurrence around her. "I appreciate you, too."

My phone buzzes in my pocket with an incoming call, but I ignore it. When it buzzes again with a text alert, I reluctantly pull it out. When I see that the missed call and message are from Pat, I click on his text.

"You're going to want to see this." I slide my phone over to Shayna.

She reads the message quickly and squeals. "My truck will be ready in two weeks?"

I slide my phone back into my pocket. "That's what he said."

Pat also said I'd better be at their pickup baseball game next Saturday. I'd debated coming up with an excuse, but since Pat is giving Shayna a deal because of our past teammateship—is that even a word?—I've begrudgingly decided I'll show up. It means I'll have to engage in awkward conversations for the morning, but I'll do it for Shayna.

I'm hoping she was so excited reading that her truck is ready that she missed the part about the game. Otherwise, I might end up with a large cheer section at a pickup game. Shayna's the kind of person who doesn't do anything halfway, as evidenced by the crew she assembled at the last minute to help me move. So, if she knows when the pickup game is, I know she'll be there with her pom-poms and a whole group to rally behind me, even though I would bet every last cent I have on the fact that not one other guy will have anyone there since it's a *pickup* game.

"I can't wait." She beams.

"Is there anything else you need help with for your truck?"

Shayna shakes her head. "I have my meeting with the lawyer scheduled, and I also ordered a new custom canopy from the measurements you sent me. You're taking care of the shelves, so I think I'm pretty much set."

"It sounds like it's all coming together."

"It really is."

I'm pleasantly surprised by how quickly the rest of the afternoon passes. Holding a conversation with Shayna is easy. I don't overthink what I'm about to say or not listen to her because I'm worried about how to respond. With her, I'm able to be fully present. It's the most refreshing and enjoyable date I've ever had. Definitely better than what I'd expected today to look like when walking into the charity auction.

I put the leftover food back in the basket and then look over at Shayna. She's leaning back on her palms, her head tilted toward the sun. It makes her dark hair take on a warm glow, and her face… I take a deep breath, needing to steady myself after being hit by her beauty. Her eyes are closed, but joy still radiates off her in droves. She has that ever-present smile on her face, but really, it's just her. She has that warm, welcoming personality that puts everyone at ease. Always down to help others, even to her own detriment. But it also makes her the kindest human I've ever met.

I'm still staring at Shayna when another strong breeze hits. Goosebumps form on her arms. If I'm chilly in my short-sleeved shirt and long pants, she's got to be freezing in the thin straps of her dress.

Why didn't I think to bring a jacket when I was planning an outdoor date? I groan, chastising myself again. I'm not built for this. Constantly thinking of someone else and anticipating their needs. "Sorry, I didn't think it was going to be this windy."

"It's fine." Her teeth chatter as another strong gust makes her hair dance in the wind.

"Come here." I wave her closer.

Shayna doesn't question me, scooting over like her life depends on it. I reach over and grab the corner of the blanket, pulling it over her lap before opening my arms to her. She leans back into my chest, her head resting just beneath my chin. I wrap my arms around her to block the wind. She sighs and melts into me.

My stomach fills with the flutters that are becoming more familiar when I'm around Shayna. Yet again, I don't flinch at her touch. Something about her being in my arms just feels…right.

Shayna intertwines our fingers. Now I'm the one letting out a shaky breath as my mind fills with flashes of a memory I'd long forgotten.

It's my sister's turn to host her weekly sleepover with her best friends, which is how I ended up driving the four of them home from Waggener's homecoming football game. No one ever prepares you for all the final things you experience as a senior. Your last first day of school. Your last homecoming game. Not to mention all the lasts to come with homecoming, prom, the final day of school, and graduation.

I'm so close to becoming an "adult," but it's a weird in-between where I'm still trying to figure out who I am and who I want to be, all while enjoying my final months of being a kid. With everyone around me talking about what colleges they're getting accepted to, I feel pressured to pursue a degree when what I really want is to be a firefighter.

I'm scared to tell my parents that I don't want to go to any of the schools I've been accepted to—or, really, that I don't want to go to the University of Louisville like both my parents did. They've never given me any reason to believe they wouldn't support me, but I'm nervous nonetheless. I'm not the best with words, and what if I say the wrong thing? What if I tell them about my plans and then don't pass the fire academy?

Shayna rustles in the passenger seat of my truck. She's been quieter around me since I taught her how to slow dance last year. And her cheeks are always red around me now, too. I hope I didn't make her uncomfortable. I was only trying to help.

"Con?" she whispers.

I briefly look over as her eyes flutter open before turning my attention back to the parking lot. The line of cars in front of me still hasn't moved. Getting out of our school lot after a football game is like our own version of The Hunger Games—*one where the odds are never in my favor. "Yeah?"*

Shayna sits up, wiping the side of her mouth. She looks at the backseat where Mallory, Alyssa, and Kelsey are all indulging in their own power naps before turning back to me and wrapping her arms around her middle. "Did you decide where you're going to college yet?"

The timing of her question is ironic, but I feel like Shayna has a sixth sense for these things. Always asking the right question at the perfect time. Always saying the right thing. Always being the picture of kindness.

I sigh. May as well tell someone my plans for the future to prepare myself for that conversation with my parents. "Actually, I think I'm going to the fire academy."

Her face quickly morphs from one of surprise to excitement. "A firefighter sounds like the perfect job for you."

I raise my eyebrows. "You think so?"

"Of course." She leans forward and knocks her arm into mine. "How did your parents take it?"

"Haven't told them yet." I shake my head. "I haven't told anyone yet, actually."

Shayna chews on her bottom lip. "Thanks for trusting me. I won't say anything, but you should tell them. They'll be happy for you."

"You don't think they'll be mad I'm not going to UofL?"

She shakes her head. "Just because you aren't following in their footsteps by going to the college they went to doesn't mean they won't be proud of you. They just want you to do what you love."

I feel the stress lift from my shoulders. She's right. "Thanks."

"Anytime." She yawns and looks out the windshield. "We still haven't moved?"

"Nope." I gesture with my thumb to her friends. "You can go back to sleep if you want. I'm not tired."

She yawns again, covering her mouth with her hand. "I think I will." She tries to get comfortable, leaning her head against the window of my truck, but she keeps readjusting every few minutes.

After I've moved a few car lengths forward, she shuffles again and huffs.

"Shayna, just come here."

She peers over at me. Her eyes are heavy, but she listens and scoots across the bench seat. I open my arm and wrap it around her shoulder. Shayna's face softens, and she immediately melts into me, resting her head against my chest. I wonder if she can hear how my heartbeat just picked up speed. I'm never this close to girls, aside from those in my family. Hopefully, she's too tired to notice.

"You're going to be the best firefighter," she murmurs. "You're always saving me."

I don't know what exactly I've saved her from, but her words have me beaming. The smile forming on my lips isn't something I'm accustomed to. If my mom saw me smiling right now with Shayna Monroe in my arms, she'd snap a hundred pictures. And also probably be frustrated that I'm smiling for a girl when I never smile for her pictures. But I don't think smiles are meant to be forced, only earned.

And I don't know what it means that Shayna's words are making me smile, but for now, I'm happy there's another person in the world who knows what I want to do in life. And the fact that she believes in me has me smiling the rest of the way home.

"Con?" Shayna whispers, pulling me from my reverie.

"Yeah?"

She squeezes my hands tighter in hers, like she's pulling from my strength to build up the courage for whatever it is she wants to say. "I know it's only for charity—that it's not real—but this has been the best date I've ever been on."

I press my cheek to her sun-warmed hair. "It feels pretty real to me."

I've been living on a high since my date with Shayna. We didn't promise each other anything when I dropped her back off at her car, but the idea of something more between us lingered in the air like the scent of freshly brewed coffee in the crew kitchen. And I'd be lying if I said I wasn't looking forward to the next time I see her.

Life has been busier than usual for the last month. Between moving and shifts at the station, plus all the time I've spent with Shayna, I've hardly had a spare moment to finish the shelves for her flower truck. Luckily, Cap gave me permission during my last shift to work on them while I'm here as long as I kept up on all my other duties around the station. I think he felt bad about telling me I was going to be in the bachelor auction, but if it means I have an opportunity to work on the shelves, I'm not mad.

I promised Shayna I'd have them ready for her approval soon, since we'll be able to get her truck from Pat's shop next week. I couldn't live with myself if I let her down. I'd pull multiple all-nighters before I let that happen.

Thankfully, today is a slow day at the station, although I guess I shouldn't even think those words. Any time you admit to a slow work shift is when the day turns into utter chaos, but today I really need things to stay quiet here so

I can finish the final sanding on these shelves in case she decides she wants them stained.

I head to the bunkroom where I stored the wood and grab the shelf I've been working on, along with a sheet of 220 grit sandpaper. I sit on the edge of the bed and begin sanding. I already worked on the shelves with my sander, but the cutouts in each one to hold the vases need to be sanded by hand. Plus, I enjoy going over my projects a final time by hand. Most woodworkers hate sanding, but the combination of the rhythmic motion mixed with the sound of the sandpaper running along the wood has always been calming to me.

As I'm working on the second shelf, I hear mumbling outside the door.

"Go on," Malone whispers, her voice quiet but commanding. "Knock."

"What if he's sleeping?" Fisher's loud voice carries, and Malone shushes him.

"He rarely naps on shift," Lieutenant Barnes says.

"Move aside." Gordon opens the door and steps into the room without any pretense. The rest of our crew, aside from Captain, stands behind him. "How was the date with your little badge bunny?" If it wasn't for his condescending tone, I wouldn't mind the question. But the way he refers to Shayna has my blood boiling.

"Don't call her that," I growl.

Gordon jerks back, holding his hands in the air. "I think the man doth protest too much."

I grit my teeth, ready to show him how I feel about his accusations, when Lieutenant Moreno places a hand on my shoulder. I startle, wondering how he got across the room without me noticing.

"She's not a badge bunny," Moreno says.

I nod along, thankful for the backup from our usually silent lieutenant. I know he chooses his words carefully, like me. Since it's usually just commands that come out of his mouth, I'm grateful he's choosing to help me defend Shayna.

Moreno shrugs, as if the answer is obvious. "She's his person."

I jerk my head to the side, wondering when my love life became a casual topic of conversation. I look to the rest of my crew, expecting someone else to rally to my defense, but the room remains silent. Malone and Fisher nudge each other and look at me with matching conspiratorial smiles. Even Lieutenant Barnes is smirking at me with a knowing look.

I set the shelf I'm sanding onto the mattress and cross my arms, waiting for an explanation.

"You told us Shayna was your sister's best friend. But let's face it, you don't look at her like she's *only* your sister's best friend." Fisher smiles. He's not wrong.

"Yeah, ever since you saved her from the flower-shop fire, it's been obvious." Malone picks at her nails. "Then when she showed up here with donuts, I knew y'all had something special."

"By your standards, does that mean every civilian you save who brings a gift by the station as a thank-you is 'your person,' too?" I ask.

"Only when you look at them in some type of way."

"I didn't look at her in any kind of way," I scoff. At least, not back then. After this weekend is an entirely different story, but they don't need to know that.

Malone shrugs. "If that's what you have to tell yourself."

"Plus, you went and visited her in the hospital after," Fisher adds.

"Because Cap told me we do that for community morale," I argue.

Moreno shakes his head. "We don't do that."

That stops me in my tracks. My mouth falls open. "Cap hazed me."

Everyone nods.

"He's done it to all of us in some way or another."

"That means you've officially been welcomed onto the crew." Fisher claps me on the shoulder.

"Then was the bachelor auction a form of double-hazing?"

"No, the LFD requested you specifically," Lieutenant Barnes responds. I know she doesn't have a reason to lie, so it must be true.

Malone's lips tilt into a grin. "But isn't it ironic that Shayna is the person who won a date with you?"

"We can't forget that she dropped a grand for it when you would've taken her out for free," Fisher adds.

Gordon laughs. "And you still expect us to believe there's nothing going on between you two?"

When I rolled out of bed on this dreary Monday morning, the last thing I expected was to be questioned by my crew like I'm on trial. I don't understand their fascination with my connection to Shayna. It's not exactly platonic anymore, but I'm hesitant to call it something it isn't yet when I'm still trying to process all my thoughts and fears. To determine if I'm fit for a relationship.

"What did you do on your date?" Malone nudges my boot with hers.

"We went to Waterfront Botanical Gardens and then had a picnic lunch at the park." I figure offering a brief, honest answer will satisfy whatever need they seem to have regarding my dating life.

"Didn't know you were a romantic, dude." Fisher claps me on the shoulder.

"That's adorable since Shayna worked for that flower shop." Malone places her hands over her heart. "Did you hold hands? Are you going to see her again?"

"He'll see her again if he's not an idiot." Gordon laughs dryly. "She's gorgeous."

Moreno raises one shoulder in a nonchalant shrug. "'Course he will. She's his person."

I grit my teeth. Looks like this is going to be the longest shift of my life.

CHAPTER TWENTY-THREE

CONNOR

THE SECOND I STEP foot in my parents' house, I'm hit with the scent of my favorite meal simmering on the stovetop: chili. Either Mallory did something to make Mom so mad that she's making a meal that she hates, or my mother is trying to butter me up.

I close the door behind me and take off my tennis shoes before quietly making my way into the kitchen. Mom stands by the stovetop, stirring the chili and boiling noodles as she sways to the country song playing over her Bluetooth speaker. I clear my throat, and she jumps. "Connie, how long have you been standing there?"

"I just got here."

She presses a hand to her heart. "I think you're in the wrong career field. You should be a mime or a spy. Better yet, a professional tip-toer." My mom shakes her head and laughs. "We need to get you some tap shoes or something. I'm getting too old for these jump scares."

I sit on a barstool and lean my elbows on the island. "Didn't mean to scare you." I look around the empty kitchen and living room. "Where is everyone?"

"Mallory is running a little late, and your father is probably playing a game of toilet golf thanks to you."

I have no regrets.

"Hole in one," my dad shouts from the half bath.

Mom groans.

I shrug. "He golfs. You scroll."

Mom gasps. "I have to see all the cute videos people make of Griffin and Mallory." She steps closer. "Did you know a fan came up with a nickname for them as a couple, and it's taken off?"

I shake my head. I don't do social media, and I definitely don't do internet searches of my sister or her boyfriend. I'd prefer to live in ignorant bliss than see a picture of them making out.

"It's Griffmallo. Isn't that so cute?"

"Sounds like a kid's toy," I mutter.

She nods excitedly. "A fan said they're as cute as a Squish-mallow, and the whole Griffmallo couple name took off. Isn't it adorable?"

I shrug. "Sure." I don't see the point, but I'm not going to argue with my mom.

She shoots me a saccharine smile. "Now we just need you to get a girlfriend, and then…"

I hold up a hand to stop her before she goes off the rails dreaming about both of her children in love, married off, and giving her grandbabies to spoil. "You know I'm not interested in your matchmaking schemes."

My mom heads back to the stove and gives the chili another stir. "But you seemed pretty happy when Shayna bid on you at the auction."

There's no way I'm about to tell her—or anyone else—about the feelings Shayna stirs up inside me. I know my mom would have the wedding planned tomorrow if I even *hinted* at the potential of having feelings for Shayna. Next thing I know, she'd be referring to us with our own weird couple name, like Conshay or Shaynor. Nothing cute about that. Do they combine last names? My mom could call us Porroe. That's even worse, like poverty-stricken fish eggs.

"She was a much better option than the woman who was eyeing me like I was her next dating victim."

Mom scrunches her nose and looks around anxiously before turning back to the stove. "That's a good point."

I don't have a chance to question her change in demeanor when my dad exits the bathroom. He walks over and shakes my hand. "Good to see you, son."

I don't know what to say because I'm the person who doubts every word, even when I'm only talking to my parents. Except, not around Shayna. "Heard you got a hole in one," I mumble stupidly.

"Sure did." Dad grips my shoulder. "Thanks again for the gift." He leans closer. "Gives me an excuse to hide out in the bathroom longer."

"I heard that," Mom says without even a glance back. Nothing ever gets past her. I swear, she either has bionic ears or a second pair of eyes on the back of her head.

"Remind me to get you some noise-canceling headphones for your birthday, honey." Dad winks at me like I'm in on the joke with him. Maybe I am, but I was never good at telling jokes, so it beats me.

She throws a dish towel at him, but there's a hint of amusement in her eyes. Even after all these years, my parents are still as in love as ever. "Drain these noodles for me?"

"Anything for you." Dad taps her butt as he walks past.

I grimace. Really didn't need to see that.

"Sorry, we're here," Mallory calls out from the foyer.

"Who's *we*?" I look to my mom for an answer to find her wearing that worried expression again.

Mallory comes up behind me, ruffling my hair. I roll my eyes and turn around to tell her I'm not a dog when I notice the other half of the *we* she was referring to.

Standing in the kitchen of my childhood home, wearing a nervous smile, is none other than the girl living rent-free in my mind.

My palms are instantly sweaty.

"Shayna," I rasp.

"Hey, Con." Her smile is a little warmer as she looks at me, but I can sense her nerves.

"Hi, Shayna dear." My mom wipes her hands on the kitchen towel before pulling Shayna into a tight squeeze. They hug for what I think is entirely too long, but they don't seem to think so.

"Hi, Mama Porter."

The glee on my mom's face is evident. Our house was always open to our friends, and she acted like a second mom to them. But the look she shoots me feels heavier, like she's thinking Shayna could just call her Mama one day and take my last name.

I look to my dad for an explanation of why Shayna's here, but he just holds his hands up. Who am I kidding? He probably didn't even know she was coming.

Mallory, on the other hand, is staring me down from across the kitchen, trying to gauge my reaction. I make sure to keep my face in check. I'm cool, calm, and collected. Nothing to see here.

"Now that our guest of honor is here, let's eat." Mom gestures for Shayna to make her bowl first.

Well, now I have my answer: This is one hundred percent a butter-me-up chili.

I let everyone make their bowls before me, needing a moment to digest what's happening. Once they've all moved into the dining room, I push up from the barstool and grab the last bowl on the counter. I fill it with a small amount of ditalini noodles—because we're a household that firmly believes noodles belong in chili—and cover it with a hefty scoop of chili. I top it off with cheese and hot sauce, then pour myself a glass of my mom's homemade sweet tea before trudging into the dining room.

I stop as soon as I enter the room, staring at the seating arrangement. My usual chair isn't just taken, it's missing entirely. Our six-person table now only holds five chairs, four of which are already taken. You can guess where the only available seat is. Yep, right between Shayna and my mother, as if she planned it from the beginning. Because she definitely planned this…I just don't know what her full agenda is.

But I guarantee I'm about to find out.

I place my glass and bowl on the table and take the remaining seat. Usually I feel uncomfortable at family dinners, even with our core four—what my mom lovingly calls our family—that I've spent my entire life around. But tonight, I feel oddly at peace—and I can't help but think that it's because of Shayna's calming presence.

Dad says a quick blessing, and everyone starts eating except Mallory, who is sitting across from me, glaring at her bowl like the chili has personally wronged her. She's never been a fan of my favorite meal, but I feel like she's being a little dramatic. She stirs her bowl, which is ninety percent noodles, eight percent cheese, and two percent chili.

I shovel a giant bite into my mouth and savor the different spices that hit my taste buds and create the perfect blend of flavors. I turn to my mom. "This is the best batch you've ever made."

She preens under my praise. "Thank you. What do you think, Mal?"

My sister takes a tentative bite. "Not terrible."

Shayna leans over and looks at Mallory's bowl. There's a hint of humor to her tone as she says, "You hardly got any chili. That's the best part."

Mallory shoots her friend a look. "Hilarious."

Shayna takes a bite. "I think it's delicious, Mama Porter."

"Thanks, sweetheart." Mom beams at her.

I feel Shayna's eyes on me as I take another bite. When I turn to look at her, she's staring very intently at her bowl. "I wasn't expecting to see you tonight."

She slowly drags her gaze back to mine, a faint blush coloring her cheeks. "You didn't know?"

I set my spoon down and lean back in my seat. "Know what?"

"That I was coming?" I shake my head, and Shayna's eyes move to my mother. "But your mom said that—" She stops mid-sentence.

I turn just in time to see my meddling mother making a fast-cutting motion with her hand in front of her neck. I cross my arms. "What did you tell her?"

My mom's eyes go wide, trying to play innocent. Dad clears his throat and shoots Mom a look that finally has her sighing in defeat. "I may have mentioned that you wanted to invite her to family dinner but were too nervous to ask, so you had me do it."

I sigh and rub a hand over the stubble peppering my chin. "When are you going to stop meddling?"

Mom holds a hand to her chest and gasps. "I don't *meddle*. I've simply suggested you call a darling young woman I met at church or a friend's neighbor's daughter who moved home." She gestures to Shayna. "Or take the opportunity to encourage you to see a good thing right in front of you."

I groan. "That's the definition of meddling."

She rolls her lips into her mouth and shakes her head. "It's not meddling when it's your mother."

"It still is," Mallory says before folding her arms across her chest. "Also, you can't just try to set my friends up with my brother."

My hand itches to reach out and hold Shayna's. I could really use her grounding touch right now. I never even considered the idea that Mallory may not approve of me dating her friend. She never told me her friends were off-limits, but maybe she didn't think she had to since I never dated anyone back in high school.

I turn to apologize to Shayna for this insane evening just as she starts to stand. "I think I should go," she says.

"Stay." The word slips out, but I mean it.

I *want* Shayna here. I wish I'd had a heads-up, but her presence makes me feel more comfortable and at home than I've ever felt in this house.

She looks at me for a few seconds. I can see the question in her eyes, asking if I'm really okay with this. I nod, hoping she can see the sincerity in the action.

"Okay." Her voice is quieter than usual, almost shy.

Thankfully, everyone seems to unanimously vote to change the topic. Mom jumps in and asks Shayna about her new flower truck, and that keeps the conversation going—and not focused on me—for the majority of dinner.

It's nice being able to eat my chili in peace, without trying to figure out how to answer my parents' questions and then overanalyze everything I said on the drive home.

Shayna nudges my leg with her foot. I turn to her and blink a few times, trying to recall what they were talking about before I spaced out. "Sorry, what was the question?"

"Did you tell them about your game next weekend?"

So, she *did* see that part of Pat's text.

"Game?" My mother looks at me with a raised brow. "What game?"

Shayna shoots me an apologetic look and mouths *sorry*.

"It's nothing." I wipe my mouth with a napkin. "Just a pickup game with some guys from the baseball team."

"Oh, I'd love to see you play again. We'll be there."

"Great," I deadpan. I'm not entirely dreading it, though. While I don't love the thought of a whole crowd showing up with lawn chairs and pom-poms to support me, I like the idea of Shayna being there.

I picture her in a brightly colored lawn chair with a wide smile on her face, cheering me on, and my stomach flutters. It's time I finally call them what they are: butterflies. She makes me feel everything all at once. Butterflies. Excitement. Fear that one day she'll wake up and realize I'm not enough for her. Thrilled at the thought of seeing her.

I don't know what to do with any of these emotions, but there is something I know how to do: play ball.

CHAPTER TWENTY-FOUR

SHAYNA

I PULL INTO THE parking lot for Connor's pickup game Saturday morning with all my besties and my lawn chair in tow. It's covered in a light blue floral pattern that makes me feel like the perfect combination of girly and outdoorsy.

I get out of the driver's seat and move to the trunk, grabbing my chair after my friends grab theirs. I push the button on the trunk for it to close, lock the car, and take a few steps toward the ball field when Mallory sidles up beside me.

"Um, since when have you had one of Connor's sweatshirts?"

Heat rises to my cheeks. I look down, trying to act like I have no clue what I'm wearing. "Oh, is that what this is?" I shrug. "I've had this since high school."

Her eyes narrow as she looks at me. I drop my gaze to my feet as we walk along the paved path, knowing I'll spill everything like a toddler with a lidless cup if I look into her eyes for too long.

"Oh, I know." Mallory snaps her fingers. "He gave it to you at his game when it was pouring. We were miserable, remember?"

I snap my head up and try to pretend like it's just now hitting me. "Oh, yeah. You're right." I shove my hands into the front pocket. "I guess I never gave it back."

"Wait, don't you wear that all the time in the morning when you're doing coffee or matcha runs?" Mallory's brow furrows. "I can't believe I've never noticed it before."

She's grumpy in the morning before she gets her caffeine fix. Plus, she's usually at school and teaching already before I'm up and about.

"Maybe sometimes." I shrug again. If I don't stop this madness, my shoulders are going to be permanently stuck up by my neck. "You know I always sleep in sweatshirts."

Mallory laughs. "No kidding, your hands are always like ice cubes." She glances over at me. "So, there's nothing going on between you and my brother?"

I pause for a moment. Having feelings isn't the same as acting on them. But with the way things went at the end of our date, I'm hoping Connor and I will act on those feelings very soon. And I'd never be able to do that without talking to Mallory first. I would never go against girl code. "Maybe we could talk after the game?"

Mal grabs my arm as we reach the field and turns to me with wide eyes. "Wait, seriously? Tell me ev—"

She's cut off by Mama Porter pulling us both into a hug. "Thank you so much for telling us about this game, Shayna. I wouldn't dream of missing watching Connor play again."

"Of course." I smile, grateful for the change in conversation. "I'm glad we can all be here to support him."

I glance around. It looks like me, my best friends, and Connor's parents are the only people here, aside from those playing in the game. Hopefully he's not mad that I let this game slip in front of his family and that we're all here, but

I don't see what's not to like about loved ones at an event to support you.

While Mallory gets pulled into a conversation with her parents, I set up my lawn chair and look out to the field where the men are warming up. I spot Connor immediately. Unfortunately for me, he isn't wearing baseball pants. It's not a secret that he's gotten more muscular over the years, so I'm sure his ones from high school no longer fit.

But lucky for me, Connor *is* wearing gray joggers that give off a sexy, laid-back vibe. It's ridiculous how irresistible men look in them. But Connor Porter in gray joggers? That's enough to scramble my brain to mush and make me say things I'd never be confident enough to utter without a whole lot of encouragement.

He catches the ball his teammate throws to him during their warm-ups, but rather than throwing it back, Connor looks over at the small crowd that's come to cheer him on. I swear, his eyes instantly find me, and everything about him softens. His frown disappears, and his shoulders fall like he's finally letting go of whatever stress was making him tense. He offers me a small wave. I smile and wave back.

Connor grabs the ball from his mitt and throws it back to his warm-up partner like nothing just happened. But the racing of my heart is evidence to the contrary.

I'm in trouble if the slightest bit of acknowledgement from Connor can send my body reeling. I'm still patiently waiting for something to happen between us, but I don't mind because my feelings for Connor Porter are the steady kind.

He's no longer just the guy I had a crush on back in high school. Learning who he truly is over the last month has been a gift. So for now, I'm content holding onto hope. I know Connor's scared because of his past, but what else do we have to live for if not for the hope of it all?

I move my chair between Alyssa's and Kelsey's, wanting to put some distance between me, Mallory, and her parents. I'm here to support Connor, and I can't do that if I'm dodging questions about whether Connor and I are a thing.

By the time we've reached the ninth inning, Connor's team is down by two runs. With fully loaded bases and two outs at the bottom of the ninth, Connor is up to bat. The first pitch is thrown high, but the second is a strike, right down the middle. Connor takes a step back and readjusts his grip on the bat. We're close enough to home plate that I can see every detail as he returns to the batter's box and looks over.

At me.

His gaze falls from my face to my outfit, and I inhale a sharp breath.

I promised him I would wash the sweatshirt and get it back to him on the plane, but I could never quite convince myself to. All morning, I debated whether to wear it. With the way he's looking at me, I'm glad I did. The expression on his face is steely. Determined.

Connor steps back into the batter's box and swings on the next pitch. I hear the crack of his bat as it connects with the ball. I push up from my lawn chair and hold my breath as the ball flies through the air. When it hits the ground behind the fence, I throw my arms up and cheer. "Yeah! Way to go, Con!"

Connor rounds all the bases in a jog. When his foot touches home plate, he doesn't pay any attention to all his teammates congratulating him. Instead, he looks over, and his eyes lock with mine. Then Connor Porter does the unimaginable in front of a crowd: he smiles.

I grin back at him so widely that my cheeks instantly hurt. I'd take all the sore cheeks just to see this man smile on a more regular basis, because Connor's smile is devastating in the most wonderful of ways. Yep, I'm completely ruined. I'm confident there's not another soul on the planet that could ever make me feel the way he does.

I hear his mother scrambling for her phone. "Oh, where's a camera when I need one?"

Alyssa nudges my side. "Looks like someone got a little close to a certain Porter on their business collab if he's letting you call him by a nickname."

Kelsey peers around her, listening in.

A blush spreads across my cheeks. I was so in the moment watching Connor that I forgot where I was and who I was around. "I've always called him Con," I say. It's true. I bestowed the nickname on him back in middle school, but there's more weight to it now after he told me he likes it when I call him that. I mean, we love a man who knows what he likes.

"And have you always shared super-charged looks across the baseball field?" Kelsey asks.

"That has been a more recent development."

Alyssa's mouth gapes. "You've been holding out on us."

"I promise I'll share everything soon." I keep my attention focused on the field as the other team gets the final out needed to end the game.

With Connor's grand slam, his team officially won. By the way our little cheering section is shouting, you'd think he just won the World Series, not a pickup game. But that's what I think it should always be like when we show up for our people at the exciting moments in their lives— we should come full force, all out, cheering our heads off, making fools of ourselves to let them know we care.

Connor jogs over, pulls his ball cap off, and runs his fingers through his damp hair. "Looks like you're my good luck charm."

As if the man couldn't become any more handsome, he puts the ball cap on. Backward. His eyes flick down to the sweatshirt before slowly dragging back up to mine, filled with amusement and a flicker of heat. "Or maybe it's just my hoodie."

I play with the ends of the drawstrings, doing everything in my willpower not to freak out that he's flirting with me. I mean, there's no other explanation for his comments.

"What about me *in* your hoodie?"

His lips tilt up in another small smile, and it's like a boost of serotonin straight to my veins. "I guess we'll have to test that theory out some more. For scientific purposes."

I nod along. "For science."

He gestures over to his family. "I'm gonna talk to my parents, but I'll see you tonight at their spring barbecue?"

"I'll be there."

"Great." Connor waves to Kelsey and Alyssa, who must've stepped away to give us our space. I didn't even notice them move—not that I would've noticed anything else when I was fully locked in on Connor. "Thanks for coming," he says to them before turning and jogging over to his family.

Kelsey and Alyssa walk back over to me as I'm putting away my lawn chair.

Alyssa bumps my hip with hers. "I thought firefighters were supposed to put out fires, but all I saw were sparks flying between you two."

I let out an incredulous laugh. "Did that really just happen?"

They nod. "Girls' night can't come soon enough." Kelsey smiles. "I need all the details."

Alyssa tilts her head. "*We* need all the details."

"You ready to talk?" I turn to find Mallory waiting behind me, a lawn chair bag hanging from her arm.

"Yeah." I place the strap of my lawn chair on my shoulder.

Kelsey threads her arm through Alyssa's. "We'll leave you to that."

I give them my car keys so they can wait in there while we talk. As they move past me, both my friends mouth *good luck*.

I'll take all the well-wishes I can get. I'm not exactly scared to talk to Mal. She's been one of my best friends since we were eleven. But I value her opinion, and if she tells me she doesn't want me dating her brother, I don't think I could be with Connor, even if it would break my heart. Let's hope it doesn't come to that.

Mallory and I walk off to the side of the park, away from the people walking from the field to their cars. "Okay, what gives?" She starts numbering things on her fingers like evidence. "You bid a thousand dollars to win that date with my brother at the bachelor auction. You're wearing his sweatshirt that you've apparently kept since high school. You just cheered for him even louder than my mother. And Connor smiled at you after his grand slam. *Smiled*." She throws her arms up, making the lawn chair hanging from her arm smack against her hip.

I take a deep breath to steady my racing heart, then tell her the truth. "I'm in love with Connor."

Her mouth falls open in complete shock. I'm just happy that she doesn't seem mad. "Shut up. Since when?"

"Pretty much since I met him." I fiddle with the strap of the lawn chair bag. "I mean, it was obviously more like puppy love back then—an innocent crush. But spending time with him getting everything ready for my business has let me get to know him for who he is now, and all it's done has made me fall for him more. Please don't be mad." I stare at her, bracing for whatever impact my words are going to have.

Her brows furrow. "Why would I be mad?"

"When we all became friends, we promised each other that we wouldn't let anything come between our friend group. No exes, no siblings."

Mallory waves off the comment. "That's just something we said when we were kids and still thought boys had cooties. Plus, Connor was a grumpy, reclusive teenager who wasn't interested in anything beyond baseball." She wrinkles her nose. "And his room always smelled like the cheddar-and-sour-cream chips he hid under his bed to snack on late at night."

I decide to take a page from her book and be bold. "It sounds like you might be holding him in time a bit."

Mallory stares off at the field, then sighs. "You might be right. I guess he's not that stinky teenage boy anymore. I think it's hard for me to see how much he's grown because that means we're all getting older." She drops her lawn chair and wraps her arms around her middle. "And if I'm getting older, then I have to think about the future. And what if I marry Griffin and I have to move to LA away from my family and friends?" She kicks her pink sneakers on the dirt, sending a small cloud around our feet. "Sorry, this isn't supposed to be about me."

I reach out and grab her hand. "That's exactly what friends are for." She squeezes my hand and shoots me a small smile before wrapping her arms around her middle again. "If you end up marrying Griffin and have to spend a lot of time in LA, we'll plan annual vacations. We'll text you so much, your phone will never stop going off." My eyes well up. "We won't forget about you. *Ever.*"

Mallory's lips tremble. "Promise?"

I nod and wipe my cheeks. "I swear on all the flowers in the world. Besides, we're all getting older. It's sad to think about, but it's also beautiful that we all are entering this new season of life that we get to walk together. We knew that we wouldn't be roommates forever." I blow out a breath as emotion tightens my throat. "It's heartbreaking to think about not coming down the stairs and seeing all my besties every morning. But just imagine all of us married and at a summer house with our husbands and a bunch of kids running around." I smile at the mental image. "That's a future we get to look forward to."

"And you want Connor to be part of that?"

"If you're okay with the idea of me dating your brother. And, obviously, if this is what he wants, too."

Mallory purses her lips. "It would be an adjustment for me to see you with my brother and not freak out seeing you hold hands or kiss or whatever." Her expression softens. "But what kind of sister and best friend would I be to come between the connection you two have?" She tilts her head and smiles. "Plus, if it all works out, you'd *officially* be my sister."

Happy tears flood my vision. "I never thought about it like that." I open my arms and envelop her in a hug.

It would've made things a lot easier if I knew Mallory wasn't holding me to that middle school promise. I wouldn't have had to suppress my feelings all these years, but I'm honestly not sure it would've changed much else.

The more I think about it, this time apart from Connor allowed us to step into adulthood and learn about ourselves. It made us who we are and allowed us to come back together at the perfect time.

When Mallory pulls back, her lips are pulled to the side like she wants to say something.

"What's wrong?" I ask.

She drops her gaze. "If you're serious about trying to see things through with my brother, I need to tell you something."

I'm instantly nauseous.

"A while back, when Connor was living in Seattle, he dated someone. All I know is that the relationship ended badly and he didn't have plans to date anyone again after that. I know you've always dreamed of getting married, and I couldn't live with myself if I had information that could save you from heartbreak and didn't warn you."

"I already know about Jillian," I say, relief flooding me.

"You do?"

"Yeah, he shared everything about their relationship with me after the charity auction. I know he has some fears around relationships, but I think we're getting there."

"Oh, good." She smiles. "That makes me feel so much better. I only want what's best for you. And if you think that's my brother, not that you really need it, but you have my blessing. Just be careful, okay?"

I nod and she pulls me in for another hug.

I step back as she reaches down to grab her lawn chair. "I should get to Daisy Mae. I drove Alyssa and Kelsey here, so they're waiting for me."

"Do they know about Connor yet?"

I shake my head as we start walking back to the parking lot. "I wanted to talk to you first for obvious reasons."

"I'm glad we finally got to talk."

"Me, too." I smile.

"I'll see you at the barbecue," she calls out as she walks toward her car.

I have a feeling this is going to be the best one yet.

CHAPTER TWENTY-FIVE
CONNOR

THE ANNUAL SPRING BARBECUE that my parents throw is probably the only event I don't mind attending and maybe even look forward to. I get to be outside with good food and lots of room to distance myself whenever I feel peopled out. As far as events go, it's a much more ideal situation than being crammed in a small house with a bunch of nosy people asking invasive questions or talking my ear off for hours straight without any avenues of escape.

But this afternoon, my stomach is in knots as Shayna walks into my parents' backyard wearing a floral dress that hits her mid-calf, as well as her usual headband. I flirted with her this morning. Well, I attempted to. I'm not sure if I'm any good at it, but I had to say something because seeing her sitting at my game in *my* hoodie shifted something inside of me.

It had me swinging for the fences with all my strength, wanting to impress her. A deep-seated desire to spend more time with her has been present ever since our time in the gardens, and seeing her at my game today only solidified that feeling. But now that she's finally here, the nerves are hitting me full force.

Shayna hugs my mom and laughs at something she says. I don't know how I haven't noticed it before, the way she seamlessly fits into my family, but I see it now. I see *her* now. The way her whole face lights up is a beacon pulling me into the light and out of my world of gray. I'd have to be blind not to notice how beautiful she is, but she's more than that. She's radiant and magnetic, pulling everyone around her into her orbit.

I'm just the guy who's lucky enough to witness it.

Shayna looks my way and shoots me a soft smile. She says something to my mother, then makes her way toward me.

"I'm happy you're here," I say when she reaches me. I ball my hands into fists at my side. That was a stupid thing to say when she's been coming to my parents' barbecues since she was in middle school.

"I wouldn't miss it. This is the perfect kickoff to my favorite time of year." She closes her eyes and takes a long breath in. "Do you smell it?"

I take a little whiff. "The burgers and hot dogs on the grill?"

She laughs. "Smell beyond the food."

I close my eyes like her and take a minute to breathe in, trying to let everything else fade away and let my senses take over. That's when it hits me. The smell of fresh air. The faint scent of flowers beginning to bloom. "It smells like spring."

"Isn't it perfect?" She gestures to the trees at the back of my parents' property. "And look at all the beautiful shades of green that are budding on the trees and sprouting up from the earth." She sighs. "You know why spring is the best season of all, aside from that?"

I shake my head and wait for her to continue.

"It's a reminder that even after the harshest seasons in our lives, something new and beautiful can come from it. That nothing is beyond restoration."

I catch the hidden meaning behind her words. That my fears aren't beyond repair. That I can grow and move past the lies into a better future. With her.

"You're brilliant, you know that? You have this eloquent way of saying things." I shake my head. "I could never sound like that, but you—" I stare at her, wondering how someone so gorgeous and brilliant is still single. "You're amazing."

Shayna blushes. "I'm just stating the truth."

"So was I."

She slips her arms around my waist and leans her head against my chest. I melt into her touch, wrapping my arms around her shoulders and pressing my cheek to the top of her head. I breathe in her floral perfume and the clean smell of her shampoo, and all my nerves fade away.

When she pulls back and looks up at me with a shy grin, I have the crazy urge to kiss her. But I wouldn't do that here. If I'm going to kiss her, I'm going to do it right—and I can't do that in my parents' backyard.

"Hi," she whispers.

"Hi."

"I don't know if I said it earlier, but you were amazing at your game."

"Like I said, it's because I had my lucky charm there." I shoot her a teasing smile. "Speaking of, where *is* my sweatshirt? I distinctly remember you telling me you were going to return it."

She pops her lips. "You know, I don't remember any such thing."

"I guess you'll just have to keep it. It seems to bring the most luck when you're the one wearing it."

Shayna peers up at me like she can't believe what she's hearing. "Who are you and what have you done with Connor Porter?"

I rub the back of my neck and don't miss the way her eyes move to my arms. "You're the one who's openly ogling me."

Her blush deepens as her eyes dart back to mine. "Who uses that word?"

"People who are being ogled."

She shakes her head. "Is that the way you were looking at me when I wore your sweatshirt earlier?"

There's no use denying it when we both know it's the truth. I shrug. "It takes an ogler to know an ogler."

Shayna laughs. "Okay, now I know you're an imposter."

"You have yourself to thank for that."

"Me?" She holds a hand to her chest.

"You're the one who insisted on helping me build my confidence."

"And you're using that confidence to…" She trails off, leaving me to fill in the blank. I can see the questions swirling in her eyes, and I don't blame her. It's not as if I have a history of flirting with her.

"Talk to you," I tease.

She quirks an eyebrow. "Is that what the kids are calling it nowadays?"

"Dinner's ready, everyone," my dad calls out from the patio, my mother at his side.

Shayna stares at me like she's waiting to see if I'm going to answer.

Before I have a chance to respond, Shayna lightly kicks at the grass. "I'd better make my plate before all the macaroni salad is gone."

My mom's macaroni salad is delicious, but the bowl is never empty. It's as if the noodles multiply after every scoop.

I should say something—*anything*. Tell her I'm freaking out. Tell her I *was* flirting but still need time to fully open up.

But I don't.

I dip my head, and Shayna looks at me for another long moment before turning and walking to the patio. I hate that it's so hard for me to confidently go after what I want. I wish I could shake some sense into myself and be what she needs, but I think I need to figure this out on my own before fully letting Shayna in. She deserves the best version of me, not scraps.

Kelsey's boyfriend, Tyler, walks up to me and claps me on the shoulder. "Sorry I missed your game this morning, man. I already had tickets to take my niece to see Disney on Ice."

"Sounds fun."

"There were thousands of screaming kids. You'd have loved it."

I grimace. I don't know how he survived that or how my sister does it every day as a teacher. They've got more patience than me. I look over and find Tyler smirking. He's messing with me.

"Anyway." Tyler inclines his head toward where Shayna, Kelsey, Mallory, Tess, Alyssa, and little Evie are piling their plates. "Is something going on between you and Shayna?"

I sputter and choke on my saliva. Tyler claps my back as I break into a coughing fit. I hold up a hand to show him I'm fine, but I still can't talk while my windpipe rebels. When the coughing has finally subsided, I clear my throat.

"Sorry about that," he says. "I didn't know Shayna was such a touchy subject."

"It's not. We're…" I trail off, unsure how to describe what exactly we are.

"I won't tell Kelsey, you know. Bro code."

I blow out a long breath. "Nothing's really happened yet, but…" It seems I'm incapable of finishing my sentences now.

"You want it to?" Tyler suggests.

I shove my hands in my jeans pockets and nod.

"Can I offer you a piece of advice?"

"Go for it."

Tyler crosses his arms and keeps his eyes on Kelsey as he says, "There will be a time when a woman walks into your life that you can't stop thinking about. Maybe she drives you crazy, or maybe she flips your entire world upside down until you're questioning everything you ever thought you wanted. But, regardless, you can't get her out of your head. You'll be at work, minding your own business, and you'll see or hear something that reminds you of her. That revelation will knock you off your feet, but that's when it's important to lean in. Don't let the what-ifs or worries hold you back. Pursue her." My eyes drift to Shayna. He grabs my shoulder and squeezes. "Don't let the opportunity slip through your fingers. It won't be there forever, man."

I know he said not to, but I can't help but think about all my fears. Shayna is practically perfect, but me? I'm still figuring out what it would mean for me to be in a relationship again. My inner critic still insists I'm not what she needs. I'm like a rocky soil in comparison to her bright, beautiful flower. I won't help her bloom; I'll only make her colors dull until she wilts.

The hurt, guarded part of me says that I'm not good for her, that I'm not enough. But I can already see how good she is for me. Shayna brings out a side of me that I didn't know existed. One that smiles and laughs more often than I have in my entire life. One that's able to speak freely around her without fear of judgment. One that doesn't have to actively search her out in the crowd because I already know where she is.

One that's starting to believe that I can't see a future without her in my life.

"What if I'm not what she needs?"

"What would you say to Shayna if she told you that she wasn't enough for you?" he counters.

"That's crazy." I shake my head.

"Exactly." Tyler looks over to where all the ladies are sitting at the long picnic table. "You have to trust that she can choose who is or isn't good for her, man."

I've never thought about it like that. This whole time, I've been telling Shayna she needs to figure out what she likes and wants—not because someone asked something of her or told her to, but because it's what she really desires.

And what if that's *me*?

Once I've made my plate, I sit across from Shayna, a few people down. I dig in, hoping a full stomach will help give me the courage I need to open up later. Talking about feelings doesn't come naturally to me, but I guess that's part of a relationship—doing the things that terrify you.

I devour my burger while the people around me listen to Evie talk about her upcoming dance recital, then the corn is calling my name. My mom's corn on the cob has been my favorite side dish for as long as I can remember. She coats it in melted butter and grated Parmesan. It's a heavenly combo but an absolute mess to eat. That's what napkins and wet wipes are for, though. I pick it up and take a giant bite, right down the center. Butter dribbles down my chin, and for some reason, I choose that moment to look over at Shayna.

She's already watching me, her lips slightly parted. I'm not much for guessing what people want without them verbalizing it, but I'm quickly learning that everything is different when it comes to *her*. It's obvious she wants to finish our conversation from earlier, and I'm not going to keep a lady waiting. I grab a napkin and wipe my chin before glancing at my plate, then back at her. She giggles and mirrors me, taking a huge bite out of her corn. Parmesan cheese dots her lips like a misplaced mustache, and I run a hand over my mouth to hide my smile at how cute she is.

I gesture with my head to the house and Shayna nods, excusing herself after quickly wiping her face with a napkin. No one questions me as I get up from the table and follow after her. When I reach the patio, I take a deep breath and shake out my hands before opening the back door.

Here goes nothing.

Shayna is pacing the kitchen when I walk inside, but she immediately stops when she notices me.

"Hi."

She smirks. "Is that how we're going to start every conversation now?"

"Should I try out a different greeting?" I dip an imaginary cowboy hat and do my best deep Southern accent. "Howdy."

Shayna grabs an extra biscuit my mom made for her strawberry-shortcake trifle and chucks it at me. I catch it with one hand before it hits me in the face. I drop it back on the counter.

She groans. "How do you make everything look so hot?"

I raise an eyebrow. Looks like I could take some lessons from her on how to be forward. And the knowledge that she thinks I'm hot has me feeling warm. I didn't know catching a flying biscuit was attractive, but to each their own.

Shayna purses her lips. "Was there a reason you wanted to meet me here, or did you just need an escape?"

Right. The reason.

"I wanted to finish our conversation." She looks surprised, her eyes a little wide and her mouth agape. "I was flirting with you." I tilt my head. "Or at least, I was *trying* to."

Shayna steps closer. I can't help but be distracted by her beauty as she looks at me in a way I never thought a woman would—like I mean something to her. Her voice is barely above a whisper when she asks, "Why?"

"Because everything felt different on our date at the botanical gardens, and then when I saw you in my hoodie this morning, it confirmed it for me. You're someone I could see myself with—and that honestly terrifies me." I run a hand through my hair. "But it also has me excited about the future for the first time in a long time. I'm not sure I'm ready for a full-blown relationship, but you deserve to know where my feelings stand." I sigh. "I don't expect you to say anything. I don't even know if you feel the same way, but—"

She rises on her toes and presses her lips lightly to my cheek, effectively cutting off the rest of my rambling. I close my eyes and memorize the feel of her mouth against my skin so that, even after she's stepped back, I can hold onto the sensation.

It was just a kiss on the cheek, but the feeling it stirs inside me is like a five-alarm fire—an intense inferno that's hard to contain. I've never felt like this with anyone else. I can only imagine what another touch from her might bring about. Probably my undoing. Because I'm completely captivated by this woman.

CHAPTER TWENTY-SIX
SHAYNA

It's *FINALLY* happening.

I'd like to thank every birthday candle and shooting star that has led me to this moment.

Kissing Connor on the cheek was risky. The last thing I want to do is scare him away, but I'd say the blush climbing his neck means I'm safe.

"In case that wasn't clear, I feel the same way." *I always have.* I keep that little tidbit of information to myself for now because it would likely send him running for the hills.

Connor brushes my hair back from my face. His touch is gentle, but the reaction my body has is anything but. A trail of flames lingers where he touched my cheekbone. My heart rate skyrockets.

"Do you have any plans after this?" When he shakes his head, I smile. "You do now, but you'll have to drive because I drove the girls, so they'll need my car to get home."

Connor shoots me the barest of smiles, but it's there. I'll never get over this moment. Knowing he's interested in me. Being the sole recipient of his smiles. I don't know how I got so lucky. "I'm in."

I glance out the back door and spot the mostly empty plates on the picnic table. "We should get out there and finish our food. We don't want to look too suspicious."

He lets out a dry laugh. "I think it's a little late for that."

I bite my bottom lip, hating the idea of being the talking point at the table. "I'll go first, and you can come back out in a few minutes?"

He nods. "Whatever makes you most comfortable."

"Thanks." I reach over and squeeze his arm. "I'll see you out there." I walk back outside, carrying a bottle of water, trying to make it seem like I was only grabbing a drink. Nothing to see here. When I approach the table, a few people clear their throats.

Oh, begonia. Unfortunately, it appears Connor was right about us being the topic of conversation.

"And that's why you should never eat without washing your hands first." Tyler wasn't the one talking when I first walked up, so I've got to give him props for the quick cover story.

"Hey, Shay." Kelsey shoots me a look that says *You go, girl.*

I unscrew the water bottle cap and take a sip as Evie looks me right in the eyes. With the most serious expression, she asks, "How was the canoodling with Connor?"

My sip goes down the wrong pipe and I cough, trying to pull myself together and digest what she just said.

"Evie," Tess chides.

"What?" Evie shovels another bite of corn into her mouth. "It's what you were talking about." She tilts her head in a sassy manner. "I thought you wanted to know."

Tess sighs and lets her face fall into her hands.

My cheeks flame as crimson as a rose. "I was just grabbing water and responding to a message from the lawyer Austin connected me with." The lawyer did message me earlier today to let me know everything was officially processed, so it doesn't feel like a total lie. If I tell them Connor and I were just talking for the last fifteen minutes, I'm not sure any of them would believe me.

"Then where is Connor?" Mallory asks.

I shrug, hoping I look casual when I feel anything but. "I don't know."

"Looks like we can ask him now." Mrs. Porter smiles at her son as he walks out of the house and back to the table. "Where have you been?"

Connor sits down and moves the food around on his plate with a plastic fork. "Just needed a minute of quiet." He digs back into his food, and conversation resumes around the table, but my appetite is long gone.

I push my plate back and turn to Mallory, desperately needing a change in conversation. "When do you get to see Griffin next?"

"He might be able to fly out in a few weeks as long as he can continue his training at home." She lowers her voice. "And I'm thinking about staying out there with him for my summer break."

"You should go." After enduring all the years of Connor living on the other side of the country, I know how sacred time is with the person you have feelings for. "Like I said this morning, we all obviously want you to stay, but I also really want you to get married to a handsome actor and have lots of gorgeous babies for me to hold."

She sighs, gazing off into the distance with a dreamy look. "He is handsome, isn't he?"

I lower my voice. "Not as handsome as your brother."

Mallory grimaces. "Okay, yeah. Still not used to that." She shakes her head. "Do you have any summer plans now that everything is coming together with your truck?"

"I want to take Daffodil to as many places as I can." I close my eyes, reveling in the dream. "Farmers' markets. Local festivals. Bridal showers. Baby showers."

"I can't wait to see you thrive. Louisville doesn't know what's about to hit them."

"Some good ol' flower power." I grin.

Mal squeezes my arm. "More like the lovely, joyful force of a woman that is Shayna Elise Monroe."

Happy tears brim in my eyes. "Thanks, friend."

"Mallory, are you making our guests cry?" Mama Porter asks.

I laugh and swipe away the tears that have fallen onto my cheeks. "Only happy tears."

"Well, that's a relief." She stands from the picnic table. "I couldn't have you crying before we all enjoy my strawberry-shortcake trifle."

By the time everyone is piling into their cars with full bellies and even fuller hearts, I'm ready for some alone time with Connor. While I loved spending the better part of the day with so many people I care about, I can't wait to pick up our conversation where we left off.

"Are you ready, Shay?" Mallory calls out, standing by my red SUV, Daisy Mae.

I jog over to her and hand her my car keys. "Would you mind driving home for me?"

"Too tired to drive?"

I glance back over my shoulder at Connor, waiting for me by his truck. "I was thinking about getting another ride home." I turn back to her and watch Mallory look at her brother.

She steps closer and gives me a hug. "Have fun, but not too much fun."

I laugh as I squeeze her tight. "I won't do anything you wouldn't do."

Mallory pulls back and shoots me a look before yelling at her brother, "Don't keep her out too late."

I wave to my friends before I walk over to Connor. He opens the passenger door for me. I know I could open it myself, but the knowledge that I never have to around him makes me feel cared for in a way no man ever has before.

"So, where are we going?" He joins me in the truck and looks at me expectantly.

"Is all your fishing stuff still back there?" I gesture to the bed of the truck. My whole plan is contingent on my assumption that he hasn't put his fishing gear away since the bachelor auction.

"Should be."

"Perfect, then take me to your favorite fishing spot."

In the fading light, Connor's smile is bright enough to light the sky as he turns onto the road. "Seriously?"

"You took me to the botanical gardens. It's only fair that I take you fishing, but you'll need to teach me how." I crinkle my nose. "And hook the worms for me."

His laughter fills the car. I wish I had the sound on video to listen to whenever I need a serotonin boost, because the results would be instantaneous.

"I use lures, but if I used worms, I would handle them for you." Connor reaches over and places his hand on my thigh.

I bite back a gasp, trying to play it cool when I would rather be squealing. This is what I dreamed of for so long that it's hard for my brain to process that this is reality.

I place my hand on his. Connor gently turns it over and intertwines our fingers. We're quiet for the rest of the drive to his favorite fishing spot, but no words are needed. The way he gently rubs his thumb across my palm says it all.

Connor pulls into an empty dirt lot and puts the car in park. "This is it."

"I was expecting some—oh, I don't know—water," I tease.

"Sometimes you have to take a small journey before you can enjoy the view."

I look over at Connor as he exits the vehicle and takes a deep breath. A soft smile forms on his lips, like he can't help but be happy when he's here. The journey we've been on that's led us to this moment has been anything but small, but I sure am enjoying the view now.

I join him at the bed of the truck to help grab the fishing gear. Connor pulls his phone out of his pocket. He barely glances at it before looking back at me. "Pat texted." I perk up, hoping this means my truck is ready. "He said we can pick up the truck Friday."

I throw my arms around Connor's neck. He wraps his arms around my waist, lifts me off the ground, and spins me. My laughter floats in the air, and I can't help but think about how absolutely happy I sound. How happy I *feel*.

My mobile flower truck is ready, which means everything will be ready in time for the booth I reserved at the Dogwood Festival. And I'm in Connor Porter's arms after I just held his hand in the car. Life doesn't get much better than this.

"I should have the shelves ready for your final approval in the next few days." He sets me back on my feet. "Is there anything else I can help with?"

I shake my head. "I meant to tell you, I had my meeting with the lawyer last week, and everything is now filed." I beam at him. "You're officially looking at the owner of Sunshine Blooms."

He rubs my lower back. "I'm so proud of you, flower."

"Thank you." My eyes brim with tears. Joy. Utter, complete joy that this is my life. That my deepest wish might just come true: to start my dream job with the man I'm falling for at my side. "I couldn't have done it without you."

It could be a reflection of the setting sun amidst the clouds casting a pink hue on his cheeks, but I swear he blushes. "You're the most ambitious, persistent woman I know. You had the strength to accomplish it yourself all along. I'm the lucky one who got to come along for the ride."

I stare at Connor in awe. This day has felt like a dream, and I never want it to end.

He takes my hand. "Come on. I want to show you part of my world."

He grabs a fishing pole and a small storage container and leads me down a dirt path between a series of trees and bushes. After a few minutes, we arrive at the river. It's a secluded area, surrounded by trees. The only sign of humans knowing about this destination is a single wooden bench planted on the bank.

"What do you think?" Connor sets down the fishing pole and container and looks out at the river.

I close my eyes, appreciating the soothing sound of moving water. "I feel at peace here."

I open my eyes to find Connor watching me with a soft gaze. "I knew you'd appreciate it." He gestures for me to sit on the bench as he grabs the fishing pole.

"What's in the little container?" I ask.

He picks it up and opens it. "This is a tackle box. It's where I store my fishing gear."

"And what gear does a person need to fish, exactly?" I want to know everything about him and his hobbies, but when it comes to fishing, I'm starting at ground zero.

"Hooks, lures, bobbers, extra fishing line, and some tools like pliers and a knife." Connor's eyes twinkle with amusement. "And obviously a fishing pole."

"I never would've guessed," I deadpan. "Will you show me how to…" I don't know the technical term, so I mimic the motion of throwing the line into the water.

"Cast," he finishes for me.

"Yes, that."

Connor grins as he grabs the fishing rod and steps closer to me. "You're going to flip the bail to an open position while holding the line against the rod." He shows me his hand positions on the rod. "Then you cast it as you let go of the line."

"What do you do after you cast?"

"You turn the reel." He motions to the side of the rod. "When you start reeling the line back in, the bail will click back over into the closed position. The trick is to reel it in at a speed that mimics natural prey. For certain fish, that means it's a little stop-and-go, but you also don't want your lure to sink to the bottom and get snagged on something."

"Sounds simple enough." I'm not sure I'll remember all the terminology, but if I can get the casting down, maybe I might actually catch something.

"The hardest part is patience." Connor looks out at the water. "Sometimes you'll be out an entire day and not catch a single thing. Others, I'll catch multiple fish within the first hour. If you have the patience to continue casting and reeling, you're already halfway to becoming a skilled angler."

"Then it's time to put my patience to the test." I turn to him. "Will you help me the first time?"

"Sure." Connor hands me the pole and moves behind me. "You ready?" I nod, and he wraps his arms around me and places his hands on top of mine.

I try to remember what he told me and flip open the doodad while holding the line against the rod. I flick my wrists forward, let go of the line, and watch it propel into the water. I bounce up and down and glance over my shoulder. "Did you see that?"

"That was perfect." His lips tilt up into a smile.

I reel the line back in without catching anything, but it still feels like a success with Connor's praise. "Your turn." I extend the rod to him.

"You sure?"

I nod. "I want to see you in your element."

He gets the lure back out in the water before I can even blink, making it all look like one effortless motion. I guess I can add fishing to the list of things he looks hot doing.

"Do you have any fun plans this week?" I ask.

"I actually have to fly back to Washington to finalize a few things with my house sale out there." He recasts the lure. "I was wondering if you wanted to come?"

I try to swallow down my fear of flying and put on a fake smile, but then I think about who's asking me the question. "In case you didn't remember, I'm not the biggest fan of flying."

Connor grins. "Congratulations, you passed the final test. You've officially graduated from People Pleasing University."

"What's my graduation present?"

Perhaps a kiss from my professor? A girl can dream.

"The ability to say no anytime you don't want to do something."

That's not a bad gift either. No more balloon animals or other outrageous requests in my future.

"And if there is something I *want* to do?"

"That's the best part. You have time to dedicate yourself to the things you like."

I deflate like a balloon with helium slowly leaking out. I thought he might catch my drift, but it seems it all went right over his head. I change the topic. "So, you aren't going back to Washington?"

He shakes his head and passes the rod back to me. "I'm hoping to spend some time this week with a beautiful woman who recently became a small business owner. You wouldn't happen to know anyone who meets that criteria, would you?"

I smirk as I cast the lure again. "I think I know the perfect girl." As I'm slowly reeling the line back in, I feel a strong tug. "Fish." I turn to Connor and squeal. "I think I caught a fish."

He moves closer to me, ready to step in if needed. "Reel it in."

Right. I turn back to the river and reel the line in, tightening my grip as the fish fights back. When the lure is almost out of the water, Connor leans down and scoops up the line. The olive-green fish flops as Connor brings it closer to me.

"I can't believe I caught my first fish." I beam. "What kind is it?"

"A smallmouth bass." His eyes move to me, his gaze soft and full of pride. "And a big one, at that." He moves to hand it to me. "You need a picture with your first catch."

I grimace. "That's okay. I don't really want to hold it."

"Just grab it where I am." He hands me the line a little bit above the fish. I grip it and pray that the fish doesn't start flopping around again.

Connor pulls his phone out. The proud look he wears as he takes the picture is adorable and makes my stomach flutter. My smile widens as I look at the real catch of the day: the man behind the phone.

CHAPTER TWENTY-SEVEN
CONNOR

Ever since Shayna approved the shelves I made for the back of her flower truck, I've been working nonstop on another series of wooden vases. I grab the latest one from my workbench and continue sanding it. I know Shayna already bought brown Kraft paper to wrap her bouquets in, but maybe she'll have a use for these, too.

As I run the sander along the wood, I can't help but smile because she's going to be here any minute and we'll go pick up her truck. I've seen her every day this week that I haven't been at the fire station, and I'd be lying if I said I wasn't falling for her.

I always desire to be around her. I think about her every night before I fall asleep, and she's my first thought in the morning. I'm attracted to everything about her, and she makes me feel more safe and more comfortable than anyone else in my life. And I have something with her I've never experienced before: an emotional connection.

I thought she needed a guy more like her. Exuberant. Overflowing with positivity. Someone with a larger-than-life personality who knows exactly what they want. Meanwhile, I'm this reserved man who struggles opening up to people and was fine being alone. But she walked back into my life and changed everything I knew about myself. And maybe Tyler was right about needing to let Shayna decide for herself what she needs and wants. And from our recent conversations, she's made it extremely clear that she wants *me*. Just as I am.

I set the wood vase I just finished sanding down and grab my phone. After opening the Photos app, I scroll until I find the picture I took of Shayna in front of the flower truck. Even though I know she was disappointed at the state of the truck, she still looked optimistic with her arms up in the air and her wide smile.

This is for her. I look around at all the wooden vases I've made over the past month. The realization hits me like the blast of a firehose: they're my favorite thing to build because they remind me of *her*. It's been her all along. Before I realized I wanted anything other than a reclusive life. Before I recognized my feelings for her.

Before all of this, there was always her.

The girl I taught how to slow dance. The girl who encouraged me to tell my parents about my dreams to be a firefighter. She became the woman who helped me find my confidence. The woman who lit up my gray skies.

I'm not sure when it happened. If it was slow or all at once. I'd like to believe I've been slowly falling for her all along but was too blind to notice.

But I see her now.

"Knock, knock." Shayna peeks her head into my shed.

"You're early." I quickly close out my phone screen, but there's no time for me to hide all the wooden vases.

"Sorry, I couldn't wait at home any longer."

"Too excited to go pick up Daffodil?" I ask.

Shayna smiles. "You remembered her name."

"She's important to you, so she's important to me."

Her bottom lip quivers. "I think I'm going to be a puddle after today."

I wipe my hands on my jeans and then walk over and pull her into my arms. I tangle my fingers in her hair. I don't know what kind of magic shampoo and conditioner she uses to get it so soft and shiny, but I hope she never stops using it. I kiss the top of her head. "Then you'd be my favorite puddle."

Shayna lets out a watery laugh and pulls back, wiping the tears from her cheeks. "Thanks. I can wait by your truck if you need to finish whatever you were—" She looks over at my workbench, her words effectively cut off. "What is that?"

If she didn't know my feelings for her were real before, she's about to. I slide my hands into my jacket pockets and walk across the shed with her. She runs her hand along the smooth wood. The current series of vases I'm creating all have the wood at a diagonal angle, forming a fun shape. It made it a little trickier to get the glass interior added to hold the water and flowers, but I was able to figure it out.

"A vase."

She glances up at me. "You make vases?"

"Funny story." I go over to my storage closet and close my eyes before opening the door. "They're actually my favorite pieces to create."

Shayna walks over, looking at the countless vases on the shelves in awe. "Con." She clears her throat like she's trying to compose herself. "These are stunning."

"Thanks." I dip my head at her praise.

"Seriously, you could sell these."

"Or I could gift them to a certain flower truck owner."

She turns to face me and tugs at the bottom of her quilted floral jacket. "You can't just give them to me. These could be worth a lot of money."

"I don't think people will want to buy wooden vases from a nobody."

Shayna reaches over and squeezes my hand. "You're somebody to me."

I can't help but smile at her statement. I have a feeling I'm going to be smiling a lot more, having her in my life. "You know, I started making them years ago in Seattle, but I didn't realize why until today."

"And why is that?" She smiles up at me, and it takes all my willpower not to kiss her. I won't let our first kiss be in my shed that smells of sawdust and wood stain. It needs to be someplace as special as Shayna—like a field of flowers or under a dogwood tree in bloom.

"They reminded me of you." I trace the pad of my thumb across the back of her hand. "And I think that made me feel like I always had a little piece of home with me."

"Con." The hazy look in her eyes and the breathiness in her tone have me second-guessing my resolve to not kiss her in here. But no, this is the place you kiss after you've already done it tens or hundreds of times.

I glance at the clock on the wall. "We need to head out."

Shayna places her hands on her hips as her face falls slightly, but she quickly recovers with a smile. "Let's go get my Daffodil."

"Gotta grab something first." I hold up a finger. "I'll meet you at my truck." I jog inside my house and make my way into the kitchen. I grab the strawberry matcha I picked up for her from her favorite café this morning out of the fridge and hurry outside, locking the front door behind me.

Her face lights up when she sees what I'm holding. "You didn't have to do that."

"I wanted to."

She takes a sip, then closes her eyes with a soft smile on her lips. Waking up a little early to get Shayna her favorite drink is something I'd gladly do on my off days if it means I can make her happy.

When we pull into Pat's Auto Body, Shayna's legs are bouncing so fast that it's shaking my truck. I reach over and set my hand on her knee, and she seems to settle at my touch. "You ready?"

"Yeah." She shudders in a breath, then lets out a dry laugh. "I don't know why I'm so nervous."

"I'd be shocked if you *weren't* nervous." I squeeze her knee. "This is a big moment."

She takes a deep breath and nods. "Okay, I'm ready."

We walk to the entrance of the shop, and Shayna tosses her empty matcha cup in the trash before grabbing my hand. I open the door for her, and she pulls me inside, still clinging to my hand like I'm the source of her strength. It's ironic because I feel like she's the one that bolsters me, but I'm happy to support her in this moment.

"Well, I'll be darned." Pat pops up from his desk, staring at our joined hands. "I knew there was something between you two. People don't look at each other like y'all do without there being some major feelings there." He points at me with a smirk like we've been in on a months-long joke together. "You got me good."

Shayna moves to let go of my hand, probably thinking I'm uncomfortable with all the attention. I kind of am, but I want to show her off even more. Let Pat know he's never going to have another shot at asking out Shayna Monroe because she's taken. I squeeze her hand, and she looks up at me with slightly raised brows. Looking into her eyes seems to be the cure for all my worries. My shoulders fall as tension leaves my body. There's nothing else. Only her.

She reaches over with her free hand and grasps my forearm. She shoots me a shy smile before turning to Pat. "Would you mind taking us to the truck?"

He sweeps his arm as if he's rolling out the red carpet for us. "Right this way."

Pat leads us through the back door of the shop, and I immediately spot Daffodil in all her yellow glory.

The moment Shayna sees her, she lets out a small gasp, immediately followed by a squeal of delight. She rocks on the balls of her feet and grips my hand and arm like she can't believe this is real.

I nudge her with my elbow. "What are you waiting for?"

Shayna lets go of my arm and steps in front of me, our connected hands between us. She slowly backs toward the truck, pulling me with her, while wearing a wide grin. The sun is perfectly positioned behind her, casting her in a golden hue. It almost looks like a halo, which seems fitting since she's the closest thing to an angel I've ever seen.

I return her smile, and we walk over to the truck. She pulls me to a stop a few feet away. To no surprise, she has tears in her eyes and a smile on her lips.

"I can't believe she's mine," she whispers.

"Well, you'd better believe it," I say.

"The shade of yellow is perfect."

I walk around the truck, taking everything in. All of the rust and imperfections are gone, leaving behind this new flower truck ready for a new, full life. "Come look at what your buyers will see at markets." I wave her over, hoping she'll like the special request I sent to Pat without her knowing.

The look of pure joy on her face when she spots the logo I custom-designed for her on the passenger door is the one I want emblazoned in my memory when I'm eighty years old and reminiscing about the past. I want to picture her exactly as she is now, filled with surprise and bliss. And I'm hit with another overwhelming realization: I want to be the reason she smiles like this for the rest of my life.

Shayna turns to me, misty-eyed. She really wasn't kidding about this whole becoming a puddle thing today. "I can't believe you did this for me."

"I'd do anything for you."

Go to family and public events. Participate in as many pickup baseball games as she wants to watch me play. Spend hours in the botanical gardens until her heart is content.

I'd do anything she asked me just to see that look of inexplicable radiance again and again.

CHAPTER TWENTY-EIGHT
SHAYNA

Thunder Over Louisville is one of my favorite things about the city. It's the kickoff event leading up to the Kentucky Derby. Next weekend is the annual Dogwood Festival, where I'll bring Daffodil and my assortment of bouquets to sell for the first time. But for today, I'm trying to stay in the moment and enjoy everything Thunder has to offer.

We already saw the airshow this morning where military-style aircraft do flybys over our city and other aircraft do fun aerobatic demos. Let me tell you, hearing fighter jets fly overhead is exhilarating. It's no wonder the day's festivities draw hundreds of thousands of visitors from all over.

Now, my friends and I are enjoying the annual home Mustangs game in Waterfront Park from the comfort of Austin's box seats. There's a concert in the stadium that follows the game. But my favorite thing about Thunder Over Louisville, by a long shot, is the thirty-minute fireworks display over the river. Everyone crams together like a can of sardines along the Ohio River to watch the night sky light up in one of the nation's largest fireworks shows.

Although, I've always preferred watching the show from the less crowded ballpark.

While I've attended Thunder every year of my life, this year is my favorite by far. Everything feels more special and magical today with Connor by my side. I know crowded places aren't exactly his thing, so the fact that he's here because he wants to spend time with me fills my heart.

Alyssa cups her hands around her mouth and shouts, "Boo!" The umpire just called another pitch thrown to Austin a strike when it was *clearly* a ball. "Get some glasses, Blue."

Connor leans closer to me, his arm brushing mine on the armrest between us. "I didn't know she was so invested in baseball."

"It's not the *game* she's invested in." He shoots me a questioning look. I press my cheek against his and whisper, "Lyss won't admit it, but she's totally in love with him."

"Really?"

I pull back and nod.

Connor looks thoughtfully between Alyssa and the field, the puzzle pieces all falling into place in his mind. "I see what you mean. The winter trivia night. Your joint birthday party. He always shows up for her."

"He bakes for her, too, whenever she leaves another one of her awful dates that are completely wrong for her."

"Well, no dates will ever measure up if she's in love with him." Connor gestures to the field. "Austin's a pro baseball player."

"That's what we've been telling her all along." I sigh. "She just needs time to see it for herself."

"Just like us." Connor reaches over and grabs my hand before hiding it behind the giant tub of popcorn we're sharing—a perk of Austin giving us his box seats for this game. I don't know that we necessarily need to hide our hand-holding since everyone here already knows something is happening between us, but the excitement of hiding our affection in front of all my friends has me feeling like a middle schooler concealing her crush. It's an adrenaline rush that leaves me craving more.

There's no hiding my smile as Connor plays with my hand, dragging the tips of his fingers against my palm in a way that feels both playful and enticing.

With a full count, Austin pulls his bat back, preparing for what Connor just told me is called the payoff pitch—one that ends in either the batter striking out, walking to first, or getting a hit. The pitch is thrown and Austin swings. The sound of his wooden bat connecting with the ball has me inhaling sharply. I think everyone in our box collectively holds their breath as we watch the ball soar over the heads of the infield players. The center field and left field players of the opposing team sprint toward the back of the field and run into each other as the ball hits the outfield wall and falls to the grass behind them.

Alyssa throws her arms up and cheers as Austin rounds first base and heads toward second. "Go, Austin!"

The left fielder scrambles to get back up and grabs the ball, throwing it to the second baseman. Austin slides into the plate just before the second baseman catches the ball. The on-field umpire slides his arms out, gesturing that he's safe.

All of us in the box hoot and holler. I turn and high-five Alyssa with my free hand.

"That was a great hit, wasn't it?" She beams.

"For sure." I nudge her with my elbow. "Speaking of Austin, have you asked him to go to your cousin's wedding this summer yet?"

Her face falls. "I don't think I'm going to."

"Why not?"

Alyssa runs her fingers through the ends of her long hair curled to perfection. Today, half of it is pulled up in a high pony, and a maroon silk scarf is tied around it for an added touch of Mustangs spirit. "It's during All-Star Week."

"Isn't that usually *during* the week?"

Alyssa nods. "Yep, Bianca and Bradley decided to get married on a Wednesday."

I roll my eyes. "They're like the human equivalent of a splinter."

She scoffs. "Tell me about it. I mean, of course the two most conceited, selfish people in the world would choose to get married in the middle of the week to make everyone take off work."

"Seriously." I eye her suspiciously. "But why won't you ask Austin if it's during his time off?"

"That's his only real break, minus a random few days off sprinkled throughout the season. I couldn't ask him to give up that precious time to come to an awkward family wedding."

"You *could*," I counter. "It's up to you, but I'm sure Austin would want to be there for you."

Alyssa leans back in her seat. "We'll see. I haven't really even convinced *myself* to go yet."

"I don't blame you."

Alyssa pulls her lips to the side. "I'm going to need *all* the updates at girls' night this week."

"About what?"

She lowers her voice. "The fact that you're holding hands with Connor right now."

My cheeks are on fire. I guess we aren't as inconspicuous as I thought. I turn back to look at the field as the rest of our friends cheer again. I tilt my head toward Connor. "What happened?"

"Cooper hit a double that sent Austin home. We're up by one run now."

I look over at the scoreboard. It's the bottom of the seventh. If the Mustangs can keep this up, they just might win one of the most exciting, sold-out home games of the season.

I relay all the information to Alyssa so she can congratulate Austin on his run later. "Also, I can't wait to tell y'all everything." I glance over at Connor, then back at her. "I'm really happy."

Alyssa squeezes my arm. "I love that for you. You deserve all the happiness in the world." She shoots me a meaningful look before turning her attention back to the field. I reach over and grab another handful of popcorn.

"What was that about?" Connor asks.

I shrug. "Just girl stuff."

"You don't have to hide anything from me, flower," he whispers. The feeling of his warm breath along my ear and neck has heat pooling in my middle and spreading out to all my limbs. I bet the color of my neck and face right now would make a wonderful shade of lipstick or blush. "I like that you want to talk about me." I swear that I feel his lips brush along my ear. "About *us*."

"Is there an *us* to talk about?" My responding whisper comes out an octave higher than normal. I'm doing a poor job of maintaining any semblance of control, but what else is a girl to do when the man she's been crushing on for over a decade's mouth is literally so close she can feel it? So close I can almost *taste* it. I'm only human, after all.

"I want there to be." He pauses, then adds, "Don't you?"

I nod so quickly I would be the perfect model for the bobbleheads sold in the stadium gift shop.

Connor's lips pull up at the corners. "I'm glad we're on the same page."

Tess's daughter Evie bounces excitedly in my lap as the band on the stage finishes their final song of the concert. This year, it was a local cover band that played everything from The Beatles to the Jonas Brothers. Evie was ecstatic that their last song was a cover of "Into the Unknown" from *Frozen 2*.

Even though they're now off stage as we wait for the fireworks to begin, Evie is screaming out the siren call part of the song. "Oh, oh. Oh, oh."

She's actually not half bad.

Evie abruptly turns in my lap. "Mr. Austin?"

He arrived in the box suite halfway through the concert after his press time and a quick shower. Austin pauses his conversation with Tyler and gives her his full attention. "Yes, Ms. Evie?"

She giggles. "Are any of the friends you play with single? You know, I still need a new daddy."

I bite the inside of my lips to contain my laugh.

Tess turns with a huff as all of our friends near enough to hear the exchange attempt to stifle their laughter. "What have I told you about asking random men if they're single?"

Evie crosses her arms. "I wasn't asking him if *he's* single. I asked about his *friends*. They aren't random. He knows them."

Tess moves across the box and kneels in front of me to look her daughter in the eyes. "It's not polite to ask that. If I ever date again, I want it to happen naturally, not because my daughter is asking a bunch of men to be her new daddy."

Evie lets out an exasperated sigh that feels much too heavy for someone who's only five years old. "Okay."

"Thank you." Tess makes her way back to Alyssa and Mallory and resumes her conversation.

I look back at Austin just in time to catch him nodding at Evie like they're in on the secret together. He mouths *I've got you.*

Evie giggles, then grabs my arms and wraps them around her. From the moment all the Long Live Girlies went and cheered her on at her dance recital in the fall, she's become our honorary niece. Getting to spend time with her and Tess as a package duo has been the biggest blessing.

"Aunt Shay?"

"Yes, sweetie?" I squeeze her tight, and she erupts into another fit of giggles.

"If you marry him"—she points to Connor, who is still sitting right next to me and very much listening to this conversation—"does that mean I get to call him Uncle Connie?"

"What?" I sputter.

Connor wipes a hand over his mouth. I can't tell if it's because he's uncomfortable at the thought of marrying me or if he's trying to hide his amusement. Hopefully the latter.

"Isn't that how it works?"

"You're one smart cookie," Connor says, because I apparently can't form words right now.

"Thanks." She grins. "You're getting married, right? That's what I overheard Mama talking about with Aunt Alyssa and Aunt Kelsey."

I really hope Connor doesn't think I told my friends we're getting married. That's one way to scare him away before we've truly begun. I clear my throat, hoping my voice doesn't come out shaky. "We're not getting married, sweetie."

"Well, not right now." Evie shakes her head, causing her cute curls to bounce around. "They said something about it only being a matter of time. I learned in school that time was in hours, minutes, and seconds." She scrunches her little nose. "I don't know what matters are."

Connor's shoulders shake beside me as he tries to hold in his laughter.

Evie snuggles closer to me, resting her head on my chest. "Can I be the flower girl?"

Oh, poppy.

A strangled laugh slips out of Connor's mouth. "Excuse me." He gets up from his seat and leaves the suite. A sliver of worry settles inside me at his abrupt departure. I hope he wasn't upset by Evie bringing up the whole marriage thing.

Evie turns to me with an innocent expression. "Is that a yes?"

I run my fingers through her curls. "Of course you can, but it'll be a while before I get married, sweet girl."

She shrugs and leans back against my chest, seemingly satisfied with the answer.

I give Evie my phone to watch *Frozen 2* on while I watch the sun set over the field. I never imagined this would be my life. Surrounded by my best friends in a box suite at an MLB game. One week out from Sunshine Blooms debuting at my first event. Being an *us* with Connor. Life has never been sweeter, and I don't know how I got so lucky.

Connor returns a little bit later with enough hot dogs on hand for all of us to enjoy, dispelling my worry about why he left. Austin ensured our suite had catered food, but nothing beats the nostalgia of eating a ballpark hot dog.

Evie hops off my lap to go eat one while I load mine up with mustard and relish before diving in. I wipe my mouth with a napkin, making sure I don't have any rogue mustard on my face, before turning to Connor. "Thanks."

He dips his head. "I remember you used to buy one at all my games."

"How did you—" I don't finish the rest of my question as the answer hits me. The only way Connor would know that is if he was watching me, too. Looking for me in the stands.

Connor shrugs, but there's a hint of a blush on his cheeks. "A lot of memories have been popping up for me recently."

I take another bite of my hot dog. "Such as?"

"Ones with you." He polishes off the rest of his hot dog and balls up the foil paper it was wrapped in. "It made me realize something." He wipes his hands off on a napkin before running them through his hair. I wish he knew he doesn't have anything to be nervous about, not around me. "I've noticed you all along, flower. In the stands at every one of my games. Across the room at events. Whenever I gave you and your friends a ride home from football games. You were always right there. In all my best memories, *you* stand out."

I place my hot dog in the wrapping on my lap and reach up to dab under my eyes with a clean napkin.

"I thought it was because you were kind, but Kelsey and Alyssa were always nice to me, too. Then I realized that I've always been drawn to you because you're you. I think all along I knew you were special, but I moved away and then thought I didn't want to date again after Jillian."

I glance around, making sure no one is within earshot, then play with the edges of my sweater, scared to ask this question but even more scared to not know the answer. "Have I changed your mind?"

Connor reaches over and wipes the next tear that falls away with the pad of his calloused thumb, a reminder of all the selfless work he does for our community. Of the flower vases he made because he said they reminded him of home—of *me*. "You've changed everything."

I lean in, ready to kiss him despite being surrounded by all our friends, not to mention his sister. But when a man goes and says something like *that*, how can I not kiss him? I'm inches away from his face when I hear the first crack of a firework go off. I startle, and Connor drops his hand from my face and moves his gaze to his lap.

I pick up the rest of my hot dog and his trash. "I should throw this away." After carrying it all to the trash can by the buffet table, I pop a mint in my mouth and return near the glass to watch the show.

I look up in awe as the night sky comes to life. Every color of the rainbow sparkles above with each crack of a firework. It's beautiful, and even more fun to watch when the Mustangs are celebrating a win.

I swear, the fireworks for Thunder get better every year. Or maybe I just appreciate all the work and planning that goes into it more as I get older. A few minutes pass as I bask in the beauty above me until I feel the hairs on the back of my neck raise in awareness. I turn to find that while everyone else's attention is on the brilliant display of fireworks, Connor only seems to have eyes for me.

I join him in the back of the box suite, away from everyone else. "You don't like the show?"

"I had a more beautiful view right in front of me."

"My backside?" I tease, trying to get a handle on my racing heart. As if I have any shot of calming down when he just called me beautiful.

Connor snickers. "I was going for all of you." He cocks his head to the side. "But that works, too."

I playfully slap his chest and he reaches up, wrapping his hand around mine. My heart pounds. "Are you ever going to kiss me?" Embarrassment courses through me. I can't believe I just blurted that out, but around him, I feel bold.

His eyes go wide before they dart to my mouth, like he's been thinking about this, too. "I've been waiting for the right moment."

"That moment is now." I tug him toward me, my lips only centimeters from his. I need this, need *him*. "Kiss me." The words come out as a plea, begging him to fulfill my request. If he does one thing I ask of him for the rest of my life, I want it to be this. A moment almost fourteen years in the making.

Connor brushes his nose against mine and wraps his hands around the small of my back. I arch into his touch and let out a shaky breath, still trying to wrap my brain around the fact that this is really happening. He pulls back enough to look into my eyes. His gaze is both soft and determined before he moves one of his hands up to the back of my neck and pulls my mouth to his.

Connor's lips are still at first, as if he's scared I'm going to jump away at any second. But when I part mine and move them against his, his resolve seems to melt away. Our mouths move together like we've been doing this for years, like they were made for each other.

I've imagined this a hundred—no, a thousand—times. But nothing in my wildest dreams could compare to the real thing. The feeling of Connor Porter's lips on mine, breathing me in like I'm his only source of oxygen.

Every stroke and press of his lips against mine is a reminder of why there will only ever be him for me. All my pent-up years of feelings go into each kiss. I slide my hands up until they're at the nape of his neck, in his hair that's gotten a little bit longer again over the past month.

I run my nails along the back of his head, and he sucks in a breath before pulling me closer for more. His kisses become more frenzied and impassioned, like he can't get enough of me. It feels like an out-of-body experience, one I want to partake in over and over again.

As Connor continues to do an extremely thorough job of kissing me under the fireworks, one word reverberates in my mind:

Finally.

CHAPTER TWENTY-NINE
CONNOR

IF I'D KNOWN KISSING Shayna Monroe would feel like *this*, I would've started doing it a long time ago and never stopped.

I didn't know what I was missing until Shayna stepped back into my life on that airplane, wearing my old sweatshirt, and changed everything I thought I wanted. Because ever since that moment, she's brought more light into my life than all the fireworks coloring the sky above us.

When she tugs at the hair at the nape of my neck again, I deepen the kiss. I would never get tired of this. Of *her*.

Nothing about this feels like a first kiss. There's nothing awkward or hesitant about it. The way Shayna's lips move against mine feels urgent and possessive, like she's staking a claim on them, branding them with her initials to let every other woman out there know whose I am. And I'm perfectly fine with that. She can stake all the claims on me. Every single one of them.

Because, in this moment, she's no longer my sister's friend or the girl I'm helping out with her flower truck. She's sunshine. The most beautiful flower. My last thought every night. The epitome of joy. The thing I look forward to most each day. She's everything.

She's *mine*.

At least, I want her to be.

I move my hands to cup her jawline and gently trail my fingers on her cheeks. She shivers under my touch and lets out a small gasp. I've always thought a woman would never like my rough hands, calloused from my workouts and my job, but I never have to worry about that with Shayna. Certainly not when she reacts to my touch like that.

She comes back in for another kiss, hungrier, like I'm the sustenance that keeps her nourished. She fists the collar of my sweater polo, the one I wore to impress her, and pulls me closer. Nothing's enough—not proximity or the number of kisses. Because I could hold her and kiss her a million times, and I'm not sure it would ever be enough.

I want this. Her. All of her. For the rest of my life.

I pull back, rocked to my core by the revelation.

I've never been so sure of anything.

I'm a firefighter. Grass is green. The sun rises every morning. And I'm in love with Shayna Monroe.

I open my eyes as I try to slow my rapid breathing and look at Shayna. She's gorgeous. The way she's peering up at me is filled with such tender affection that it steals my breath away. I never thought anyone would look at me like that, like I'm her whole world. My eyes dart down to her swollen pink lips that have me wanting to lean right back in for another taste.

It may be true that nobody's perfect, but she's perfect for me. Every ounce of my body aches to be near her again, but a quick glance over at all our friends has me rooted in place. Shayna must have the same thought as she looks over at everyone—who, thankfully, are all still watching the fireworks show—then buries her head in my chest.

"I can't believe we just did that," she whispers.

"It was a long time coming." I wrap my arms around her and press a final kiss to the top of her head. But nothing about this is final.

It's only the beginning.

I almost didn't come to family dinner tonight, but I figured it would be suspicious if I didn't show up since we live in the same city. Mallory probably would've shown up at my house and dragged me here anyway. Especially with the way she kept glancing at me whenever I was talking to Shayna at the game yesterday.

Now she's staring me down across the table while I'm just trying to eat my honey-garlic salmon in peace.

I wish Shayna could be here to hold my hand and ground me, but I know I need to fill my family in on everything first. Though, I guess I probably should've talked to Shayna about that, but it's not like we did very much *talking* last night.

Mom and Dad are discussing how great last night's fireworks show looked from their spot along the river, but Mallory is still looking at me.

I set my fork down. "What's your problem?"

Everyone immediately quiets and looks at me.

"Me?" Mallory cocks her head. "I was about to ask you what *your* deal is."

I frown. "I'm just trying to eat my salmon."

"No." She shakes her fork at me. "You know that's not what I'm talking about."

"You're going to have to spell it out for me." I can't think of anything I did to upset her.

"You haven't told us about Shayna at all."

I sputter, feeling flustered. This wasn't how tonight was supposed to go. I had a whole plan to tell my family during dessert, like an extra little treat in addition to Mom's banana pudding.

"Don't even try to deny it. I've seen the way you've been looking at her lately." Mallory stabs a piece of broccoli with a fork. "Oh, and the way you were making out with her during the fireworks."

Mom squeals. "You and Shayna kissed?"

I blanch, keeping my attention on my sister. "You saw that?"

"Everyone did." Mallory drops her fork with the speared broccoli and crosses her arms. "Tess had to cover Evie's eyes."

Am I embarrassed that my first kiss with Shayna was on full display in front of our friends like we were a museum exhibit portraying off-the-charts chemistry between a man and a woman? Yes.

Do I hope Evie isn't scarred for life? Also yes.

Do I wish it had happened somewhere a little more private? Obviously.

But I won't apologize for it because that wasn't the kind of kiss you regret for a single second. No, it's the kind that stays seared in your memory. The kind that artists write love songs about.

"I didn't plan on anyone seeing it. I honestly forgot everyone else was there."

Mom gasps and places her hands over her mouth. "I never thought I'd live to see the day. My Connie's in love."

"Who said anything about love?" Mallory furrows her brow. "What I want to know is this: What are your intentions with Shayna?"

I roll my eyes. "Who are you, her dad?"

"He's not here at the present, so I'm enacting my duty as her best friend to grill you until you're more charred than a well-done steak."

I throw my hands up. "Okay, what do you want to know?"

"Hm, I don't know." She taps her bottom lip. "Maybe an explanation for how you went from saying you don't want to get married or even *date* anyone to kissing one of my best friends who very clearly wants a husband and the whole shebang?"

"The whole shebang?" I repeat, raising an eyebrow. She narrows her gaze. Okay, no joking. Got it. "Sorry." I place my hands on my thighs and squeeze, trying to calm the nerves running through my body. I'm just talking to my family. No need to stress. "Things have…changed."

"You expect me to believe that you randomly woke up one day and decided you wanted to settle down with someone?" Mallory purses her lips.

Mom leans in, looking entirely too invested in this conversation, while Dad continues eating his dinner like this is just normal table talk.

I shake my head. "Wasn't random, and it's not just someone. It's Shayna."

Mom squeals again, but Mallory's expression doesn't change.

I sigh. "Every time I saw her, she'd do or say something that slowly chipped away at the future I thought I wanted."

"Then?" she prods.

"Then, one day, it hit me." All the stress leaves my body as I think about Shayna. "I realized I'd been falling for her all along."

"That's so sweet," Mom coos. "Both of my kids are in love." She turns to Dad. "Can you believe it, Todd?"

Dad scoots his empty plate back and rests his elbows on the table. "That's great, Angie."

"He didn't say anything about love." Mallory still appears hesitant with her furrowed brow.

I shrug. "I'm not going to say something to you that I haven't gotten the chance to tell her yet."

Mallory snorts. "Probably because you were too busy playing tonsil hockey."

"Because I've been waiting for us to be alone," I correct, though she isn't *entirely* wrong.

"So you can make out in front of all your friends but can't tell her you love her in front of them?" She quirks her head. "Make that make sense."

Dad grabs his empty plate and heads to the kitchen. "On that note, I'm going to grab dessert."

"Trust me, I would much rather have been alone, but when a woman you like asks you to kiss her, you kiss her." I look down at the table for a minute. My stomach knots at the thought of sharing my deepest insecurities with my mom and sister. I know they love me, but it's hard for me to open up. I squeeze my thighs again, trying to distract myself from my anxiety as I say, "I want to tell her how I'm feeling, but I'm scared."

"Why are you scared?" Mom's voice is full of concern.

I finally look up, meeting her gaze. "There's someone I need to tell you about." Her expression falls. "Mallory already knows the basics, but I think it might help me to talk about it."

"Okay." Mom shoots me a sympathetic smile. "We're here for you, Connie."

I take a steadying breath and tell them about Jillian. I try not to leave anything out, from how we met to what she said to me when she ended things. Once I've laid it all on the table, I let out a shaky sigh.

"I'm so sorry you've been holding all that in." Mom sniffles. "That you ever believed anything that horrible woman said was true."

"I think part of me always thought I wasn't enough, so when she said that, it struck a nerve."

Mom dabs her napkin under her eyes. "Why would you think that?"

I drop my gaze to my lap. "You two are outgoing, always seem to say the right thing, while I worry over every word and feel like the black sheep of the family."

My mom leans forward on her elbows and waits for me to meet her gaze. "You're perfect just as you are. You hear me? There's nothing wrong with you."

"Yeah, who would I call a caveman if you weren't reserved?" Mallory deadpans. Mom shoots her a look. "What? Just trying to lighten the mood. Obviously, we love Con Con the way he is."

"I want to believe that. But how do you know that I won't ruin another relationship?" I frown. "I couldn't forgive myself if I let Shayna down."

"Spoiler alert: We all make mistakes," Mallory says. "No relationship is perfect, but if you're committed to Shayna, you'll make things work. She's not like this *Jillian*." She says the name with such vehemence that it makes me scared for all Jillians in the world. Her eyes darken. "I'd love to find her and tell her exactly how her snide, untrue comments make me feel."

"It's in the past at this point." I'm worried that if I don't call her off the hunt, she actually would find her, and that's the last thing I need. "I just don't want to repeat the same mistakes again."

"You know how I know that you won't?" Mom asks. I shake my head. "Because you're having this conversation with us. You're asking the hard questions. That already tells me you care enough about Shayna to not let your doubts keep you from the future you want." She looks at me emphatically. "The future you deserve."

I blow out a breath, taking in everything they've said. They're right. I can't let the lies of someone who barely knew me hold me captive. It's just like Shayna said—the right person will appreciate me for who I am…and that's her. She sees me exactly as I am and doesn't try to change me.

And I can't wait to let her know that I want to be all in.

"I need to tell her I love her," I mumble.

Mallory slaps the table. "It's about time."

I turn to my sister. "And you're okay with us being together?"

Surprise flits across her features. "You want my permission?"

I shake my head. "I want your blessing. Because if things turn out the way I hope they do, Shayna could be your sister-in-law one day."

Mallory's resolve crumbles. She presses her lips together, and I swear I see actual tears in her eyes as she scoots back from the table and runs over. I brace myself for a punch, but she flings her arms around my neck and hugs me.

I pat her gently on the back. "I'll take that as a yes?"

She nods against my neck. "I always wanted a sister, and now you're telling me I get to have one of my besties as one?"

"We still have to date, but I can't see myself with anyone else," I admit. "And as long as Shayna is on board."

"Of course she will be." Mom dabs under her eyes with her cloth napkin. "Oh, I think my heart just might burst."

Mallory returns to her seat and wipes away a few tears of her own. "I know you're my brother and all, so I love you." She points a finger at me and narrows her eyes, looking absolutely terrifying. "But I will destroy you if you hurt my best friend."

"I can't promise that I'll never hurt her, but I'll spend every day doing my best to make her happy and take care of her."

Her face morphs into a wide grin. "Seriously, though, you have to marry her, okay? That would be the dream."

"Any more questions or objections?" I ask, and they both remain quiet. "Great."

With the busyness of the week ahead, I won't get a chance to see Shayna again until the Dogwood Festival next Saturday. I already miss her, even though I just saw her last night. When I want to spend as many waking minutes with her as possible, a week feels like an eternity, but the promise of supporting her at her first event will help get me through the next six days.

I dig back into my salmon just as Dad walks back into the room. "Sorry about that. Had a long game of toilet golf, if you catch my drift." He raises the trifle dish he's carrying that's filled to the brim with layers of banana pudding, vanilla wafers, freshly sliced bananas, and whipped cream. "Who's ready for dessert?"

Mom groans. "Literally none of us, Todd."

I bite back a laugh as my family dives right back into their usual conversation as if nothing happened. This evening was the first time I've felt truly at ease around them. I still don't love being the center of attention, but at least I didn't question every word I said and was more of myself.

And I can't help but think it's all because of the prettiest, flower-loving brunette. She makes me want to be the best version of myself. Although I'm sure I could live a hundred years and never measure up to her.

But I will do my best to be the man Shayna deserves.

CHAPTER THIRTY
SHAYNA

"Thank you for the lovely bouquet," I scream-sing the lyrics to the titular track of Taylor's newest album that's playing on vinyl.

My besties and I walk into the kitchen, which I took over as my own personal workspace today. The countertops and kitchen table are covered with clean buckets filled with water, flower food, and all the flowers I harvested this morning from the greenhouse at the flower shop. If all goes well at this event, I'll plan on using my contacts to order a larger variety of blooms in the future from other vendors. But for tomorrow, they're all homegrown in the flower shop's greenhouse that, luckily, wasn't touched by the fire.

"Shay, they're beautiful." Alyssa leans close and smells one of the buckets of roses.

Tess sidles up next to me. "How do you feel about your opening day?"

"Excited but also slightly terrified," I admit. There's always a risk when opening your own business that it won't succeed. I could show up to the festival tomorrow and not sell a single bouquet, but I choose to hold onto faith.

A girl doesn't survive a fire and get gifted enough money to purchase and renovate her own mobile flower truck for no reason. Selling flowers is more than a job. It's my purpose. A way to spread joy and love to the world, one bouquet at a time. So, regardless of how things go tomorrow, I know I'm doing the work I'm meant to.

"I don't think you'd be human if you weren't nervous." Tess threads her arm through mine.

"I hope you're proud of everything you've accomplished. Daffodil is the most adorable flower truck I've ever seen," Kelsey says.

I smile, thinking about how far my truck has come in a little over a month. "The cutest."

"We'll all be there for you tomorrow. No matter what." Alyssa slings her arm over my shoulder and pulls me into a side hug.

"Yeah, and I'll chase people down to sell bouquets if needed." Mallory smirks. "You'll be sold out before you know it."

I laugh. "We don't want to scare the customers."

She shrugs. "There's nothing wrong with a healthy dose of persuasion."

"It is when it's *your* kind of persuasion." Kelsey nudges her.

Mallory holds a hand to her chest in mock offense. "Whatever could you mean?"

"You literally just said you'd chase people down. I don't even want to think about what you'd do to get people to adopt puppies from my future dog rescue."

Tess bumps my hip with hers. "It would probably look something like the scene in *The Proposal* where Sandra Bullock is running around holding the puppy above her head."

I laugh at that mental image.

Mallory shakes her head, but there's a hint of a smile on her lips. "Okay, enough about that."

"Yes." Alyssa turns to face me. "What still needs to be done for tomorrow?"

I move farther into the kitchen and grab my checklist because sometimes a girl just needs a physical list to cross things off to feel accomplished. Winston comes running behind me with his tongue lolling, like he wants to help, too. "I think just about everything's done. I already got all the payment options squared away for tomorrow and stripped all the flower stems, so if y'all want to hang out with me while I arrange the bouquets, I would love the company."

"Are you—" Mallory presses her lips together, turns to the other girls, and points at me. "Is she crazy?"

"Oh yeah, she's definitely crazy if she thinks we aren't helping," Kelsey says.

I shrug. "I don't want to make y'all work on girls' night."

"We wouldn't have it any other way." Alyssa steps toward me with open arms, and the rest of the girls quickly follow suit.

I hold back tears as I'm engulfed in a giant group hug. We may seem like an unlikely group with our different personalities and interests, but we're connected by the most important thing: sisterhood. "I love y'all forevermore."

"Forevermore," they echo back.

When they all pull back, Kelsey salutes me. "Okay, tell us what to do."

I explain the flower combinations I had in mind, including an assortment of bouquets inspired by the different Taylor eras, then show them an example arrangement.

"I'll make any final adjustments and wrap them in the Kraft paper. I want you to have fun with it." I smile. "It is girls' night, after all."

I shove the worry down that this is too much to ask of them. Over the last month, Connor helped me realize that it's not only okay to set boundaries, but that it's okay to ask for assistance. It doesn't mean I'm not enough. It means we aren't meant to live this life alone. That we don't have to burn ourselves out when we have our chosen people around us and helping carry the load.

Mallory moves over to the vinyl player, and soon enough, the nostalgic intro of "Welcome to New York" is floating through our kitchen. She smiles over at me. "Since *1989* is your favorite album, I figured this would be the best pump-up music."

I shake my booty to the rhythm and the girls jump in, laughing and moving to the beat with me. Tess grabs my hands and twists back and forth with me as I watch Kelsey, Alyssa, and Mallory attempt to do some type of triple twirl. This is it—peak girlhood. And I wouldn't trade it for the world.

When the next track starts playing, Mallory sticks her pointer finger in the air and waves it in a circle like she's rounding up the troops. "All right, ladies, let's get to work."

Everyone spreads out around the kitchen and starts making bouquets. I station myself in front of the roses, peonies, and daisies and start building a bouquet. I'll fill in the gaps later with some baby's breath and maybe some white asters.

"Time for happies and crappies." I don't want us to miss out on our Friday night tradition just because they're helping me.

Alyssa shakes her head. "No, time for you to give us an update on everything that's been happening between you and Connor."

I squeal. "We kissed."

"Oh, we know." Tess fans her face with the bouquet she's making. "That kiss said he would love you forever and hurt anyone who got in the way of your happiness. Like hungry and possessive, but not in a toxic way."

"Okay, ew." Mallory shuts her eyes and cringes.

"Wait, y'all saw that?" My face heats as I remember all the feelings that coursed through me during that kiss. I can almost feel the stroke of his strong hands on my face. The way his fingers tangled in my hair. The confidence in every press of his lips to mine.

They all nod.

"I went to kiss Evie goodnight that night and she tried to open-mouth kiss me." Tess doubles over and laughs so hard, I think I see tears in her eyes. "I asked her why she was doing that, and she said she wanted to be more like you."

"Ranunculus," I sputter, mortified. "I'm so sorry."

Tess uses her shoulder to wipe the tears spilling onto her cheeks on the sleeve of her shirt. "Don't be. It was a good teaching moment."

"Don't always do what you see other people doing in public?" Kelsey teases.

"Exactly."

I groan. "I'm never going to be able to face Evie again."

"She probably won't even remember it next week. She's always coming home with crazy stories about all the kids in her class." Tess picks up a peony. "Who knew there was so much drama in kindergarten?"

I try to shrug it off as Alyssa brings us back to the topic of conversation. "Tell us all the details, Shay."

Mallory lets out a small sound of disgust. "Nope. Please spare me the details about making out with my brother."

"Not about the kiss. I know you shared a little bit with us at the last girls' night, but I want to know the whole story. When did you know you had feelings for him? When did you find out he had feelings for you? Is he always so stoic and brooding, or is he different around you?" Alyssa adds another lily to her bouquet. "I need to live vicariously through you now that Tess and I are the only ones left in the single ladies crew."

I take a deep breath, bracing for their reaction. "I've kinda had a thing for him since we all met."

They all gawk at me. Mallory even does a good job of feigning surprise since she already knows everything.

"I never did anything because of the promise we all made to each other to not date each other's exes or siblings. I always told myself that if Connor ever showed interest in me, I would just talk to Mallory about it, which is why I wanted to talk to her after the pickup game." I add baby's breath to my bouquet, then turn and look at it from all angles to make sure it's perfect before I continue talking. "It just turned out that he didn't return my feelings for about fourteen years."

"You've been holding this in for over a *decade*?" Tess squeaks. "Girl, you're way more patient than me."

"I didn't feel very patient." I laugh. "But it was definitely worth the wait because at Thunder, he told me he wants there to be an *us*."

"We're so happy for you." Tess grins.

"I mean, I'm a little upset you kept your crush a secret for over a decade"—Kelsey shoots me an annoyed look—"but I also understand why you did. Mal can be scary when she's mad."

"I prefer *intimidating*, thank you very much," Mallory deadpans.

"I promise, no more secrets," I say.

Alyssa fiddles with her half-made bouquet like she has a secret of her own, but I'm riding on too much of a love-drunk high to say anything right now.

"As for the brooding and stoicism, Connor's more reserved than anything." A blush climbs my cheeks. "But he's different around me. More talkative and thoughtful and so sweet."

"I can't wait to see y'all together tomorrow." Alyssa grabs eucalyptus from a bucket.

"He's working an overnight shift into the morning, so hopefully he's not too exhausted." I wrap my finished bouquet in the brown Kraft paper.

"He'll be there no matter what." Mallory sounds sure.

"Miss ma'am." Alyssa shoots her a look. "Do you have insider information?"

Mal's face gives nothing away. "I can neither confirm nor deny—"

Kelsey groans. "Oh, come on. You obviously know something."

"My lips are sealed." Mallory mimes a fake key in front of her mouth before tossing it over her shoulder.

Everyone laughs, and we dive into our happies and crappies of the week as we continue arranging all the bouquets. By the time we finish at one in the morning, I'm feeling extra thankful for my friends. There's no way I'd be getting any sleep tonight without their help.

As my head hits the pillow, I drift off to sleep with a smile on my face. A future with Connor finally feels within reach. My friends are all caught up on the details of my relationship. And I have my first event for Sunshine Blooms to look forward to. My whole world is blooming, and I couldn't be happier.

CHAPTER THIRTY-ONE
SHAYNA

"Happy opening day." My old boss, Shirley, takes slow steps toward me with her arms open wide. I meet her halfway and fold into her embrace.

"How did you get here?" I pull back and look at her smiling face. Shirley can't drive and is a major germaphobe who is scared of any mode of transportation she deems unsanitary, like airplanes, taxis, or buses. But she always trusted me, so when I worked for her, we would close up shop early and I'd take her to her weekly book club or any doctor's appointments. She even started having her groceries delivered to her doorstep every Monday morning after I taught her how to use phone apps.

"The bus," she answers.

My mouth falls open. "You took public transit for this?"

"I took public transit for *you* because I had to come tell you how proud I am of what you've done." She gestures to the truck behind me. "This is amazing, and I can't wait to see the flower legacy we built continue to live on in your new business."

It's impossible to miss the meaning in her words. The flower legacy *we* built. Her never-ending trust and faith in me is truly the reason we're here today. That Sunshine

Blooms was ever even a possibility. "I never would've been able to do any of this without you."

She pats my cheeks with her wrinkled hands. "I never had children or grandchildren, but I had you. And that's more than I ever could have asked for."

Tears sting my eyes and she pulls back, wagging a finger at me. "Now, don't you cry before the day has even begun. You've got flowers to sell." She loops her arm around mine and walks back with me to the truck. "And beautiful ones, at that."

I take a deep breath to calm my emotions. "They're all from the greenhouse."

"I'm so happy you can still use that space." Shirley looks around, and I turn to see what she's looking at. My people have been showing up all morning to help me with the setup. There are all the Long Live Girlies, my parents and sister, Tyler, Evie, and even some of my friends' parents are here. All to support me. Everyone's even wearing the same Sunshine Blooms shirt that Connor gave me for my birthday, a surprise he apparently arranged with my sister.

My heart is overflowing with gratitude and joy. I think the only thing that'll make the day better is making my first sale.

Connor hasn't arrived yet, but he already helped me so much with the truck and the beautiful shelving, so it's not like I expected him to assist with all the setup this morning. But did I think he'd be here bright and early anyway? Absolutely. I'm sure he's just taking a quick nap after his shift, though. Working twenty-four hours straight has to be brutal.

"Where's that strapping young man that saved you in the fire?" Shirley asks, seemingly having the same thought as me.

I purse my lips. "How did you know I even knew him?"

"I still get the daily paper, and I have eyes and ears everywhere, Ms. Thousand-Dollar-Bidder."

"You and your book club ladies should try actually reading a book rather than gossiping," I deadpan.

Shirley takes a step toward the truck, getting a closer look at all the bouquets. "But then how would I keep up on all the town's hottest news?" I shake my head as she continues. "So, where is he?"

I shrug. "He worked until seven this morning at the station, so he's probably taking a power nap, but he promised he'd be here."

She takes my hand and gently pats the back of it. "Then I'm sure he will be, dear." After a quick glance at her watch, she sighs. "I know the festival hasn't started quite yet, but I need to take off. Any chance I could buy a bouquet before you officially open?"

"Anything for my generous benefactor," I tease.

"Oh, pish-posh. I'm no such thing." Shirley waves off my comment, then looks at all the bouquets before selecting the one I knew she'd pick. One with only sunflowers surrounded by sprigs of lavender. She smiles at me. "You know I've always loved this combination." She reaches into her purse, and I hold up a hand.

"I can't let you pay me."

"You can—and you will. I told you that I wanted to be your first customer, and I meant it." She looks at the chalkboard pricing sign I have set up on the curb and pulls out twenty-five dollars from her wallet.

I reluctantly take the money. "Thank you."

"No, thank you." Her eyes glimmer with unshed tears. She pulls me in for another hug. "Remember to take lots of pictures so you can show me later."

"I will. Thanks, Shirley."

Mr. Porter walks her back to the bus stop while I take a few pictures and videos of the flower truck to post on my new business social media pages later. Everyone who came to support me also takes turns getting group photos with me, starting with my family, then a large group photo, and ending with a Long Live Girlies picture.

They pull me into another group hug after my sister takes the picture.

"We're so proud of you." Alyssa pulls a friendship bracelet from her pocket and hands it to me. "We all made you a little something."

I turn the bracelet over in my hand. Between all the white and yellow beads are the words *Sunshine Blooms*. "I love it." I slide it onto my wrist.

"Have I mentioned how cute that skirt is?" Kelsey says. "It's very on brand for you."

I run my hands along the hot-pink skirt covered in a fun darker pink floral pattern that Alyssa gave me for my birthday. I paired it with a white tank top, tucked in, and a cropped jean jacket, then topped off my look with some braided sandals and my pearl-studded headband. I even tried curling my hair, wanting to do something a little extra. I know the curls will fall out within a few hours like they always do, but at least it will look cute for pictures.

"Thanks. I love y'all." I look over at Mallory. "Have you heard from Connor?"

Her expression gives nothing away, but I see a hint of worry in her eyes. She shakes her head. "I tried calling, but he didn't answer."

"He probably slept through his alarm," Tess says. I grab onto her positivity like it's the life raft keeping me afloat.

"But hey, look at how amazing your setup looks." I appreciate Kelsey's attempt to distract me.

Alyssa points to the parking lot. "Looks like people are starting to arrive."

"We won't hover too much, but just wave us down if you need help with anything." Mallory squeezes my arm.

The girls head to other booths. I watch the time on my phone change to eleven.

Connor didn't show.

He's always on time.

Anxiety swirls inside me at the thought of something happening to him. It's unlike him to not show up without texting or calling.

I do my breathing exercises to stay calm. I can't afford to freak out right now. He's fine. He just slept through his alarm. His crew also could've been called onto another fire. Or he's getting cold feet about being an "us" in public.

I shove those thoughts deep down, refusing to think about any option other than him oversleeping. I plaster as much of a smile as I can manage on my face. I can't afford to be sad right now. This is supposed to be one of the happiest moments of my life. A day I look back on when I reflect on the beginning of Sunshine Blooms.

But it feels wrong celebrating it all without the man who helped me get to this point by my side.

CHAPTER THIRTY-TWO

CONNOR

"Can you drive any faster?" I grumble, anxiously tapping my foot against the floor of the fire engine cab. Hit the horn. Blare the siren. Flash the lights. Something—*any-thing*—to get me to Shayna as fast as humanly possible.

I planned on telling her today that I love her. Instead, I've missed the majority of her first event with Sunshine Blooms. She's probably sad and confused, maybe even mad. But she could never be as furious as I am with myself.

I usually bring my phone on calls and keep it in the rig, but I forgot it for our final call of the shift. It was an awful house fire caused by an explosion from a gas leak. Luckily, everyone was able to get out before the explosion, thanks to their smart thinking by calling emergency services when they smelled gas. But the call lasted way longer than my shift was supposed to—I glance at the time on the dash—and even went over two hours into the time of the Dogwood Festival.

And of course I don't have my cell to call or text Shayna and let her know where I am. That I'm safe and just running late. My family is all there, too, and I know my mom must be freaking out. Fisher offered me his phone, but I'm a little embarrassed to admit that I never bothered memorizing any phone numbers aside from my own. I'll be rectifying that soon, but for now, I just want to get to Shayna.

"She'll understand why you're late, man." Fisher socks my shoulder.

I know how gracious and understanding Shayna is, but I can't help but beat myself up over the fact that I'm already letting her down. This is what I was afraid of. Not being enough for her. Not being able to be the man that shows up for her.

"We're nearly there, Porter," Lieutenant Barnes calls over her shoulder from the driver's seat.

I return to bouncing my knee and try to think about what I'm going to say to Shayna. After a few more turns, we finally pull into the parking lot.

Barnes turns and shoots me a rare smile. "Go get your girl." She reaches up and tugs the chain hanging from the ceiling of the cab. The air horn blares, and people hurry to move out of our way. I shrug off my jacket and hat, but decide it will be too much work to take off my suspenders and turnout pants. Hopefully, I don't smell too much like smoke.

The fire engine rolls to a stop. I get out and hang onto the side handle, scouring all the rows for her yellow truck. When I finally spot it a few rows away, I jump down and maneuver my way through the crowd of people and booths.

When I reach Shayna's row, I immediately spot her looking like a floral goddess in her pink skirt, surrounded by the remaining bouquets. Seeing a lot of the vases empty brings a smile to my face. *That's my girl.* I knew she would succeed at whatever she put her mind to, and seeing our city come out and support her new business is a beautiful thing.

I jog toward her. When I'm close enough that I think she can hear me, I call out, "Flower."

Shayna turns in my direction, and a wide smile breaks out on her face. That's a good sign. She meets me halfway and throws her arms around my neck as I crush her against me.

I cling to her and immediately feel more at ease. Everyone says that I saved her, but really, she's the one who has saved me. "Sorry if I smell like smoke."

"I don't care." She stands on her tiptoes and burrows her face in the crook of my neck. "Are you okay?"

I press a kiss to her temple. "Great, now that I'm here with you."

She pulls back and looks me over, trying to determine if I'm injured in any way.

"There was a gas leak explosion in a residence at the end of my shift that we just finished." I run my hand through my hair that's still damp from sweat. I got it cut again this week so that I would be looking fresh for Shayna's big day, but I guess that's probably not noticeable now either. Everything about this day has gone horribly wrong. I wish I could start the day over and do it all correctly. "I forgot my phone at the station. I would've called otherwise."

Shayna cups my cheek and I lean into her touch. "You don't have to explain. You're safe. You're here now. That's what matters."

"How can you be so understanding?" My jaw ticks. "I wasn't here for you."

"But you were." Her smile is soft. "You were here in the beautiful craftsmanship of the shelves you built and the galvanized vases you bought with me. You were here in the logo on the truck." She looks up at me and bites her bottom lip. "And you were here in all the wooden vases you made, which I completely sold out of in the first hour."

My eyes go wide. "What?"

She sucks in a breath. "Please don't be mad, but I kind of snuck into your shed yesterday when you were at work and loaded up all your wooden vases in my car to sell today."

My mouth falls open slightly as I try to process her words. "And they sold?"

"Every last one." She gestures to Daffodil's passenger seat. "Well, except for the one in there. I couldn't bring myself to sell my favorite one." I peer in the window and see that it's the one she caught me making. "Are you mad?" I turn back to find her wringing her hands. "I just wanted to help you feel more confident in how good you are at what you do, and I think selling out really shows how talented you are." She taps her purse. "I actually have a whole list of people who saw other customers carrying your vases around. They were disappointed when I told them I was sold out, but they gave me their contact info in case you wanted to make more or show them more of your work."

I take her hands in mine. "How could I be mad at you? You're amazing, and I'm honored you believe in me that much." I let out a disbelieving laugh. "I still can't believe you sold out and got me a waitlist."

"You better believe it, Con." She squeezes my hand. "No. Believe in *yourself*."

I lift one of her hands to my lips and kiss her knuckles. "With you by my side, I do." I notice that a customer seems to linger near the flower truck. "Do you need to go?"

Shayna shakes her head. "I'll get Mal to cover it real quick." She waves at my sister over my shoulder.

I know the second Mal is here because she punches my arm. "What's the point of a cell phone if you're not going to answer it? You know Mom is freaking out."

"I'll explain everything later, but for now, can you cover for Shayna so I can talk to her?"

Mallory's face softens as she realizes what I want to talk to Shayna about. "Fine. I'll text Mom and Dad that you're okay, too, but you owe me." She approaches the customer with a cheery grin, ready to help her friend make a sale.

"That was easier than I expected." Shayna laughs.

"She has her days." I lead her away from the crowd to a more secluded area under a dogwood tree in full bloom.

"What did you want to talk about?" She rocks on her feet.

I take a deep breath and dive in. "Helping you with your truck started out as a favor to my sister, but it quickly became what I looked forward to most every week. I honestly only feel like I'm me when I'm with you. I thought I was fine being alone, but now that I've had a glimpse of what life with you is like, the future I thought I wanted feels lonely." She squeezes my hand and smiles up at me, encouraging me to continue. "I know I was trying to help you figure out what you want in life, apart from what anyone else asks of you. But the truth is, you're the one who helped me come to the biggest realization of my life: there's nothing I want more than you."

Shayna wraps her arms around my neck and pulls my mouth to hers. The kiss is gentle and sweet, just like her. The feeling of her lips on mine after I just laid my heart bare breaks the dam inside of me that I worked so hard my entire life to build, hiding all my feelings and emotions. They come flooding out in a rush as I cradle her face and turn the kiss into something more, deep and full of emotion.

I move us backward until her back is pressed against the tree trunk. I keep one hand on her face and settle my other on the bark as I put my all into showing her just how much she means to me.

I'm breathing hard when I finally pull back. When I see her swollen, thoroughly kissed lips looking perfectly pillowy and the hazy look in her eyes, it nearly has me leaning in for more. But I need to finish this conversation. Make sure she knows where I stand.

I run my finger along her jawline, and she shivers at my touch. "Have you decided what you want, flower?"

Shayna trails her fingers along my suspenders, just like she did after the bachelor auction, and snaps one against my pecs. She beams up at me with a flirtatious grin. "Still you. It's always been you."

I press a kiss to her forehead. The tip of her nose. Her cheek. The hollow spot beneath her ear. Before finally allowing my lips to meet hers again in a whisper of a kiss. "Then you should know that I plan on marrying you one day." She gasps, the sound full of awe. "But for now, will you please be my girlfriend? Because I want to date you for the rest of my life."

A single tear falls onto her cheek. I swipe it away with my thumb. "I can't think of anything else I'd rather be more than yours."

I pull her into my arms and hold her tight. My girlfriend—those are two words I never thought I'd say again, but everything about them feels right when it comes to her.

We head back over to the flower truck, and Mallory raises her brows when she sees us. "Looks like you two had a good *talk*." Her emphasis on the last word makes me roll my eyes.

"You can talk to my girlfriend later," I say.

My sister's eyes go wide as she squeals. "Girlfriend?"

Shayna nods and leans her head on my arm.

"I'm sure she'll tell you all about it," I assure my sister. "But I'd like to buy a bouquet now, if you don't mind."

Mallory squeezes Shayna's arm before saying to me, "Shop away."

When she leaves, I turn to my girlfriend. "Which bouquet is your favorite?"

"You'd probably expect it to be an all-yellow one, but I really love this one." Shayna leads me over to a bouquet of red flowers with yellow centers. "These are Gerbera daisies. I thought they were too beautiful to mix with anything else."

I lift it out of the vase. "They remind me of you."

She blushes. "How so?"

"They're vibrant and cheerful, and they add a splash of color to life. Just like you."

Shayna's eyes go misty. "I think that's the nicest thing anyone's ever said about me."

"There's a lot more where that came from." I hand the bouquet to her. "For you. And I'll pay for them later when I get my phone back."

She smiles up at me like I just handed her Taylor Swift concert tickets. "No one's ever given me flowers before."

I rear back in shock. "Really?"

"I guess everyone thinks a florist doesn't need flowers when they're surrounded by them all day and can make themselves a bouquet."

"You deserve a fresh bouquet every week." She sniffs the flowers, and her lips pull into a content, closed-lip smile. She looks so peaceful like this. So happy. Because of me. "Maybe every day," I amend, because I would buy this beautiful woman flowers every day for the rest of my life if she'll let me. "I love you, flower."

Shayna wraps her arms around my neck, and I cradle her against me, careful not to crush the bouquet. The look she gives me when she pulls back is one I add to the list of mental images I want to hold onto forever. Her hair wild from our time kissing under the tree. Her grin wide. And her eyes full of love and affection for me. "I love you."

I return her smile, wondering how I got so lucky to have landed someone so stunning. How I found someone who knows me deeply and loves me despite my flaws.

I'm honored to support Shayna and her business, a legacy she'll leave behind one day.

As for me, if the only thing I'm ever known for is loving her, that's a life worth living.

EPILOGUE

SHAYNA

One Year Later

In my wildest dreams, I wouldn't have dared imagine this life for myself. Not because I didn't want it, but out of fear that reality would never measure up. That I would forever wish for a fever dream and forget to live in the moment.

But here I am, at the Dogwood Festival for the second year in a row, with abundantly more than I could ever ask for.

Sunshine Blooms has reached heights I hadn't thought possible in just a year's time. After I had a few videos go viral on social media last summer, business has been booming. Customers travel from all over the country to the markets I attend just to buy my Taylor Swift era-themed bouquets or craft their own. I was also booked solid for all the weekends I had available on my website, bringing Daffodil to countless bridal showers, weddings, and other events.

Ever since the festival last year, I've been selling Connor's wood pieces at any market I attend. Everything from his original wooden vases to window planters sell out every time.

I smile over at Connor as he sets another load of wooden vases near my truck. His lips tilt up in the grin that has become like second nature to him now, at least around me. My chest swells. I knew what happiness and joy were before I was Connor Porter's girlfriend—I never get tired of saying that—but my life is immeasurably better with him in it. Each day I'm filled with a deep, undeniable, ever-present feeling of joy, knowing he's mine.

I walk over to Connor, and it feels like I'm floating, forever on cloud nine around him. "You really outdid yourself this time, Con."

He kisses my cheek. "It's because I had *you* on my mind."

"I'm not *always* on your mind?" I tease.

"Oh, you are." He smirks. "But I really wanted to make something that I knew you'd love."

I wrap my arms around his neck and press my lips to his. He places his free hand on the small of my back, drawing me closer until I don't know where I end and he begins. My heart skitters as he deepens the kiss, my pulse erratic as I breathe him in. I don't think I'll ever get used to this. *Him.* And I don't think I ever want to.

A lifetime of stolen kisses in crowds sounds like perfection.

When I pull back, he rests his forehead against mine. "You're going to be my undoing, flower."

I smile up at him. "Then I'd say my goal of ruining you from ever wanting any other women is a success."

Connor shakes his head at my antics. "I think we're way past that." He lets go and moves back to the truck.

I tilt my chin and soak in the sun's warm rays beaming on my face. It's the perfect day. A balmy sixty-five degrees. Clear skies. A festival with my flower truck. Time spent with Connor. I couldn't ask for anything more.

"Shay?" The tenderness in Connor's voice catches me off guard. I open my eyes, finding him in front of me, shifting on his feet as he holds one of his vases.

"Why are you so nervous?" I laugh. "Trust me, no one is going to notice if there's the tiniest imperfection in the wood—only you can see that."

His face remains neutral at my teasing.

I tilt my head and raise an eyebrow. "What's wrong?"

"I'd like to buy a bouquet for my fiancée." Connor takes a step closer and turns the vase around. "That is, if she'll have me?"

A gasp escapes my lips. Etched into the wood are the words *will you marry me?*

It's only four little words, but the meaning they carry is monumental.

"Flower, I've known you for over half of my life, and while I didn't realize it then, I was slowly falling for you all along. I love how kind and thoughtful you are. That you would do anything for anyone. You light up any room you walk into, and I love seeing how others are naturally drawn to you. You're the best girlfriend, daughter, sister, friend, and honorary aunt. But, most of all, I love who you are in the small moments. How you show up to the fire station with donuts as a thank-you to the people who were literally just doing their job saving you."

I release a shaky breath as he continues, trying to soak in every moment. Every word.

"How your presence alone makes me feel safe to open up and share my thoughts and feelings without any fear. That you're the same person when no one's watching that you are all the time. You're truly the most generous, considerate, empathetic, and optimistic person I know, and I'm simply the man that's lucky enough to be known and loved by you. While I know I'm not perfect, I promise to spend the rest of my days being the best possible version of myself for you."

Connor drops to one knee. He sets the vase down beside him and reaches into his pocket, pulling out a black velvet box. A single tear falls from his eye as he looks up at me and whispers, "I love you." He clears his throat before a teasing smirk tilts his lips. "I think it's time you officially take the Porter name that you've been doodling since the sixth grade."

A laugh bursts from my lips. I'm going to kill Mallory for telling him what I recently told her in confidence. After I say yes, that is.

He flips open the box, revealing a round diamond with a sunburst halo of glittering diamonds around it, making it look like a flower, all set on a white gold band. It's not only beautiful…it's *perfect*. I couldn't have picked a better ring if I'd gone shopping for one myself.

"Shayna Elise Monroe, will you please marry me?"

Happy tears drip onto my cheeks as I nod. "Yes." I bend down and fling my arms around his neck.

He effortlessly catches me—thanks to his deliciously strong muscles—and presses a kiss to my temple. "I can't wait to marry you."

I pull my head back just enough to plant my lips on his. I keep it short and sweet this time, since I hear lots of cheering around us. We've had enough kisses in front of an audience. But what can I say? When you love someone as much as I love this man, all fear of PDA goes out the window.

Connor stands, pulling me with him, before carefully slipping the ring onto my finger. It's a perfect fit, just like he is for me.

I reach down, pick up the vase he made, and hold it to my chest. "I'm keeping this forever." I can't even imagine how long it took for him to carefully carve each of the letters.

Friends and family run over to us, and my family pulls us into a hug first.

"Welcome to the family, Connor," my mom says.

"Yeah, it took you long enough." Reagan laughs. I smack my sister's arm. "What? It's true. You've loved him for, like, *ever*."

I can't argue with the truth. The second they let go, we're engulfed in another hug by Mallory. Unshed tears shine in my friend's eyes. "We've always been sisters, but I can't wait for it to be legally official."

"Me either." I squeeze her tight.

Over her shoulder, I watch as Connor gets rocked violently back and forth by Mama Porter as she exclaims, "I can't believe my boy is getting married. My prayers have finally been answered."

He shoots me a wide-eyed look that pleads *Save me*. I let go of Mallory before going over and hugging their parents. Mama Porter turns her full attention to me. "Oh, Shayna dear. You're the best daughter-in-love I could've asked for."

Her comment has me tearing up faster than I do when I cut into an onion. "I'm honored to have you as my second mama."

We're both in tears, holding each other, until Mallory steps in and pulls me away. "Okay, enough of this little sob fest. You have other people who want to congratulate you."

I wipe my face with the back of my hand. After I've accepted my final hugs from Connor's parents, I'm swarmed by the Long Live Girlies. I hold out my ring for them to see, and they all give just the reaction I was hoping for.

Alyssa gasps and grabs my hand. "It's stunning."

"Literal perfection," Kelsey agrees.

"Is that a flower?" Tess asks. I nod. She tears up. "That's the sweetest thing."

"He'll probably deny it, but I helped him pick it out." Mallory smirks. "I had to make sure my future sister got what she deserved."

I would've taken a paper ring, but I can't deny how stunning it is.

Kelsey places her hands on her hips. "You two can't forget about us now that you'll be related."

"Are you kidding?" I pull them in for a hug. "Y'all are stuck with me for life, whether you like it or not."

"Forevermore," they say as we cross our arms, making hand hearts with each other in a little circle. It's been our version of a pinky promise since middle school.

"Forevermore," I echo back.

Loud shouts from behind me have me turning around just in time to catch Connor's crew surrounding him.

"Porter's getting married!" Fisher yells, and the rest of his crew clap and cheer. He looks around until he spots me, and a devilish spark dances in his eyes. Oh no.

The next thing I know, he's lifting me into the air. Once my butt is settled on Fisher's shoulder, I turn and see two of the other guys from the station lift Connor onto theirs. His lips lift in a genuine smile. I'm sure his mom is snapping tons of photos for evidence, but he doesn't seem to care, because his hazel eyes are locked on mine. He gives me a *what can you do?* shrug.

"To Porter and Shayna," Lieutenant Malone says.

"To Porter and Shayna," everyone says before they finally set us back on our feet.

Connor pulls me into his arms. "I'm sorry for all of this. I said I didn't want to make it a big deal, but everyone insisted."

I shake my head, smiling at him. "Don't be. I wouldn't change a thing."

He leans down and kisses me, making everyone cheer again. Someone even wolf-whistles. Probably Fisher.

When Connor pulls back, I'm in a love-induced haze. A perfect bubble that can't be popped. He glances at his phone and turns to address our family and friends. "It's selling time, so we'll see you all back at my parents' house later for our engagement barbecue."

Everyone offers their final congratulations and clears out, leaving room for customers. Connor moves to finish arranging his vases and window boxes as I tend to the flowers. As I adjust a bouquet of daisies, my fingers instinctively ache to pluck the petals, evidence of the daisy game I've played for years, trying to let fate decide if Connor loved me or not.

But there's no need for me to play it anymore, because I already know the answer. I catch his gaze, and the full smile he gives me sends my heart soaring like a butterfly bursting from its cocoon.

He loves me.

Read a bonus scene about Connor and Shayna before they get engaged when you sign up for my emails at https://dl .bookfunnel.com/d1bn16hkn9

Keep reading for a bonus epilogue!

BONUS EPILOGUE
ALYSSA

"Y'all go ahead, I'll catch a ride home with Austin." I know he's going to be beating himself up over the lost game, and it's my duty as his friend to cheer him up.

Kelsey holds one clenched fist above her head and moves it around like she's about to throw a lasso.

I squeeze her side, and she squeals. "Okay, I think you had one too many bags of cotton candy."

"Don't tell Frankenstein." Kelsey giggles. The nicknames she has for her doctor-boyfriend are nauseatingly adorable. "He thinks cotton candy is bad for me."

"That's because it *is* bad for you. It's pure sugar."

She shakes her head. "As I've told him, it's good for the soul, and that's all that matters to me."

I sigh. "I wish I had your metabolism."

She smacks my butt. "And I wish I had your booty. Seriously, how much Pilates does a girl need to do to have that perfectly sculpted—"

Shayna steps forward and loops her arm through Kelsey's. "Okay, girl, time to go."

"Watch out for her," I call after them and Mallory as they walk toward the ballpark's exit. "She's on a sugar high."

"We've got her." Mallory turns and waves. "Have fun with your *man*." She wiggles her eyebrows suggestively.

I offer a half-hearted wave back before heading to the waiting area for the players' loved ones. I flash the body-guard-slash-bouncer—I'm not sure what his exact title is—a smile and the VIP key card Austin gives me every season. "Hi, Henry." He's truly the largest man I've seen in my life. I'm five-foot-eight, but he towers over me and has the shoulders of a professional linebacker. I've always called him Hank the Tank in my mind. I'm not sure he'd appreciate me saying it aloud.

Henry remains stoic as he scans my key card. "Ms. Cartwright." He opens the door for me.

I step into the tunnel. "Have a wonderful day, Henry," I call over my shoulder in my cheeriest voice.

He grunts in response before shutting the door. One of these days I'll get a smile out of him.

I walk through the tunnel, saying quick hellos to a few of the family members and wives of players I know. Instead of waiting with them for Austin to find me after he leaves the locker room, I head out the exit leading to the private parking lot. Whenever they lose a game, Austin does press, showers, and heads right to his car so he can go home and work out his frustration through baking or binge-watching one of his favorite shows. Since today's loss ended with him striking out, I'm guessing it will be a baking *and* binge-watching kind of night.

The second I step into the covered outdoor lot, the summer humidity hits me full force. I quickly spot Austin's white Ford Escape in his assigned parking spot and walk over to it. I've only been waiting for a few minutes when

Austin walks outside. His head is down, and water drips from his hair like he just finished showering and couldn't be bothered to even run a towel through it. He must be in really bad shape.

"Hey," I say, not wanting to startle him. It would be extremely difficult for a crazed fan to get into this area, but I wouldn't put it past someone who wanted to see a professional MLB player bad enough to sneak their way back here.

Austin tilts his chin up at my voice. "Hey, Lyssa."

I offer him a sympathetic smile. "You'll get 'em next time, Slugger."

He sighs. "I lost it for the team. Dawson was on third. All I needed was a solid hit to send him home and tie up the game."

I place my hands on my hips. "Do you blame Fletcher for not catching the ball that was hit right at him?" Austin shakes his head. "Because if he had caught that ball rather than ducking, that would've been the third out y'all needed in the top of the eighth. Then the Mallards wouldn't have scored those last two runs that let them win the game." I reach out and give his arm a reassuring squeeze. "You can't pin the whole game on yourself just because you were the last up to bat."

Austin pulls me to him. With my face just under his neck, I'm hit with a whiff of his cologne. The spicy hints of amber fill my senses, then mellow into a sweet vanilla. It's perfect. It's *him*. I inhale the smell before I realize what I'm doing.

He's my friend. That's all he can be. I can't have him catching me sniffing his cologne.

"Thank you," he whispers as he squeezes me.

"Anytime." I pull back, needing some fresh air to cool me down, but I'm just met with the stifling humidity of summer in Louisville. *Not helpful.* "Could you drop me off at home?"

"I have a better idea." His lips tilt up into a half grin, like my efforts to cheer him up partially worked but he's still not fully over the loss. "Want to try out the new raspberry–white chocolate chip cookie recipe I found and watch *New Girl*?"

I really should say no. Spending so much time with an insanely attractive man who stuck me firmly in the friendzone isn't good for my heart. But I'm a glutton for punishment.

I nod. "Always."

♡ ♡ ♡

You won't want to miss Alyssa's book, I Wish He Would—a friends to lovers, baseball romcom.

ACKNOWLEDGEMENTS

All the glory to God! Thank you for putting a love of stories in my heart and for giving me the words to write this story.

Wade, there are never enough words to thank you, so I'll just say this: Thanks for being the man of my dreams. None of my MMCs could ever measure up to you. Thanks for all the quiet things you do to support me and all the out-loud ways you attempt to sell my books everywhere we go. I love you forever!

Thank you to my besties for surprising me with flowers, an endless supply of Dr Pepper, my favorite candy, and words of encouragement when I was facing what felt like an impossible deadline for this book. Thanks for being my real-life Long Live Girlies! Y'all are the best!

As always, a huge thank you to my beta readers, Kathryn, Kimberly, Meredith, Sara, and Steph. Thank you for reading this story on an expedited timeline. Your suggestions truly made this book a thousand times better! Connor wouldn't be the MMC he is in the final draft without your brilliant minds. Y'all are the absolute best, and I never want to write a book without you!

Annah, thank you for your encouraging comments and excitement for this book! I'm forever grateful to have you as a critique partner and friend. You're the best!

Thank you to my brilliant cover designer, Melody Jeffries. Every time you create a cover for me, it's my new favorite. Thank you for bringing my vision of Connor and Shayna to life. Your talent and creativity amazes me, and it's always such a joy to work with you!

Thank you to my wonderful editor, Caitlin. Your encouragement and kindness means the world to me. Your edits, as always, helped this story shine!

Thank you to my talented proofreader, Alicia Whitaker. Thank you so much for your attention to detail. The thorough feedback you provide is so appreciated.

To all my sweet readers, I know so many of you were anxiously awaiting Shayna's story. I hope you enjoyed reading it as much as I loved writing it. You make every hour spent on writing worth it. Thank you for reading this book and making my dream a reality!

Finally, thanks to Taylor Swift for writing songs worth writing love stories about.

ABOUT THE AUTHOR

 Amanda Schimmoeller is a closed-door romance author who writes sweet love stories for readers who love happily ever afters. Her books are filled with banter, heart, and characters you can't help but love.

She loves Dr. Pepper, salty snacks, and binge-worthy tv. You'll find her plotting her next great love story and living out her own fairytale in Tennessee with her husband and their dog.

Connect with Amanda at www.authoramandaschimmoeller.com